# The Mystery of Tony the Goat and other Tales

Copyright © 2018 by Jim Studer

All rights reserved. No part of this publication may be reproduced, stored in a retrieval system or transmited in any form or by any means, electronic, mechanical, photocopying, recording or otherwise without the prior permission of the publisher or in accordance with the provisions of the Copyright, Designs and Patents Act 1988 or under the terms of any licence permitting limited copying issued by the Copyright Licensing Angency.

**Text Design by:** Liz Dwyer

**Cover Design by:** Miranda Rice

**ISBN:** 978-0-692-16511-9

Also by Jim Studer:

*The Road Taken*

# The Mystery of Tony the Goat and Other Tales

Jim Studer

DEDICATION:

GARY STROEING
&
MIRANDA RICE

# Table of Contents

1. Forward
2. The Mystery of Tony the Goat
3. Ancestry.Calm
4. Mama's Boy
5. The Man Who Loved Horses
6. So Much to Pray for
7. Boxcars and Beer
8. The Pen
9. You Can't Scare Me Away
10. Zenith
11. The Girl From Ipanema
12. Only the Best
13. Sideways to and from the Falklands
14. What's a Penny Worth?
15. Billy and Bobby: Or What They Found
16. Gramps Strang
17. The Bench
18. Another Gotcha, Katchia
19. From A-Bomb Drills to Lockdowns
20. What to do with Astrid
21. The Old Man

# A Must-Read Forward

For as long as I can remember, I would see people I didn't know very well. If they seemed interesting and I never found out their story, I made up a history for them. Interesting people had to come from even more interesting backgrounds. After I published *The Road Taken*, I needed a new writing assignment. At the age of seventy I rediscovered my old habit of giving life to characters I didn't really know. Then I found just as much fun in creating entirely new characters. I enjoyed my new hobby, short stories.

I followed the advice of other writers that I had passed onto my students, "Write what you know." I know about growing up in Central Minnesota. I know some of it's history, like St. Cloud, Stearns County, Wright County. I heard many stories that were supposed to be historically accurate, but hearing them many times over taught me that history, lore, and gossip seem to get all mixed together. The stories were never exactly the same.

Having spent eighteen years as a student, thirty-seven more as a teacher, and a total of forty-eight years as a speech coach, I learned a little bit about students, teachers, parents, and those who ran public and private education.

I know a little bit about travel and places outside of Minnesota, having stepped in forty-five states, six Canadian provinces, and thirty-four countries of the world.

I take all of this and blend. Then I throw in my imagination. Stir some more. Let it stew while riding hundreds of miles on a stationary bike. And, at least twenty stories spill out.

In the stories some of the places are real. Some of the characters are real people—they didn't mind being a part of the story. Other characters and places are a combination of many characters and places. I hope the splicing produced a hybrid that readers will find interesting. Except for the few who know, all characters and plots are the product of my mixed up mind.

Readers will probably note that many of the protagonists are old. It is not my age, now seventy-three, that draws me to them. At least four of them grew out of my youth. They are based on people I found fascinating. Later in life I was frustrated by not having found out more about these rich personalities. Since I couldn't uncover more of their real histories, I gave them my romanticized biographies. I hope you find them to your liking.

A few of my readers who test drove some of these stories said they were frustrated because the stories left them hanging. Good. I want the readers engaged in the characters and plot. I want readers to reach their own conclusion using their intellect and imagination.

Perhaps this comes from the short story I read when I was thirteen or fourteen, *The Lady or the Tiger?* by Frank Stockton. At the end of the story the hero has to choose a door. Behind one is a beautiful lady, behind the other is a ferocious tiger. That is where the story ends. Stockton said after the publication of the story, people begged him for the answer. Which door did the lover choose? Stockton took the answer to his grave. I hope the reader finds answers in those stories on which I haven't put my ending. I know my answers.

I have many people to thank for helping me put my hobby into print. Miranda Rice does the most for me. As I am computer challenged, she does all the typing. Beyond that she's an excellent editor who has helped make this a better book than it might have been. She is the cover artist and did the illustrations. Without Miranda there is no book.

Gary Stroeing has been an avid encourager and test driver of all the stories. He has provided motivation. My sister, Margie Stroeing, and niece, Kristen Vosberg, have lent their help. Kristen is an excellent proofreader. Thank you to all.

All the mistakes in the book are mine.

If you enjoy these stories and haven't read *The Road Taken*, please do. The book is nonfiction, but the subjects are the same: Central Minnesota, the classroom, and travel.

If you have at least three favorite short stories, let me know which ones they are. Thanks to my editor, Miranda, I have a Facebook page. She keeps me informed.

I have had fun writing, I hope you have fun reading.

# The Mystery of Tony the Goat

The funeral for Aunt Genevieve was bigger than expected for a woman of ninety-five. She had outlived her generation, and the better part of a few others. Many of my cousins attended as well as many people we had grown up with on our visits to our grandparent's house near the village of Maple. After the Requiem Mass and internment in the cemetery behind the church, we headed to the church basement for the usual lunch of hot dish, ham and cheese sandwiches, dill pickles, lime-Jell-O laced with slivers of carrots, and bars in a variety of chocolate. Because of the many people, it was hard to get around for the usual visiting that was part of the ritual. Many of my cousins and I, all now in our 60s and 70s, adjourned to Al's Saloon across the county road from the church.

All had, and some still, lived in the area. I spent summer weeks on their various farms near my grandparents, whom I also visited for weeks at a time. I knew the entire group fairly well.

There were a dozen or more of us gathered to exchange stories about Aunt Genevieve. We marveled at her great memory. She knew the entire family's birthdays, weddings and funeral dates. There were stories of her attempt to control everyone's life, stories of her eccentric stinginess. We only got saltine crackers for snacks when we visited. These stories led to other stories of strange people we remembered.

Janey piped in with, "Do any of you remember Tony the Goat?"

That got our attention.

Someone said, "Too bad Genevieve can't speak from the grave. If anyone would remember him, she would. I am sure she had stories."

Cousin Jake joined in, "Wasn't he the guy with the horses and buggy and that strangely dressed women we saw once in a while on the gravel road in front of grandpa's house?"

"Sure, I remember them," Mitch chimed in. "Only you got it wrong. He drove a big old, odd looking car, or maybe it was a truck. Or maybe it was a grafting of the two. It had a long hood with mounted headlamps. There was no top, as I remember. The windshield rose straight up and the wipers were attached top down. The side windows in front and back formed a transparent three sided box. What appeared to be a rumble seat in back was covered with a canvas at a forty five degree angle. Above that, I think, was a rolled up canvas that could cover the top."

"Yes," chipped in Miranda, "the car looked like a glass caged box sitting behind that long shiny hood. It reminded me of a WWII German command car the generals rode in in all those movies. I read about those cars with the huge oversized tires, mostly white walled," Miranda would know. She was known for her exactness, attention to detail and memory. Of course her PhD in English attested to brains and independence. Everyone questioned her on the value of a PhD in English.

She went on to describe the lady in the vehicle. "She sat in front. Her back was ramrod straight. Her head was always facing forward. I never saw her turn it when we yelled hello to them. On top of her head, I remember, sat a square black pillbox hat with feathers in it. She was wrapped in a black shawl.

"Tony wore what seemed to be a black sawed-off Abe Lincoln stovepipe hat. I always thought it was begging to reach higher. He had on a tweed jacket and a brightly colored tie, or maybe it was an ascot? Both hands were on the steering wheel, and he sat as erect as she. I don't think either touched the back of their seat."

Everyone agreed with all that and added other details.

Cousin Jake said, "I wonder if she was his wife? Or live-in lover? Or sister? Or perhaps his private secretary?" Then he laughed.

We also remembered that as kids we asked all the usual questions about them: Who were they? Where did they come from? Where did they live? Why do they act so strangely? Do they speak English? Why do they keep goats? I remember my grandparents telling us not to be so nosey, to leave them alone.

"They are just people who are a little different and want privacy. They are good people and we should respect that."

"Didn't they live somewhere towards St. John's Abbey?" asked Christina. "My dad used to work at St. John's, and I remember him saying he often saw Tony out there with the monks."

"What? Was he trying to join the monastery? Hey, maybe then his lady friend could join him at St. Ben's and become a nun." This was Herby's attempt at humor.

"No." Christina countered, "My dad said Tony was real handy, especially with paint. He did odd jobs around there."

I jokingly replied, "It was just after WWII. Maybe he was secretly helping the monks restore old painting treasures from Europe that the Church rescued from the Nazis. The Nazis raided churches and museums. Pope Pius XII was supposedly on good terms with these marauders."

Miranda laughed, "You have been reading too much Daniel Silva, Gus."

"Too much?" I retorted, "Not enough, he's good! Seriously, Tony didn't live near St. John's. He lived in this very township near the old Irish one room school house on township road 138. My dad used to stop there in the fall of the year to get apples from Tony. I didn't recall how my dad knew him, but I remember stopping there. I was about nine years old.

"My brothers, sisters, and I were not allowed out of the car. I can picture a house with old grey boards that had never been painted. There was an old falling down barn that looked like it came from the same extended family as that of the house. To one side of the barn a couple of well-groomed horses roamed in a pen. On the other side of the barn about eight or ten goats browsed away at anything and everything in their one acre pen. Those were the only live goats I had ever seen.

"The rest of the five acres supported a variety of apple and plum trees. Running among the trees were a dozen or so strange birds that looked like an amalgam of pheasant, peacock, and a short necked goose. My dad said they were guinea hens and cocks. A few people raised them for food, but mostly for pets or just animated adornment. They were colorful in shades of black, teal, gold, and red."

"Ah," Miranda shouted, "the feathers in her hat."

Cousin Janey said that she and her brothers and sisters thought Tony and his lady were Gypsies who had been kicked out of the clan and had come here so no one could find them.

"They stole Gypsy treasure and used it to buy their house, horses, goats, and car. We used to sit around in the winter and make up stories about Tony the Goat."

The rest of us remembered having seen Gypsy caravans from time to time in the 1950s. All their wagons and horses drew our eyes. Of course any sightings of Gypsies produced stories of pick pocketing, burglary, and kidnapping. We were scared to death and happy when the caravans moved on.

Miranda said she had the answer to Tony and the lady. She beamed, "I recall having read about WWII German prisoner of war camps in Minnesota, north of Bemidji. Escape was uncommon, but it did happen. Most escapees were quickly recaptured, but not all. Once four of them stole a boat and headed down the Mississippi River hoping to reach the Gulf of Mexico. They had no concept of the size of the U.S. compared to Germany. After days and days of hiding, they knew they had succeeded when they rowed onto a huge body of water. They came ashore and were captured. They had reached Lake Bemidji."

Liz butted in with, "I'll bet Tony was one of those who did get away. He kidnapped a young maiden; they fell in love and eventually settled here among the many German Americans. To keep their age a secret they posed as an elderly couple." Then she winked at me.

Jake, with a few beers doing most of the talking, called Miranda and Liz hopeless romantics who had read too many novels,

"We ain't that gullible."

Miranda smiled.

"No." Shouted Lee, "Ya got it all wrong. They weren't Romani, Gypsies to you unlearned, they was Basque exiles." Lee had traveled the world many times over, often hinting CIA. He had seen all, done all, and knew even more than Miranda. We knew all this because he told us, and told us, and told us.

He rambled on. "Ya see, the Basque, who live in the Pyrenees Mountains were a closed group who were known for their fierceness and feuds. Tony and his concubine ended up on the losing side of a feud and escaped to the good ol' U.S. of A. You said Tony raised goats. The Basque are sheep people—goats are close enough."

Everyone laughed at Lee and said he had drunk too much barley pop. Rosco didn't laugh.

He rose and seriously declaimed, "Lee, you got it wrong. Goats ain't sheep, but the Greeks love their goats. The Greek mountains are chock full of goats. Tony and his wife were in the Greek underground when the Germans overran Greece during the Deuce. He helped the Allies defeat the Axis. He must have been hated by the Nazis. I'll bet that after the war the still active Nazis put a price on his head. The U.S. State Department relocated Tony to the U.S. and set him up here. Tony raised goats, therefore, feta cheese—a Greek must. I remember my uncle once told me that Al at this very bar said that whenever Tony came in here he asked for Ouzo. Why would anyone except a Greek drink that black licorice turpentine?"

Later the liquid post burial wake of Aunt Genevieve broke up, and we fanned out for our homes. I hoped there were enough designated drivers to go around. I wasn't worried about me. Diet Mountain Dew didn't have much effect on my driving. Before I got into my car, Janey walked over and said,

"That got me all riled up about Tony the Goat. We've got to find the answers to who he and she really were." I agreed, and we set a follow up phone call to pursue it further. Meanwhile, each of us was to make calls and try to dig up more information.

As I drove home, I thought of my cousin Monica who had not been with us at the saloon. She and her sisters grew up near Tony's place. I called her and told her about the saloon gathering and the dissection of Tony the Goat. She said she didn't remember much about him other than in winter he always got to the one-room school house and got a fire going in the wood stove. It was always warm when the teacher and kids arrived. He also brought in a fresh bucket of water each morning. Monica said she would call her sisters and some old neighbors and see what they remembered. I made other calls to people who might have remembered Tony. I didn't reach anyone but talked to machines and left messages requesting information.

• • •

Days later Monica called and said she found an old neighbor who remembered Tony. The neighbor thought the lady was Tony's wife. She also recalled that they always seemed to be short on money and often had to sell a goat, apples or plums for cash. She remembered one Christmas when her dad had butchered a couple of pigs. He took a ham and some side pork to Tony's door to give to them as a sort of Christmas gift. Tony refused the meat and said they did not accept charity. The neighbor and his family wondered if maybe it was because the meat was pork. Tony and his lady spoke with an accent, but then again over half of the country spoke with one accent or another. Some spoke no English at all in the '50s.

Monica's sisters recalled the stories that followed the pork refusal. Kids and adults alike had them as WWII Jewish refugees. No one could recall having seen their bare arms. Surely, they were hiding tattoo identification marks.

Most of my other calls came up dry. But, one old neighbor remembered that as a kid he often saw Tony take the horses and buggy to the nearby town of Avon. The lady would drop him off near a little café where the Greyhound bus stopped a few times a week. The bus ran from Minneapolis to Fargo and points in between. Tony would not be seen for days, and then she would pick him up and bring him home. Another returned call reported that Tony and the woman sometimes drove off in that "motorized contraption," disappearing for days and on rare occasions weeks at a time. He recalled that the neighbor across the road complained about having to feed the horses and goats. This was between 1949 and 1955.

Janey called me a week later, "I have some good stuff, why don't we meet for lunch at the Lake Wobegon Café, exchange intel, and plot our next move." I asked if disguises were advisable.

The hamburgers were great, but the coconut cream pie was better. I told Janey all of the stories I had collected. After the one about the strange absences, she suggested that maybe both of them were mechanics for the Chicago mob.

"Oh, a mom and pop hit team," I said.

Janey said her visits and phone calls produced "good stuff." One person told her that she was sure Tony was on the run from what was left of the Capone gang. Tony was over fifty when he lived here. That made him old enough to have worked for Capone in the '20s and '30s. Janey pointed out that Capone was known in this area back then for having made trips here to sample moonshine, buy it, and arrange delivery. So it was possible Tony could have gotten to know the area then.

"However, I may have found the most disappointing answer to the mystery of Tony the Goat. As I was asking any and everybody about Tony, I received a letter in the mail, no return address. It gave me a local phone number but no more. The person I called said she was a relative of the neighbor who lived across from Tony. She told me that her relatives owned the farm. She said Tony did hired-man type of work on the farm. Tony was good with horses and helped in planting and threshing. He drove the horses they were still using, repaired farm equipment, painted, fixed fences, and picked rock. He did such work for others as well, but he never wanted for his wife, goats and horses."

"His wife?" I blurted.

"Yes, she told me Tony had married a widow who was losing her farm some twenty miles away. The widow's deal with the bank was settled with her getting the five acres with the shabby buildings and the bank getting a 120 acre farm, a good house, and several fine outbuildings.

"So, I was told there is no mystery at all. But the women asked why I wanted to know and who you were."

"She knew of me?" I shot back.

"Yes, she said she had heard some old guy and his sexy cousin was poking around concerning Tony. She was curious about what we had uncovered. She wants to meet us and hear the stories about Tony.

"So, if you are game, we have a two o'clock visit set for tomorrow."

"The game is still afoot," I insisted in my best Sherlock style. "And why am I old and you sexy?"

. . .

The next day in Janey's car we followed the directions the lady gave. We arrived at a narrow dirt driveway, a quarter mile down from Tony's old place. Actually, it was more of a seldom used path that led into a maple woods. About fifty feet into the woods we passed through a sturdy-looking, open gate that had a huge chain and padlock dangling from it. Three quarters of a mile farther in we found a three story brick mansion and attached three car garage. A woman who looked to be in her seventies met us at the door before we could use the brass knocker. She invited us into a solarium on the southeast side of the house. Windows, floor to ceiling, comprised the south and east sides of the room. The windows, we were told, were tinted and sensitive to the light, controlling the heat in the comfortable room. The view overlooked the slope of a deep ravine with the silver water of the creek flickering through tree leaves. Oriental carpets covered much of the maple flooring. We were seated in very comfortable and expensive armchairs forming a semicircle facing the breathtaking view. The walls featured tapestries and oil paintings. A long maple coffee table stretched in reach of the four chair ensemble. Sweating, ice filled, cut glass tumblers filled a tray on the table. Bottles of water, iced tea and a variety of soft drinks, including Diet Mountain Dew, awaited opening.

After we sat down the woman asked what our research about Tony had produced. She seemed to enjoy each tale. Then she told us that the farm across the road from Tony wasn't owned by the people for whom he worked. They only rented, but part of the rental arrangement was that the farmer claimed to be the owner with a mortgage on the place. The family who actually owned all the 600 acres, and later Tony's five, were a most private people. They had this house secretly built in the 1980s at considerable expense, bringing in and removing equipment, materials, and workers who remained on site until completion. The remoteness of the site deep in the woods muffled any sounds of the actual labor. Few knew of the house, and the core of the wooded area was fenced. The family still used the house, but never after the snows settled in. The agricultural land and farm house were still rented out.

"The family has always been wealthy; and is from out of state, but our travels and business ventures made us aware of this beautiful area. We liked it so much we purchased the land a long time ago."

We learned little else as we depleted some of the drinks on the maple table. Then as she ushered us to the door she said, "I hope that you have now satisfied your curiosity. Mystery solved."

Janey and I found a local tavern and rehashed our visit. Things were off about the women, Janey offered. She wore a wig and she really didn't seem to move like someone the age she claimed to be. I, too, had felt something was off kilter. The feeling I had seen this woman before kept popping into my mind. Her voice was one I had heard before. I knew voices from all my years of working as a speech teacher. The almost familiar face, the voice—but I had no frame to put the picture in.

Janey further added that the story of Tony the woman told us at the house was almost word for word the story she had told on the phone, like it was scripted, rehearsed. Then we discussed the secretiveness of the land ownership.

"You know," Janey said in a surprised voice, "what about claiming to be a relative of the farmer across the road? That was never explained, and she never gave us a last name; she said to just call her 'Gina'."

We left it at that and headed home. On the drive home I kept seeing the women's face and hearing her voice. Then her hands invaded the picture. I had seen those hands before. As I cruised down the freeway, I focused on the hands. I now realized that Gina's hands were not those of a seventy-year-old woman. They looked to be the hands of a woman much younger. If the hands didn't belong to a woman of that age then the face shouldn't have either. Could make-up have turned a much younger woman into a seventy-year-old? Why not?

Now I had to spin my memory banks in search of a younger woman with the same somewhat narrow face and nose. The Gina we visited seemed about 5'6" and about 130 pounds. All the way home that face haunted me, but no ghost appeared.

• • •

A few days later while playing poker in the card room at the local harness track, the inside straight flush my memory was trying to draw to was filled. I would not be beaten on this memory.

I had played poker with Gina, but not the Gina Janey and I had visited.

On the Fourth of July weekend, a few weeks after Aunt Genevieve's funeral and the beginning of the search for Tony the

Goat, I was on my way to play poker. On that holiday weekend the freeway out of town on a mid-Friday afternoon was jammed and barely moving. I got off as soon as I could and wandered back roads to get to the card room at the harness track.

An hour or two of playing brought a young woman to our table. Women playing poker are not uncommon, but most were older than this one. She appeared to be in her late thirties or so. She was in excellent physical condition, attractive, streaky tinted blonde hair, and a short skirt that emphasized long shapely legs mounted on steep, wedged, three inch sandals. With the sandals she appeared to be about 5'10." She sat down at the table with a full tray of chips. Now seated, her tight fitting, low-cut, cotton top presented an eye catching view for the seven males at the table. I am not sure what type of view was presented to the lone grandma at the table. The short skirt and low-cut top kept eyes off her face. Perhaps, by design?

As she played, the males at the table engaged her in conversation. She said she was on her way to the casino in Hinckley to play Keno which was not possible at the harness track. She loved numbers and numbers loved her. She claimed many big Keno wins. The holiday traffic was too much for her, so she got off to wait it out here in the card room. I thought it strange that a lover of numbers would want to play Keno, a game so house friendly.

Her bronzed body aroused chatter about how she obtained such a tan. Few Minnesotans achieved such a deep natural look. "Oh, I spend half of every year in Arizona and the summer and fall here." I asked what type of career allowed for such flexibility. The smile disappeared.

"I don't work and I don't talk about how I can afford my leisurely and luxurious life style."

No more questions about her personal life followed.

She played for an hour or so. An experienced and competent player, she left four chips shy of a full rack. "I guess, the traffic has loosened, and I hear the numbers of a Keno machine calling."

The memory of her hands drifted back. One of my habits at a poker table is watching people's hands. The hands don't tell me as much as a player's eyes, but hands fascinate me. I watch how some players shuffle their hole cards, ala the TV poker studs. I am amazed at the time players must have practiced the dexterous methods of manipulating piles of chips, no doubt meant to intimidate other players into thinking they were dealing with an experienced professional. I had watched the women's long slender fingers. The clouds disappeared. Old Gina's hands and poker playing woman were one and the same: a pair of Ginas.

When I got home I called Janey and said we needed a second look at Gina.

"This time we are going unannounced."

The earliest Janey could do it was next Wednesday. We agreed to meet at Al's Saloon where all of this started.

Next, I called my brother-in-law, Gray. I had been telling my sister Magrit about our quest to find the truth about Tony the Goat. Magrit had memories of Tony also. Both she and Gray were curious. I knew Gray had connections at the county courthouse and could easily research the plat books for Tony's shabby farm as well as the farm across the road. Gray said he was on it.

On Tuesday, before my meeting with Janey, Gray called with the land search information. Both plots of land were deeded to various corporations. All had generic names that suggested nothing about who they actually were. My sister and Gray looked up the corporations on the internet and found all had been incorporated in Delaware. The earliest was 1919. The boards of directors all had generic names of Jones, Smith, Brown, etc. These produced thousands of hits on the computer for the likes of John Jones, Al Smith, Bill Brown, etc.

• • •

Wednesday I met Janey at the saloon. I told her the result of my poker playing memory research and the deed research Gray had conducted. I had even more news. Yesterday, I had taken my car into the dealer for a 10,000 mile oil change and complete new car inspection. The head mechanic called me into the work bay, gave me a hard hat and told me to follow him. My car was on a hoist. The mechanic pointed to a small metal container on the chaise. He asked if I had put it there. I hadn't. He then removed the magnetic box and showed me the inside. He looked closely at what was inside, and said he believed that the small glass bead was an expensive GPS device, not something that could be found at RadioShack. The device could track the whereabouts of my car via computer.

We headed for Gina's mansion in Janey's car. When we got there, we found the gate locked. The call box near the gate was dead. While we cursed our bad luck, a car came down the crooked path. The driver unlocked the gate, drove through and relocked it. The sides of the car had a Twin Cities realtor's logo and phone number with a Twin Cities 612 area code. We identified ourselves and said we came to visit Gina.

He said, "Well, I don't know any Gina, but I can tell you that the mansion and all 605 acres are for sale."

"Who owns it?" Janey asked.

"I really don't know. My company is dealing with an East Coast law firm."

"Can we get in and look the entire house over; who knows, we may want to buy it," I asked.

"There's really nothing to see. The mansion and garages have nothing left in them, not even dust. The place was thoroughly cleaned. It can be yours for three and a half million."

We passed on the offer and the agent drove off. We decided to go back to the saloon and sulk. Janey got this weird look on her face and ducked out of sight. I walked around her car. All I could see was her denim legs sticking out from under the car. After much movement, the agile grandma crawled out with a metal box in her hand. From it she produced a glassy chip and asked, "Did the GPS thingy they found on your car look anything like this?"

**M**axine Schafer didn't know it, but a September dip in Lake Superior rechanneled her life. As was custom for many University of Minnesota Duluth (UMD) students the fall semester was validated by a renewal baptism in Gitche Gumee. Maxine followed her friends, dove deep after reaching the Ice House and shot up into the duct that led to a much warmer cement slab atop. The Ice House was the place to chill in the refreshing, deep blue waters, bask atop the warm cement and perhaps show off flashy trunks or a new bikini obtained in the summer away from the refrigerated city of Duluth.

Max had swum to, dove under and into the Ice House conduit many times since her freshman year. On the first try of her junior year, she slammed her head into the top of the chute. When her friends noted her failure to pop out onto the slab, one of them went back into the pipeline. She retrieved an unconscious Max.

A 911 call, paramedics, and an ambulance ride to St. Luke's hospital brought her to doctors. The doctors found her unconscious, unaware of the world. Three days later she opened her eyes and asked, "What happened? Where am I?"

The nurses told her the what and the where. The doctors told her she was the owner of 24 stitches in her newly shaved head and possessor of a pint of Red Cross blood. The doctors informed her parents, brother and sister that MRIs, CAT scans, and other neurological tests could not find any abnormality beyond a concussion and the gash on her head. Her brother, Booth, said she always had a hard head. Her sister Gabby chided her about trying to deposit her brains in the Great Lake as an offering to the gods. Her dad asked her why they call the cement chunk in the harbor the Ice House.

Maxine said she asked that of other students. None seemed to know, so Max, the academic, researched its history. She learned that it was the remains of a pier that was constructed in the 1870s by one Harrison Bentley. No one seemed to know why it was called the Ice House, perhaps because it was constructed and anchored in the icy waters of the lake. The only part of the pier remaining was the far end, poorly anchored in thirty feet of water. The brick and concrete remains were tilting to the northwest. The shifting of the block, some twenty yards from shore, apparently created the crack that produced a submerged duct. Since the sides above the waterline extended ten or more feet, the only way to the top for a swimmer was down, under and up through the passageway. After the pier was abandoned, it became known as Bentley's Mausoleum.

The history of the Ice House lecture completed, her mother sensed that in spite of the girl's exuberance in telling her story, she was holding back information. Max's parents questioned the doctors and nurses further. They followed up with her friends. Finally, Mrs. Schafer, alone with her daughter, said, "Maxine Elizabeth Schafer, there is more to your story. I can tell when you are holding back. You are acting like you did when you wrecked your sister's bicycle and like you did when you covered up for your brother's misdeeds. Both times I got the story out of you. Now spill it!"

Maxine Elizabeth Schafer's face grew stern. She turned her head away from her mother. Minutes passed.

"Well?" commanded her mother.

"Okay. I'm scared. While I was out, gone, unconscious, whatever, I had this dream, vision, hallucination, I don't know. It seemed so real. I was in an old house, dressed in clothes that women wore in Little House on the Prairie. I had a chain of some kind on my left ankle. I was chained to a double bed that had an old brass rail for a headboard on a wooden framed bed. The mattress seemed to be made of straw or hay. I was looking out an open window. I had a rifle in my hands. You know, Mom, I don't like guns. I haven't shot one since Grandpa tried to teach me and I got scared because of the noise and the kick. I refused to shoot anymore. But there I was aiming out the window at a man dressed in bibbed overalls and a plaid shirt. Mom, I shot him. I shot him three times.

"I then looked at my chains, and they were gone. I remember the big oak dresser that was by the bed, maybe five feet high. There was a calendar on the closed bedroom door.

"Mom, it was all so real. I get sick to my stomach every time I think about it." Maxine's body was shaking. Sweat beaded on her forehead as she burst into tears.

Maxine's story produced several sessions with a psychologist. A tox screen cleared her system for drugs, especially the hallucinogenic type. While all the doctors and specialists were intrigued, no one had an answer, most of all Maxine. Two days later she was released from the hospital. She returned to her apartment and resumed classes with a whole sea of catching up to do.

Along with her black bikini, Max returned with other baggage—midnight haunts. The old version of the shooting returned, now accompanied by new scenes. She was still clothed in a cotton dress with an apron splotched with spills and splatters from cooking, baking, and cleaning. The movie in her head showed her stripping off the apron and dress to dawn men's pants and a button-down work shirt.

In another rerun Max was clearly focused on the calendar. The top half read in big black letters 'SHEPERD'S LAKE MERCANTILE.' In smaller print underneath was 'If you need it, we have it.' On the lower half was the blocked-out month of April, 1887. April 6th was circled.

The name Sheperd's Lake and April 6th were branded into Maxine's consciousness. Sitting in class she saw both. Sheperd's Lake kept gnawing at her. Then her addled brain clicked. Didn't her speech coach, Stuart August, often mention such a place and tell stories about it? Wasn't it somewhere near where he grew up in Wilson County? August, everyone called him Gus, was in his seventies and still coaching high school speech. He had been more than a coach for her. He was someone she could ask for help.

"Gus," she asked on the phone, "do I remember it right? Somewhere around Middleton where you grew up, there was a place called Sheperd's Lake?"

"Yes, it's about 15 or 20 miles from Middleton. There really isn't much there anymore. Only the old store, now converted into apartments, a bar, and an old blacksmith shop now faking it as an antique shop. The Catholic church, St. Bridgette's, still offers comfort and hope. There are many farms and family homes scattered throughout the area."

"Gus, you always said you would do anything for me as long as it was legal. I think you meant it. Gus, this is so hard for me to ask, even harder than learning to call you "Gus," but I think I need your help. If I come home to my parent's house over President's Day weekend could you take me to Middleton to the newspaper office? I checked. It will be open on Monday. I can't believe I'm asking you to do this. It's so hard."

"Max, what time should I pick you up?"

Maxine and Gus arrived at the Middleton Time's office at 9:30 the following Monday morning. Max told him to go visit friends or relatives while she researched the morgue for April of 1887. Gus, who had visited her in Duluth after her knock on the noggin, learned even more on the trip to Middleton. He learned about the additions to the evolving dream sequence. Gus told Max he was there to help and pitched in on the microfiche search of April 1887.

A dusty hour later the murder of Herman Partch emerged from the celluloid. His body was found on the edge of a swamp inaptly named Sheperd's Lake. The body was discovered a half mile from his farm house. Coyotes and other scavengers had feasted on the remains, but a pocketbook attached to his bib overalls by a small chain was enough for the Wilson County coroner to declare that it was Herman Partch. He had been missing for three weeks. He was last seen on April 6th.

Further newspaper articles named his wife, Maxine Partch, as a suspect. Maxine Schafer smiled at seeing the name of another Maxine. Herman Partch had been rumored to have a habit of beating his wife. With no evidence to back the suspicion of Maxine Partch having done what a spirited woman would like to do, no charges were filed.

From the Time's office the two moved on to the Wilson County History Center. Old records and the center's resident visitor, Arnie Vogel, who had a fascination for history of small Wilson County towns, unveiled the story and lore of Sheperd's Lake. Before the place was baptized with that name there was only a Catholic church, St. Bridgette's, on the four-mile-wide isthmus separating The Tamarack Swamp from a much smaller marsh. The area had been settled mostly by Irish immigrants in the 1840s. Polish newcomers and later Germans followed. They cleared forest land and farmed.

In the 1850s the Red River Ox Carts blazed their Forest Trail around The Tamarack Swamp and passed in front of St. Bridgette's. The ox carts hauled freight between the Dakota Territory from what is now Fargo to St. Paul. The carts and yokes were in constant need of repair. A call for blacksmiths and wheelwrights was ever present. This led to blacksmith and carpenter shops across from the now well-traveled road in front of the church. In the tradition of Wilson County, a tavern soon followed. Then came a general store. A creamery moved in followed by a second saloon. The new town was attracting a population. The mercantile put in a request to house a U.S. Postal window.

The growing hamlet needed a name before the Post Office would honor the request. The land north of St. Bridgette's bordered the swamp that was wet most of the year. There were a few holes, maybe ten or fifteen feet deep, scattered throughout that always held water. Most likely they were spring fed.

Sometime around 1840 the land closest to the swamp supported a flock of sheep and a shepherd. For the most part the shepherd lived a hermit's life. He did some trading with the local Indians and later some of St. Bridgette's parishioners.

In the 1850s the shepherd mysteriously disappeared. A few months later a body was found on the marsh. Apparently, the shepherd was murdered. The sheep roamed the woods, fields and swamp. Some were hunted by local farmers and a few remaining Indians. The rest died during the hard winter.

Local lore stated that the ghost of the shepherd haunted the swamp, which became known as Sheperd's Lake. The community adopted that name to satisfy the U.S. Postal Service.

After the Civil War and the pushing of the Great Northern Railroad from St. Paul to the Red River in the north, the ox cart freight business became obsolete. The railroad, while following most of the ox cart trail, didn't arc around The Tamarack Swamp. It pushed right through. Sheperd's Lake traffic dwindled. A budding town now worked to maintain its population. It remained viable until the great depression. After the Volstead Act was repealed, killing off much of Wilson County's Minnesota 13 industry, most of the hamlet's businesses failed. Today, besides its loaded folklore history, all that is left is the church and, of course, the original tavern doubling as a convenience store. The carpenter shop became a junk or second-hand store.

Max and Gus left Middleton. With her head enriched with a new view of Sheperd's Lake in April, 1887, Max returned to school. The murder of Herman Partch, the Sheperd's Lake Mercantile and the new Maxine in her life, suspected of killing her husband, added grisly new grist for milling new nightmares.

Max had to know more. She got her brother and sister working on the Schafer family tree. Both were instructed not to let their parents know what they were up to. Max didn't want them to know about her continued nightmares and her sudden interest in ancestry. She was afraid her mother would haul her off to a shrink. This was an unusual fear for someone majoring in Psychology. Perhaps her double major in Women's Studies overruled. The world needed more strong, independent women.

Gabby and Booth traced the family ancestry back several generations. They found that their father's side came to Minnesota from Bavaria just before World War I. They traced their mother's Irish side back to St. Louis County in Northern Minnesota. But records before 1912 were nonexistent.

Max's dreams generated new variations of the shooting and the farm house. The fuzzier the data she fed into her grey matter, the more her brain demanded more and clearer input. As hard as it was to ask, she again called Gus whom she had been updating on her dream state. "Gus, I looked at your school's spring break schedule. It coincides with mine. God, this is hard for me, but I need your help again. Could we go back to Wilson County. I just have to know more about Maxine Partch and Sheperd's Lake. You know so many people there. Can you find me some help?"

"More nightmares?"

"Yes, more nightmares. And they want to become day-mares. I must have answers."

A return to Sheperd's Lake was arranged. Gus combed his memory for the names of people who might be of help. A call to his cousin, Janey, provided a lead. Melvina Jansky, a ninety-six-year-old who was said to know more of the history and tales of Sheperd's Lake than anyone, was still alive. Folks claim that while Melvina knew a lot about the area, her history and lore merged into lore-story. She grew up on a farm that had been in the family since before the Civil War. Melvina's mind was as sound as the granite that Wilson County was famous for. She resided in an apartment in an assisted living complex, Maple Haven Rest. Gus phoned and asked if she might be interested in telling what she knew about Herman Partch and Sheperd's Lake. Melvina said she would love to meet with him and the young lady he spoke of. "I haven't been this excited since I thought Donald Trump would be impeached," she gushed.

Melvina's conniving brain was always churning out new ways to use her knowledge of the past for personal gain, or to escape the boredom of her "old crones home." She gathered two of the crones, Davidine Schulte and Lucile Malaly, both a younger and sprier eighty-six. They were as giddy as Melvina to rehash the tales of Sheperd's Lake and the Partches.

Melvina returned the call and told Gus she had enlisted help in the quest for the "skinny" on Herman Partch and company, but there was a price to be paid. "We will talk over a long lunch at the Palace of Pizza in Middleton. We will require transportation from Maple Haven and demand a gigantic pizza and beer, much beer." Gus agreed.

On Saturday, March 17th, Gus with Maxine Schafer aboard taxied the three dowagers to a pizza feast. After all introductions and the formalities attached were concluded, Melvina said, "We just don't get anything this tantalizing at Maple Haven, they feed us like babies. I vow to never let applesauce touch my lips again." Gus suggested they order two family size pizzas, half of one to be pepperoni and sausage for him, the remaining one and a half be anything the historians wished. He said that all leftovers would be boxed for transport back to Maple Haven. The queens ordered almost half the toppings on the menu and each a different craft beer. Maxine, a rarity among the youth of the nation, didn't eat pizza. She ordered a brownie sundae and a glass of chocolate milk.

"While we wait," Melvina declared as she sipped straight from the bottle of Beaver Island, "we will begin with Sheperd's Lake. It isn't a lake at all, never was. It's just a fen, deep in some places. It has some water in it all year. It's called Sheperd's Lake because there was an old Irish shepherd who lived there in a hut."

Davidine interrupted, "It was no dog, it was a man, so they say. Not a dog but a man."

"No, Davidine," Lucile corrected. "The man was a shepherd, he kept sheep. He was from Ireland. I don't know if he had a dog, but if he did around here it would have had to have been a German Shepherd."

"Anyway," said Melvina reclaiming the floor, "he had sheep and lived on the edge of the fen. Don't give me that look, Davidine. A fen is a swamp. He tended his sheep, trapped, hunted and traded with the Indians. This was in the 1830s or 40s. He had no claim to the land. He was just a squatter."

Now Lucile took the floor. "You see, not long after he disappeared Patrick Dunleavy, another Irishman who was buying up land, claimed the area. My grandad said he had killed the sheep man and ran the sheep into the swamp or slough or, if you wish, Melvina, the fen. In the 1850s they found some bones near the swamp—excuse me, the fen. Some said it was Indian bones, others said it was the sheep man. That's when they began to call the watery patch Sheperd's Lake."

Max asked the ladies how they knew this 150-year-old story. Melvina took claim, "What you hear is the legacy of our three families who resided near Sheperd's Lake for over six generations. Isolated families talk among themselves and communicate the history to others."

Lucile cut her off, "They gossip."

"Share the history," countered Melvina. "We all came from large families and all three of us have steel trap memories. Once a story trips the spring-steel jaws of the trap, nothing escapes."

Now Lucile took the witness stand. "Donleavy claimed eighty acres of that land and, by law, had to erect a house on it. He did so, a house close to 'the fen' and later added a barn. The barn is gone, but the house is still there. He put one of his sons on the place. He had six sons before his wife died in childbirth. The second wife bore him two daughters and she also brought a daughter with her."

Feeling left out, Davidine forged in, "Can you believe it? That daughter had no father. Not like Jesus and the Virgin Mary, but I mean, she wasn't married and would never say who the father was. Such goings on."

Melvina retook the witness stand. "The girl, Maxine, was a wild one."

Maxine Schafer's eyes fired large at the name, but before she could react the food arrived.

After another round of beer and the consumption of over half the pizza, Maxine Schafer asked to hear more of the girl Maxine. Davidine, never shy to stir the flames, said, "She was a wild one. She said women's clothing was too restrictive. She wanted a shirt and pants. When her step father forced her to work the farm in a traditional waist shirt and skirt, she would peel the outer garments and work in her underwear. The neighbors noticed. Gossip ran like the creek, downhill."

"Dunleavy then packed her off to the convent at age thirteen," chimed in Lucile.

Melvina drowned her out with, "The convent at first was able to control her. She learned to read and write quickly, too quickly for some. They said she was preaching her own gospel. She wanted nuns to be given more power by being ordained priests. Then it was that priests and nuns should be allowed to marry if they wished."

Davidine added with a blush, "She even said the nuns should be able to have children even if they couldn't marry. My aunt Delia told me that. Such scandalous notions that child had."

Melvina went on to say that the bishop got wind of the free-thinking preacher and told the Mother Superior that Maxine's mouth had to be muzzled or the convent would be sanctioned.

That got Maxine tossed out. It was back home to Dunleavy's farm. Promises of more money to both the convent and the Dioceses was of no avail. Now at seventeen, Maxine was back to hoeing the garden and slopping the hogs.

Lucile said, "Of the many things she learned in the convent she never learned to shut her mouth. When the family dragged her off to church on Sundays Maxine was preaching her own sermon to all the young girls of the parish in the churchyard after Mass. She was instructing the unmarried girls with the methods she learned in the convent on how to avoid pregnancy without avoiding the act that caused it."

Melvina, on her third bottle of Beaver Island, couldn't avoid the direction the conversation was taking. Instead she joined in, "Then she tried to convince the girls that if they wanted children there was no need to marry. 'Look at my mother.'"

By now Maxine Schafer was using her cell phone to record the historians' mine of feminist thought.

Davidine picked up the yarn, "So now Dunleavy's problem multiplied. The conniving scamp—I know many more vulgar terms for him, but conniving scamp will do—that scamp invited Herman Partch to have a beer at Sliver's Tavern. He knew that Partch was tired of working as a hired hand and wanted a farm of his own. He had eighty acres at Sheperd's Lake with a barn and a ramshackle house that he wanted to get rid of. The constant ghost stories about the old shepherd drove the son off the farm."

"Yes," Lucile plowed in, "now he had a way to get rid of the farm and a heretic witch of a step daughter. He offered the farm, buildings and step daughter to Herman Partch. Partch, they say, almost broke his wrist signing the deed and almost killed his horse racing to the courthouse to register it. They say he wasn't in much of a hurry to get to the altar, but a deal was a deal."

By that time three bottles of beer for each was gone, three fourths of a pizza were boxed and ready for home. The three yarn spinners were no longer able to tie the threads of the tale in a straight pattern. Maxine and Gus deposited the trio back at Maple Haven.

Weeks later, Max was back to asking. "Gus, it's getting easier to ask for help. Can you arrange a return visit to the three fates who hold the strings to Maxine Partch's story?" She went on to tell Gus of more dreams. "I'm sitting on a bed writing on some kind of notepad, the pad is on top of a box about the size of a cigar box my grandpa used to have. Only this box is made of tin instead of cardboard. I just have to know more. Could that have been Maxine Partch doing the writing?"

Gus made the arrangements. Melvina said the big three would be elated. The management at Maple Haven put a damper on things a bit and said no more field trips to Middleton. Gus hedged a bit on his promise. He brought Middleton to them. Maxine Schafer, a large family style pizza, and a six pack of beer arrived at the retirement center.

The yarn spinners greeted the visitors with smiles, hunger and thirst. The meeting took place in the dining room. "What do you want to know this time?" Davidine queried while stuffing a square of pizza into her mouth.

Maxine Schafer asked to hear about Maxine Partch after her marriage. "Did she have access to pen, ink and paper?"

Lucile responded first, "My grandmother, every time we road near that old house, would tell us that Mrs. Partch used to drop penned notes out her bedroom window urging women to abandon their corsets. Grandma said that Mr. Partch forced his wife to wear one to church on Sundays. The corset was from her clothing stock that the rich Dunleavy women wore. Partch, like the Dunleavys, wished to show off his prized livestock in the best fashion. Well, one exceptionally hot day during the Harvest Picnic at church, Maxine Partch complained about being confined in clothes that didn't allow her to breath. After a trip to the far outhouse Maxine Partch paraded through the grounds swinging her corset over her head, showing off more of her body through her mangey undershirt than was respectable. Grandma said all the men stood agape and the women were amazed that she could shed her corset without help."

Melvina wondered, "Did she shed her skirt, too, like she was said to have done when working the fields? I don't know that I blame her for embarrassing old Partch. I always heard that he beat her, and for punishment at times he chained her to the bed."

Maxine Schafer interrupted, "That's interesting, but did she ever write things other than the notes tossed out the window?"

"Well," Melvina countered, "hunters and trappers who roamed the woods and swamp near the house claimed to have found notes about her being chained and even starved. But no one ever raised an issue about it. My great uncle Jake used to say, 'A man's wife was his property, and none of it was our concern.'"

"Where could she have gotten writing materials?" asked young Maxine.

Lucile happily answered. "They said she robbed the convent blind when she got tossed. Her suitcase was chuck full of rosaries, prayer books, a harmonica, pens, ink, notepads, candles and even a nun's habit, wimple and all."

Maxine Schafer's next question was what had happened to Maxine after Herman's body had been found. She said she read in the old newspapers that Maxine Partch was suspected in his death, but there was no evidence.

Lucile thought that Maxine was granted ownership of the farm and that a crooked lawyer arranged for a quiet sale that left Maxine with a little money.

Melvina said, "My great aunt Ludmila claimed to have a letter or two from Maxine who had disappeared after the farm sale. She said Maxine was living in Duluth and using her mother's maiden name Daly. She was working as a domestic in some rich household there. Seems her highfalutin ideas of a woman's place didn't get her beyond household chores."

Maxine Schafer quietly said. "She had to support herself, didn't she? Jobs for women were a scarce commodity then."

This time Max and Gus left the fate spinners sober.

• • •

Max's dreams continued, more scenes of note writing in the bedroom. Max saw herself writing then putting the pads in the cigar box. The tin box was a deep rich brown and on it was a dark green tobacco leaf. On the leaf printed in bright white was Durham's Best. As she held the closed box, she heard a fading voice repeat, "Find the tin. Find the tin. Find the tin." She awakened shaking and in a sweat.

The latest nightmare triggered another call to Gus. "I'm coming home over Easter. On that Saturday I need you to take me to that Sheperd's Lake farm house. Bring a crowbar, hammer, and nails. I'll tell my family I am helping you on a research project you are doing in your old hometown area. I don't want them to find out what I am doing. If they find out about my continued dreams and lack of sleep, my dad will want me to change schools and move back home. My mom will want me to receive professional help. I won't go. I don't want to do battle with her."

"That's a psych major talking about avoiding a shrink?"

"I know. Let's just say I'm stubborn.

• • •

The two arrived at the old Partch hovel. Amazingly the place still stood. Maybe it was because for almost a hundred years nobody would go near the place because of stories of strange sounds and ghost sightings. Some were said to be of the old shepherd, others were said to be of Max Partch. Even reveling teenagers had stayed away.

Maxine said, "Here's what we're going to do. Let's start in the bedroom, the one I keep seeing in my sleep. We look for possible hiding places, remove floorboards, moldings, or even wall boards if necessary. We replace whatever we can. But we don't leave until we find that cigar tin."

First the decrepit old high dresser was examined. Then baseboards were removed and replaced. A storage closet was disassembled and partially restored.

Then Max wanted the old bed moved. No mattress or bed clothing remained. The brass bed posts were gone. A series of old planks made up the bottom of the bed. The floor underneath revealed two loose boards. Gus pried them up. They found an old oil cloth with something wrapped in it.

Like a starving cat, Max pounced on it and ripped the oil cloth off. Bingo, a rusty tin box. Three notepads with handwriting on each lay in wait. Max put the cover back on the box and said, "Let's fix this up and get out of here before anyone comes to see what we are up to. I don't want anyone to find this."

They adjourned to a nearby village pub for lunch and to examine the looted treasure. Max read aloud as she decoded the almost illegible remains. "I took paper, pens and ink from the nuns. They owed me for the four years of toil I gave them. I want to record the ugliness of my life as a purchased slave of Herman Partch. When someone finds this, I want them to know how he beat me, chained me and starved me. If I ever get the chance I will kill the bastard." Max stopped reading and put the cover on the tin box.

"I knew it, I just knew it. I'll take this back to school and read it all. Then I will decide what to do." Gus noted that Max was all smiles. He told her that he hadn't seen her smile in months.

"I couldn't before. Now I can."

The following Wednesday an excited Max called Gus. "I had another dream—a good one. The woman that seems to be me sat on the edge of the old wooden bed we moved. As I, or she, I don't know which, sat there, I could hear a voice say, 'Thank you.

Now clear my name. I will trouble you no longer if you do.'

"Gus, I read the rest of the diary. She did shoot him. In the last pages she tells how one day Partch was careless after he came home from hunting squirrels and left his rifle and shells next to the high chest. Gus, she waited at the window, and just like in my vision she shot him three times. Now what do I do?"

"Maxine Schafer, it's time you got published." Gus had been thinking about this since last Saturday. He had a plan. He contacted the editor of the Wilson County History Center's magazine. She was interested.

He drove up to Duluth the following Saturday and asked Max if she would edit Maxine Partch's diary, selecting enough to tell the woman's story. Then she would use it in an article that would reveal to the world the story of Maxine Partch and the other characters of Sheperd's Lake. The article would vindicate Maxine Partch in the death of Herman Partch with the lines from the diary:

*April 6th a.m.*
*If I don't shoot him now I most certainly will die of his brutality, a long, slow, painful death. I am a woman. I am human. I have rights. I shall kill him in self-defense.*

*April 6th p.m.*
*I opened the window and rested the rifle on the sill. Partch was coming up from the barn. I took careful aim and fired. He dropped to one knee. I carefully fired again. He was now on both knees and cursing me as he always did. I fired once more and left the window.*

*April 7th*
*I freed my leg from the chain. I looked for Partch's body. I couldn't find it. I guess the .22 rifle was not enough to have finished him before he crawled off like a wounded dog. I saw the blood trail headed for the swamp.*

*Now I must pack clothes and food and walk as far as I can. I will stop first at the house of a shady lawyer my step-father used and arrange to get some money for the deed to the farm. I know the lawyer will steal most of it, but all I need is enough to get away from here. I will walk, hitch rides where I can, and head for Duluth and hide in the port city. It should be big enough. I hope to reclaim my mother's maiden name of Daly.*

*Whoever finds this please tell the people of Sheperd's Lake I am not a murderess. I am a woman who will survive.*

The Middleton Time's picked up the article published by the History Center in August. The headlines read: UMD COLLEGE STUDENT CLOSES 130-YEAR-OLD COLD CASE
A picture of Maxine Schafer holding a tin box filled with notepads accompanied the article.
The second week in September, Max invited Stuart August to Duluth. She had him drive her to the harbor. There she peeled off her outer clothing exposing the black bikini she wore a year ago. She walked into the cold water and swam to the Ice House. She disappeared and soon re-appeared crawling out of the hole in the top of the cement slab. She stood on the top of the Ice House and shouted to Gus,
"Now I know what and who I really am."
She dove into the cold blue of Gitche Gumee and swam to shore. As she wrapped herself in the blanket Gus held for her, she looked up and said. "I'm not just the solver of 100-year-old mysteries, I am the descendant of a true pioneer feminist. Come, let's go to a coffee shop and I'll tell you what I did."
Over coffee for Max and Diet Mountain Dew for Gus, Max continued, "This summer while working and taking a summer school class, I did research. I searched the birth records at the St. Louis County Courthouse from 1892 to 1912. I found several Daly's but only one with no father listed on the birth certificate. In

1898 there was a record of Maxine Elizabeth Daly born on November 19th. Yes, Gus, my birthday also. You can always leave it to a feminist to do what men have done forever, name a child after herself.

"Then I went to the Register of Deeds office on a hunch. My mind wouldn't let go of the idea. I searched for property deeds for Maxine Daly. I started in 1898. It didn't take long. In the spring of 1899 a house on South 12th street in Duluth on a 60-foot lot was deeded to Maxine Daly, no mortgage. The clerk told me that meant it was a cash transaction. I checked the history of the property. For years it had been owned by Harrison Bentley. On the tax records it was listed as rental property. In September of 1898 it was sold to a company called A Safe Future. That company sold it to Maxine Daly.

"I then searched the Duluth News society pages from the late 1890s for anything to do with Harrison Bentley. I found him in a story about a Port City Gala hosted by Bentley featuring the governor of Minnesota, David M. Clough. Bentley and the governor were pictured being served a drink by a maid identified as Maxine Daly. She was a strikingly beautiful woman.

"You see, I found me. I am a solver of crime puzzles. I am a feminist from a long line of feminists. And I am a psychologist who brings calm to my ancestor."

# Mama's Boy

"What a jackass. You're as dumb as the damn gravel I push around working construction. You think I care about what you want? No stupid, stumble bum like you is going to tell me how to act."

"Larry, you should be ashamed of yourself."

"Steadly, you should be ashamed of *yourself*, wasting my time. Who the hell needs history? Get a real job, you dumb son-of-a bitch."

Those words filtered through a collapsible wall that divided the two small classrooms. All activity stopped in my room. My students, wide eyed, looked at me posing a question; "Are you going to let that go?" They knew that such an outburst in my classroom would end in a trip to the principal's office. But the outburst was not directed at me and wasn't in my classroom. We continued on for a while, but again the loud voices from the other side invaded us.

"What's it to you if I stand up and pass gas. Didn't you yourself tell us of the great history of gas passers? You're as ugly as the smell in here."

"Please, Larry, you don't mean that."

"God, what does it take for you to get it? You gutless worm."

"Larry, please see me after class. Now, class, let us get back to today's lesson."

The eyes in my classroom had been bouncing from the talking wall, to me and then back to the wall. I'd had it. I marched out and knocked loudly on Mr. Steadly's door. A student opened it. I stepped in and declared, "Someone in here has all the detention I can give for continuously interrupting my class."

"Who?" boomed the same loud voice that had pierced the wall.

"You," I said. That's the first time I had met Larry.

After school I wrote up the incident for the principal. Larry Buggs got three one hour after school detentions.

The next time I encountered Larry was in my speech class a year later. We had quarter rather than semester or yearlong classes. I liked the idea. Kids could goof up, get behind and fail, but only one quarter was wasted. A new quarter, a new start. Of course, it was a lot of work for the principal to schedule, but Mr. Kennedy spent hours and hours making it work, "For the good of the kids." as he stated. Kennedy was the best principal I ever worked for. Since speech was a required class, Larry couldn't avoid me.

Teaching public speaking was a joy for me. Speech is such a valuable skill, and helping students learn how to face and overcome one of the most dreaded fears, performing in public, gave me great satisfaction. One of my standing rules in all my classes was, "No one had the right to make fun of, insult, or hassle anyone in the classroom." This was even more emphasized in a speech class.

This was merely a dare for Larry. While one of the brightest and most attractive girls in school gave her speech, Larry made faces at her, flashed obscene gestures and openly laughed at her. It took him less than thirty seconds. Larry was shown the door and warned that next time he wouldn't return.

A few weeks after Larry's return one of our more challenged boys was struggling to speak to us about his 4-H rabbit raising project. Larry, evidently bored or disliking the concept of having the meat of a French Lop for dinner, shouted, "I wouldn't eat that, you must be nuts." Larry was sent to the principal's office and was not allowed to return that quarter. The speaker was too devastated to continue. A week later, the rabbit raiser gave a painfully delivered but enlightening speech on those huge rabbits.

Later in the year Larry showed up in my required writing class. Larry's behavior for the first weeks was acceptable. Then he received a mid-quarter fail notice. He blew his stack. "You mean I have to write all the papers in order to pass?"

"Yes, if you want credit for the course, you must complete the entire course."

"But, look. I have C's on the papers I wrote. Just give me F's on those I didn't write. The average will be a D. I pass."

"No, Larry, you don't pass. You get an incomplete until you do all the work. If the incomplete stays, it turns into an F."

His profane outburst earned him another walk down the hall. Larry's return to class was highlighted by his performance in a peer writing evaluation group—all male. I guess Larry didn't like a suggestion on how his essay might be improved. He took a swing at a serious boy who actually wanted to help Larry be a better writer. The skinny little guy was quick and ducked Larry's punch as I stepped in. Larry was asked to step out again. This time he didn't return.

I worked to know more about Larry. I talked with the counselors, some other teachers and several students. The verdict from the kids suggested that Larry was not really a bad guy. He was a big, strong kid who resented any challenge. If challenged, he demonstrated his power as king of the hill. If left alone, he gradually ignored the other kids, but he liked to be looked up to. The teachers responded much the same. Those with little classroom discipline were challenged until they surrendered to Larry's rule. The hard cases who had classroom control, Larry avoided or ignored. He seemed to have a sense of Darwin's law of the jungle: survival of the fittest.

Larry avoided my classes after the writing incident. That is until he banged into my room just before the middle of his senior year. "I have a problem," he mumbled.

"How can I help you?"

"I need four quarters of English in order to graduate, two each quarter."

"What's the problem? You are bright, you're not lazy unless you choose to be. You can do it."

His head hung, "Yeah, but the only way I can schedule it is to take three of the classes from you, two next quarter and one the last. Every time I take one of your classes you throw me out."

"Why do I do that?"

"Well, I get in some kids face or in your face and you toss me. I really don't need to graduate. I have a full-time job starting in June with the construction company my dad works for. I am already working every weekend now. Part-time I make almost as much money as you do. I looked up what you make. You must be nuts to work for so little.

"I am really good at working a Cat. I can push gravel and stone better than those other guys. I have the touch. Next year I'll make three times what you make. Next winter I'll be laid off and sit in my fish house all day, catching walleyes and drinking beer. The best part is I'll collect unemployment while I do it. You can't even collect unemployment when you are off in the summer. I don't need a diploma."

"Then why do you want to graduate? You just showed me you don't need it."

"Oh, it's my mother. She wants me to graduate. Says she will cry her heart out if I don't. Hell, I give her enough grief as it is. So, I guess I'll do it for her if you let me."

"Larry, what if I came out to your construction site to throw rocks at you while you work your Cat. What would happen?"

"I'd pound you."

"You sure?"

"No, I guess the foreman wouldn't let me or if I did, I'd lose my job. But my boss and the company would have you stopped."

"Then I would come back the next day and throw more rocks."

"Okay, the company would have you tossed in jail and file a restraining order in court. You know, you have no right keeping me from doing my legal job and earning a living."

"I see. Now tell me what gives you the right to disrupt my classes by throwing stones at my students and me. Don't they have the right to learn, and don't I have the right to teach and earn a living? Larry, if you stay out of my hair and let me do my job, then I'll stay out of your hair and allow you to learn."

"You mean if I behave and not mess with other kids, you'll pass me?"

"No. If you don't mess with me or other students *and* do all of your work, all in an acceptable academic manner, you will earn passing grades."

"Deal."

The two quarters passed smoothly enough. Larry did all his work and earned two solid C's the 3rd quarter. Once or twice in each class Larry would get bored or feel the need to roar. I would look at him sternly and say, "Larry."

"Yeah, I know. I know."

On the last day of Larry's final class, he had a test to take. After writing his name at the top, he filled out about a fifth of the test. He got up and approached my desk. "If I flunk this test will I still pass?"

"Yes."

He handed me the test and said, "I'm done here."

Walking to the door he turned and came back. He held out his hand to shake. I did. "You know, Mr. August, you're not such a bad guy. At last, I did something right for my mother." He headed for the door.

I said, "You're not such a bad guy yourself. I hope Mama is happy." He smiled and left.

## The Man Who Loved Horses

The bobbing hat in the ditch aroused curiosity. My sister, Magrit, and I crept down the ditch on my grandparent's side of the road. We lost sight of the hat but gained the sound of a rhythmic *swish, swish*. Gathering all the nerve five and eight-year-olds could muster, we crested the ditch onto the gravel road. In the far ditch we saw an elf swinging the long curved blade of a scythe felling the grass of the ditch, swathe after swathe, *swish, swish*. The elven man continued swinging the crooked wooden handle, two pegs mounted on it for hand grips, the sun reflecting off of the shiny steel blade. The scene mesmerized us. Long we stood on the road watching patch after patch of long grass and weeds cut down by the perpetual motion of the razor sharp blade. The crooked man, the crooked handle, the glimmering blade, and the falling grass continued south in the valley of the ditch.

  The elf finally noticed us, smiled, waved, and stroked on. We waved back and retreated to the house of our grandparents.

  Later we saw the man on the road pushing his wheelbarrow. The barrow, except for its steel front wheel, was all wood and, like the diminutive man, was old and weathered and tiny. It had no sides, but a headboard angled over the front wheel. The two wooden handles fenced the man in between them as he had lifted the barrow bed off of its rear wooden legs and pushed it north along the side of the road. The hay across the bed was neatly stacked higher than the head of the barrow pusher. The *click, click* of the steel wheel on the gravel extended the rhythm of the day.

The stooped man appeared to be less than five feet tall. As with so many his age, his physical stature shrunk with the passing years, but as we were to find out, the man himself was larger than life. He had snow white hair that glistened as it mushroomed out from under his woolen cap with its short visor. His well groomed mustache extended a drooping inch on each side of his face. The rest of his face was covered in a grayish, stubbly beard that seemingly didn't deserve the attention of the 'stache.

His denim-bibbed overalls, worn and tattered, covered a yellow and orange flannel shirt, sleeves rolled up to the elbows. A canteen, which had been on the headboard of his wheelbarrow, now hung from his neck by a leather strap. A pitch fork and wooden rake topped the load.

My sister and I attacked our grandma with questions about the elf. "How come he is so small? Why does he cut weeds in the ditch? Where does he live? How old is he?" She told us he hayed the ditches for a mile or two around to feed his horse. He lived a quarter of a mile up the road in the back of the old Corner Tavern and General Store.

"You mean that old shack near the falling down barn?" I asked.

Our grandma smiled and said, "Yes."

Our wide eyes prompted her to ask if we wanted to walk up there and give him a small loaf of bread, some coffee cake she had baked, and a few onions.

"Onions!" My sister squealed in surprise.

"Yes, he likes onion sandwiches."

This was perfect, now we could see more of this little mystery, see where he lived, and maybe see his horse.

The old house hadn't been painted for years, maybe not since it was built decades ago. The elf, Frank Povlitzski, as grandma had informed us, was standing in the doorway, leaning on the top of a two part door. The top of the door was open and swung back against the side of the house. He smiled. We shoved our offering towards him and said our grandma thought he might find use for some "goodies."

He opened the bottom of the door and waved us in while relieving us of our offerings. The old house had been reduced to one room. There was a wooden table and three mismatched chairs. He motioned for us to sit while putting grandma's gifts on the table. On one end of the room was a bed neatly covered with a brightly colored patchwork quilt. Three or four cats were pouncing on and off the bed, scampering in and out of the still-opened door. A Franklin stove stood a few feet from the wall. It had a stove pipe going up and bending to go out through the back wall. A square two-by-six wooden frame enclosed the base of the stove. It was filled with gravel, a fire precaution. An old, blackened tea kettle and a cooking pot rested on the stove. Nearby on a wall hung a cast iron frying pan. I remember seeing a wood pile alongside the house near the door. The floor seemed to be dirt, covered with wooden pallets. These in turn had several woven rag rugs scattered atop.

In broken English he asked us our names and said his friends called him Frank. He hoped we would be his friends. We said we saw him cutting hay. He asked if we wanted to see his horse. We did.

The barn was in even worse shape than the house. It too was populated with cats. There could not have been a mouse or rat within a mile of the place. The horse was an old and gray gelding. "This is Kuba. He not so smart, but he got a good heart," Frank said it in his best English.

"Where did you get him?" We asked. He said a nearby farmer was going to send him to the glue factory. Frank asked him for the horse.

"Kuba is my friend."

This is how we got to know the man who loved horses. Years later I heard how Frank Povlitzski talked to, walked, rubbed, and waxed a horse for forty-eight hours. The vet gave up on the sickly horse, but the owner wanted to save the gentle old gelding, which his daughter dearly loved. Someone suggested that if anyone could help a horse survive, make it want to live, Povlitzski could. He loved horses, but more importantly horses loved him. This was long before anyone had heard such words as "horse whisperer."

The farmer sent for Frank. Frank asked for horse blankets, horse liniment, curry brushes, water and to be left alone. He wouldn't let the horse stop moving. He led, pushed, and cajoled the horse to walk. Once the horse would lie down it would have been all over. Frank rubbed and curried the horse, kept it warm with blankets, but his soothing talk, all in Polish, kept the horse on its feet. He even sung softly in the horse's ear.

The horse must have understood Polish, for it survived. The owner asked what he owed Frank, "For Kuba, five bushels of oats in December."

Over the years I heard many such stories. They went all the way back to when Frank just arrived in the county, sometime after 1900. If a horse had colic, just get Frank; hours later he'd have convinced another horse to live.

Years after our first encounter with the little elf, my sister and I continued to ask my grandparents and others many questions about him. We were fascinated by this man who seemed to belong in a story book rather than the dirt floor shack up the road.

When Frank arrived in the area he had little trouble in finding work as a hired man on the many farms, especially in spring and summer and through the harvest seasons. He became a popular choice because of his hard work, but mostly because of his way with horses. Very few tractors could be found in the county. Horses were used for plowing, cultivating, harvesting, and hauling. As long as Frank had horses to tend, he was a happy man. Unlike many other hired men, Frank had less of a problem with the bottle and never when a horse needed his attention. Horses loved him. He kept them happy and healthy. Farmers loved him. The horses worked hard for Frank, and Frank saved many a farmer a vet bill or the cost of replacing a horse. Frank was health insurance for horses. No one knew where he came from, and he ignored all questions of his past.

In the fall after the harvest Frank cut wood, pruned orchards, repaired machinery and harnesses. He knew his services were in demand, except in winter. No dummy, Frank made sure that a farmer could be sure of Frank's labor for the following year by keeping him on over the winter. For winter work his only charge was room and board. The rest of the year he needed only a few dollars a month for necessities—the occasional pair of overalls, a shirt, socks, shoes, snuff money, and most of all, treats for horses, anything sweet. Peppermint candy was a favorite.

Whenever Frank had some place to go he walked. Frank was well known and liked by most. Often, he didn't have to walk far. A passerby would offer a ride. Sometimes he asked the farmer he worked for to borrow a horse to ride to church or a dance. Frank was a regular at St. Columba's Catholic Church. The church was largely of Irish worshipers, but as the years had passed the Germans and the Polish of the area were tolerated. Frank sat in the back pew. Of course if a horse needed his attention Frank was in a stall instead of a pew on Sunday. Over the years the uppity men and women of the parish, the moneyed folk, began to complain about Frank's horse liniment and manure smell. Mostly they complained because he paid no pew rent. They wanted him banned from Sunday mass.

There was no need. Frank got wind of the talk and he began spending his Sunday mornings with his horses. He figured that most of the horses he knew were better Christians than those who attended St. Columba's to sit under the stained glass windows they had to pay for.

Years after Frank's death, I had asked if Frank had ever married or had ever had a lady friend. Great Auntie Frances said that during the years that he worked as a hired man, including a few years at Great Uncle Jake's, Frank would walk a mile to the Maples' dance hall. Sometimes he would borrow a horse or a horse and buggy to travel the five or six miles to the Spunk Lake Ballroom or to the Blue Moon Dance Hall. He never had much luck with the ladies, Auntie Frances said, "Maybe it was because he was shy or because of his broken English, but more likely it was because he smelled too much like the horses he loved."

She said, "I remember one gal saying Frankie would rather rub his horses with liniment than cuddle with a gal. What girl wanted to ride a horse or go in a buggy when so many swains had access to a car or truck? His best chance for a roll in the hay was with a horse. No, Frank's one and only was horses, and they loved him. He was luckier than many people who don't know how to love or be loved in return." Auntie Frances proved to be a wise, old philosopher.

After WWI, tractors began to appear on a few farms. Men returned from the war and fewer hired men were needed, yet Frank was always able to find work. The legend of his magic with sick horses grew. Frank was always in demand. However, after WWII the times were catching up with him. First, as after the last war, men returned to work and by now tractors were becoming common. Fewer and fewer farmers kept horses. By 1946 age began to catch up with Frank. Even he didn't know how old he was for sure. He was sure he was past seventy.

After WWI Frank could not find regular work. With no Social Security for him, and certainly no Medicare, a man like Frank was at the mercy of the community. Communities then were sometimes actually communities and tended to their own. That is, except for those holier-than-thou Pharisees who still wanted Frank banned from St. Columba.

At least, in the case of Frank Povlitzski, some members of the community responded. They responded enough to see the man had a place to live and something to eat. The owner of the Corner Tavern and General Store said he could live in a dilapidated dirt floor house back of the bar. Occasionally farmers hired Frank for small jobs or to tend horses in need of special care. Frank was paid a little money for his efforts, but more often and more importantly he was offered preserved fruits and vegetables in Mason jars. Frank became a gardener himself, growing some potatoes, carrots, onions, cabbage, and spinach. He was forever finding fallen limbs and abandoned pieces of wood, stockpiling for the winter. Sometimes the owners of horses that Frank had cared for brought him a load of wood.

Not long after Frank had moved into his "retirement home," he was asked to care for a horse with colic. Frank's walking, talking, and singing kept the horse on its feet, and it survived the attack. While working with the embattled horse, Frank noticed an old horse in a nearby stall. When he asked about the old gelding, the farmer said he was going to destroy the useless old horse. When asked what the farmer owed Frank for his work with the colicky horse, Frank said if the farmer ever wanted him back, he needed the old gelding as his payment this time.

That is how Frank became the owner of his own horse. He then talked the tavern owner into letting him use the falling down old barn to stable his horse. Frank may not have been glib tongued when it came to the ladies, but he was a real Daniel Webster when it came to getting shelter and more for his new friend. The next day Frank walked to the farm and led his companion to a cleaned out stall in the old barn.

Frank knew people almost as well as horses. He knew which ones to ask for each item required for the upkeep of his new dependent. In a few months Frank obtained a water tank, horse trough, two ten gallon cans for water, a scythe, a whet stone, a small wooden wheelbarrow, a little oats, and some hay. A few responded to Frank's request for help and came to restore the tottering barn and winterize it the best they could. Frank's persuasiveness on behalf of his new horse succeeded far beyond his ability to convince any lady in years past to ride his horse and take a tumble in the hay.

Now the eighty year old elf had a dependent. He staked out the horse everyday up until November. Frank found fresh grass, weed, or field stubble. He honed his scythe and cut the ditches; he used a rake, pitch fork and the wooden wheelbarrow to fill the barn for winter. Some neighbors paid Frank for work with a few hay bales and a bustle or two of oats. Some of the same was donated. Frank's new life was devoted to keeping his horse.

"I named him Kuba. In Polish we say he is a Kuba if he is a tricky boy up to no good. I think Kuba tricked the farmer into giving him to me. I know Kuba is tricky. He knows when I have an apple for him or some peppermint candy. He follow me and try to put his nose in my pocket. He tricked me into giving him what he wants. I am tricky, too. I know how to get what I need. Kuba and me, we be tricky together."

After Magrit and I met the friendly Pole, we went to say hello whenever we saw him cutting the ditch. He smiled and said hello, but said, "Now I have work to do. See you later." I think Frank knew that a short visit was not enough for us kids. He seemed to know that we would beg grandma for something to take him later when he had wheeled his load to the barn. Frank liked grandma's home baked bread and her coffee cake with poppy seeds, which they both called *much*, a Polish word. Frank's smile was the biggest when, in a wagon, we lugged a kettle full of grandma's chicken noodle soup—she made her own noodles. Frank would say to tell grandma *dziękuję*. Then he would ask us how we were. How was school? Did we like cats? Sometimes he would show us his treasures: a shiny old horse bit, some polished stones and a few other items. He had these in a large shoe or boot box. There were a couple of large envelopes in the box as well. These he never showed us.

Our visits went on for several years. We continued to ask more people about Frank Povlitzski. Our grandparents were not the only ones who had a hand in Frank's welfare. Of course, Auntie Frances never charged him rent. But others helped as well. On the occasion Frank got sick or hurt while working, Dr. Baum seemed to appear, or someone drove Frank to town to see him. Dr. Baum's gruff bedside manner couldn't compare to Frank's stable side manner when it came to horses. I don't know if the good, gruff doctor sent a bill or if someone else paid it. The same was for any medication needed. I guess this was old fashioned Medicare.

A pair of old boots, used overcoat, mittens, old quilt, stocking cap, and anything else useful to Frank often found its way to his door on Christmas or the Feast of the Three Kings. Even a few pieces of peppermint candy would show up. The candy never passed Frank's lips, but was deeply enjoyed by Kuba.

When we visited grandma or grandpa in spring and summer, my sister and I often saw Frank in his garden and we would help him weed and hoe. Later we helped pull up the carrots and onions and dig the potatoes. Frank had dug a root cellar and fashioned a heavy door to cover it. We helped him bury many carrots and some potatoes in the sandy bottom of the cellar. Frank said later he would cover the stuff with straw so it wouldn't freeze.

We told grandpa that man must really like carrots. He had more carrots than anyone else. Grandpa laughed and said, "You know, horses like carrots, too."

Over the summer and into fall there were always stories told with a smile about raided gardens and apple orchards. I asked grandpa why no one seemed eager to put a stop to this. Again that laugh and smile, "Maybe it's just an elf shopping for his love's Christmas gifts."

As the year passed, Frank's age began to catch up with him. Neighbors and old employers provided more and more help. More wood was dropped off. Meaty hot dishes showed up every few weeks, and a pail of oats or a bale of alfalfa or clover would appear. Frank's garden shrank, but carrots always topped the harvest.

Kuba died in the spring of 1954. As Kuba got older and slower, Frank spent more and more time with him. The last year Frank slept more nights in the barn with Kuba than he did in his own bed. On April 24th, during a heavy rain, Frank slogged through the muddy yard and entered the Tavern, sat down on the short bar stool usually reserved for him, and said, "Kuba died." He put his head on the bar and cried. The bartender set up a glass of the under-the-bar jug of local moonshine, the best. Several glasses later Frank was passed out, head on the bar, snoring.

The moonshine was a good sedative. Frank woke up laying in his own bed, covered with his quilt. Out of habit he went to the barn. When he found Kuba's empty stall, he remembered and headed for the back door of the Tavern. He was told that Kuba's former owner had the horse removed and buried out back of the barn. Frank asked for a marker for his Kuba.

As the leaves of fall turned to their glory, Frank Povlitzski, too, was returned to his glory. After his horse died Frank was often heard to mumble both in Polish and broken English, "No Kuba, why live?"

In spite of opposition from the snobs of the parish, Father Stangler said a Requiem Mass for Frank and preached a sermon worthy of the man who loved horses. Father also ordered him to be buried in the far corner of the cemetery behind the church yard. An

inexpensive flat marker was sunken in to ground level so a mower could pass over it. The marker read:
FRANCIS POVLITZSKI
18?? – 1954

My sister Magrit and I were taken to the funeral by my grandparents. Later we walked up the road to watch as the locals cleaned out Frank's house. As we watched, a neighbor who knew us and of our friendship with Frank, handed us the boot box Frank had shown us. "Frank told us to be sure we gave these to his little friends when the time came." We looked inside to see the shiny horse bit, a part of Kuba's halter, the pretty rocks and two big envelopes. We were also given his wooden wheelbarrow.

We often took out Frank's treasure as we talked about him, but as we grew into our teens and then into adulthood, the box got put away, forgotten.

Years later when Magrit and I were visiting our mother, we got to talking about the friendly elf. My mother retrieved the box. The smaller of the envelopes contained letters written to Frank but were all in Polish. We didn't even look into the second envelope, figuring it was of the same, but we enjoyed telling Frank stories.

I took the small envelope home. My ever curious mind lead me to the Slavic Languages Department at the University of Minnesota. I paid to have the letters translated. They turned out to be from Frank's relatives. They wondered how he was doing. They said he was not to worry. No one made any trouble for them when Francis ran away from his cavalry unit. Frank would be happy to know that the sergeant Frank had beaten up for abusing the horses was finally put in the stockade. No one blamed Frank for defending his horses.

The translator asked if I noticed that the letters were addressed to Frank in Saratoga Springs, New York. I hadn't. On Christmas Eve of that year, as our family gathered at our parents, I told them what was in Frank's letters. I asked my mother if she could get the box, and we would all look at the second envelope. It was larger and chucked full of newspaper clippings from the Saratoga Springs Gazette, all dated in the 1890's. One had a headline: FRANCIS POVLITZSKI- JOCKEY OF THE YEAR- 1898.

The article said, the 5'1" – 112 pound jockey was in his eighth season at Saratoga Raceway. He was a Polish immigrant who came to the raceway as a groomsman and hat rider. He soon became an apprentice jockey. He was now the track's top money winner and reigning Jockey of the Year for four years running. Everybody liked the good natured, shy, "Hard working Pole."

Other articles traced Frank's Jockey of the Year awards. At the bottom of the pile of articles was one with a headline: POLISH PRINCE DESTROYED. The article related that Frank Povlitzski's favorite horse, third year running Horse of the Year, Polish Prince, stumbled out of the gate, fell and broke a leg. The articles further stated that Polish Prince had to be destroyed, but jockey, Povlitzski, walked away unscathed.

Apparently, Frank kept walking. As I sorted through the clippings again I found another article that indicated Frank never took another mount that season. In fact no one knew of his present whereabouts.

We now had a more complete story, a story that, for my sister and me, began in a ditch in front of our grandparent's house in 1951. The story for Frank began in the 1860s in Poland, then to the Polish Calvary and to Saratoga, New York, and from there to the farms near Maples, Minnesota. The story ended in a cemetery behind St. Columba's Church.

Years after the Christmas Eve newspaper gifts, Magrit told me we were going for a ride. I got in her car thinking it was a fall drive to look at the leaves. Instead it was a trip down memory lane to the cemetery at St. Columba's. She walked me to the far corner of the graveyard, stopped, stood and smiled. I looked down. Instead of a flat marker above Frank's grave, I saw a small granite stone in beautiful Cold Spring red. Etched into it was:
FRANCIS (FRANK) POVLITZSKI
1865 – 1954
THE POLISH PRINCE

In front of that stone was a beautifully etched horse in the same Cold Spring red.

50

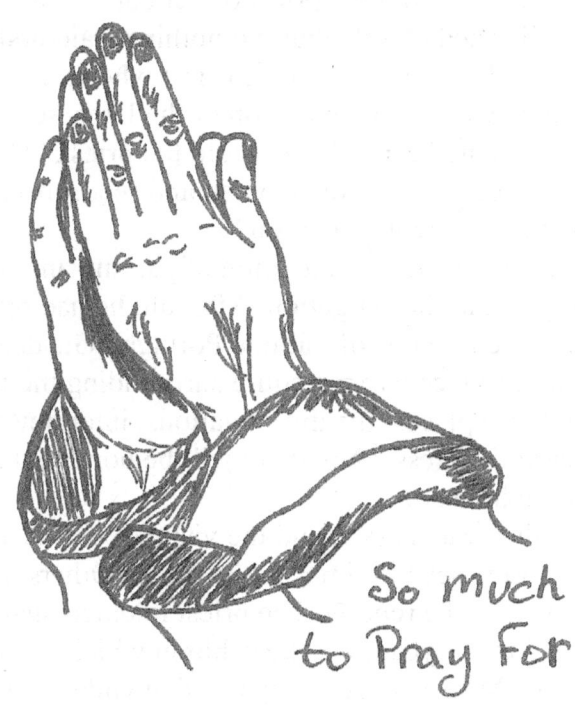

So much to Pray For

In Polish, she prayed, "Dear Blessed Mother, guide me in my actions. As you must know I continue to have visions, see things. Sometimes I see things before they happen and sometimes while they happen. This time I saw the Polish man from Crossing shoot the German. I fear for the soul of Leopold Polanski. I pray he will seek forgiveness. Please guide me. What am I to do?"

The old lady didn't know if she was blessed or plagued by her visions. For a long time she told no one. When Mary, the mother of Jesus, appeared several times, she felt she must tell the parish priest at St. Sophie's in the little town of the same name. She had mentioned her visions to some of her relatives; but all they did was tell her she only had dreams, that none of this was true. Still, she knew the visions were real. Many of them came in the daytime when she was wide awake. She guessed her relatives were afraid that others would make fun of her, and them.

Finally, she told the priest of her conversations with the Virgin. He listened closely, but did nothing, said nothing. After more visions she went back to the priest who relented and said he would seek advice from the bishop of the Diocese of Middleton. The bishop listened carefully and told the priest, "Go back to your parish; keep council with the woman and report back to me if and when you have more information."

The bishop had no intention of passing any of this along or conducting further investigation. After all, he had read about the hassles that the Bishops of Fatima, Portugal, Guadeloupe, Mexico, and Lourdes, France had to endure surrounding the Blessed Mother visions in those places: the investigations, interviews, and then the clamoring of the press. "No, there will be none of that here," he said aloud to himself.

As the years passed and the visions continued, the old woman reported several times to the priest. Others in his parish began to believe the reports. The priest relented again and said a Mass or two every year near the cabin in which the saintly woman lived. The Masses were always well attended. The priest never reported any of this to the bishop. The bishop had heard about the Masses but was content as long as none of this went beyond St. Sophie's and the neighboring area.

However, the new vision about the shooting in Crossing troubled the old lady. After all, she was Polish and so was Polanski. She feared for his soul, and her Polish pride demanded she help this man who shared her heritage. She kept many Polish customs: she spoke the language of her birth; she kept old traditions; she hung her Christmas tree upside down. She knew that pride was one of the Seven Deadly Sins, but she was sure the Good Lord understood the need to keep her Polish traditions, and help all people, but especially the Polish. She was sure the Virgin wanted her to help.

She did not trust the priest at St. Sophie's to help her decide what to do. She would walk to a neighboring town and speak to the priest there and ask for his help. On an early spring day she set out in the mist, cold, and damp at six in the morning. She dressed her almost eighty-year-old wiry frame in a long cotton dress and draped an old moth-eaten woolen cape around her. She tied a babushka around her head and pulled a woolen knit cap over it. She wore her brother's old work shoes. Her gloved hands made use of her willow cane with one hand while her rosary dangled from the other.

As she trudged the seven miles to the parish house of St. Columba in Maple, she prayed eight rosaries to the Lady of her Visions, all forty decades, "Hail Mary, full of grace…" She prayed for the soul of Leopold Polanski. She prayed that the priest would heed her request to drive her to see the Sheriff of Wilson County. She prayed her skinny legs would stand the test of the journey. She offered up her pain toward those goals.

Five hours after setting out, the old lady knocked on the parish house door. The housekeeper answered and demanded to know what she wanted. The old lady's voice cracked as she spoke, "Could I please to have a glass of water, and could I see Father Toole."

"I'll get you the water, and as for the Father, I don't know if he has time. Give me your name and where you are from."

With the information in hand the housekeeper set off for the back of the house. The old lady was sure she heard the crying of a baby come down the stairway from the second story. She full well knew of the rumors of a baby, the housekeeper, and the priest. But the old lady paid no attention to rumors, for she knew that the county was rumor-chucked with stories of a wacky old Pole who talked with ghosts, the saints, and perhaps the devil. Others spoke of her talking to God Himself. "No, rumors were not to be heeded."

Fr. Toole entered the sitting room and asked what he could do for her. He had recognized her name and was aware of the stories of the visions of the Holy Mother. She told him of her long walk and her vision of the shooting in Crossing: that she "had seen Polanski shoot the German, Huntz Goering."

She asked, "Would ya please to take me to see Sheriff Fennon Flarehty? You are Irish, he is Irish. If you ask him he will see me." Father Toole responded as asked, and after giving the old lady a cheese sandwich and more water, they set off in Fr. Toole's Model T.

Flarehty listened to the supposed vision of a shooting in Crossing. He had heard of such from his deputies. The gossip had gravitated from the now legally reopened bars of rural Wilson County, to those of the county seat in Middleton. The bar telegraph worked with telepathic speed.

Flarehty didn't want to add grist to the rumor mill. At the same time he couldn't let the festering story go unchecked. He feared the FBI would resume snooping in Wilson County. Since the repeal of the Volstead Act, the FBI and Treasury men used any excuse to avoid budget cuts. They were familiar with Wilson County's moonshining habit of the Prohibition Era, which had ended more than a year earlier. However, the distilling of Minnesota 13 and its inferior cousins had not. Elected peace officers and county attorneys had a financial interest in keeping cheaper, non-taxed, high quality liquor flowing via the cooking of Central Minnesota corn.

Just as the telegraph tree from the Sheriff's office to the various sugar sellers, shiners, and runners was still active, a reverse system of snitchers kept Flarehty informed of the activities in various hamlets of the county. He made a call to set up a fishing trip to Blanchard Dam for catching crappies and various other things. Axel Hildegaard, one of the few Swedes living in Crossing, drove to the Mississippi River to catch some needed cash as well as his beloved crappies. By the time Flarehty got there, the handyman carpenter had already used his twelve foot cane pole to land more than his limit of the shining black and silver pan fish.

Sheriff Flarehty used his new rod and reel, but mainly fished for information. "Ya, dar vas a shooting. Dis here Polack, Leopold Polanski, gut shot the German, Huntz Goering, on da main street ov Crossing."

Flarehty asked, "Who is this Polanski?"

"He vas not a goot farmer and not the bess moonshiner. Day say he tryt many times to steal a boiler, or copper tubing, and even once a still from Huntz. Ya see, Huntz by dat time hat tree stills hidden under tree straw stack blown pig barns on da far en of his pig yard, near vere da tamarack svamp on part of his farm. Ya know, dat pig shit can mask any smell. Oh, boy, dem Feds quit looking for Goering's cookers."

"So why did the Pole shoot Goering?"

"Goering say to everyone in town Polanski vas a poor teef. Day say Huntz look for Polanski's still dat vas deep in dat same tamarack svamp. Ya see, Goering vas on one en of da svamp and Polanski vas the udder.

"One guy tolt me dat a couple a times ven one ov dem tryt to steal from da udder, shots rung."

Flarehty asked to hear more about Polanski. "Oh, vait a second. Look at my cork, down and avay. It must be a big crappie." Axel Hildegaard struggled to land his big "crappie." When he did, Flarehty said, "That looks like a largemouth bass; it must be five pounds."

"No, I tink it's a big, Svedish crappie. I can't keep bass, da season is not open yet. Dis Svedish crappie vill be a meal for the vife and kits."

Flarehty, fishing for more information, agreed it was one hell of a crappie, and again asked for more on the Pole.

As Axel roamed up and down the river bank swinging his cane pole into the current and onto the quiet bays, he rambled on. He explained that Polanski was just a good guy. Not much of a farmer, but he could make his bank payments with the help of his still. His shine couldn't get the higher prices of his neighbor, but was enough to get the payments made. Even today, he sold enough to keep the bank away. "Day say he got a'nuff money in da goot days to bury some in coffee cans in his yart. He hope da kits and vife vith her garten don't dig up dem cans. He got tree kits and a vife, Marlys, I tink."

"Okay, tell me about Goering."

Hildegaard figured he didn't have enough fish yet, so why not tell the Sheriff more, "Goering vas a goot pig man. Before Volstead he hat a 120 acre farm. He vorked hart and vorked his tree kits and vife harter. He knew how to make his own viskey from his grandat. Now in 1935 he hat a 320 acre farm and owned tree smaller farms in da county."

As Flarehty trailed after the nomad fishermen, he got his fancy shoes wet when the Swede, now shoeless, waded into the river to try for bigger "crappies," and to irritate Flarehty. Flarehty asked Axel, "Who ran those farms and how did he get them?" Hildegaard told him that his two sons and a son-in-law operated the farms. Goering's kids were more like slaves. He treated them like the sharecroppers in Dixie. The kids never seemed to have any money after Huntz took his share. The kids hated him even more than his wife did.

"Ya ask how he got dem farms and his more acres? Dis here Depression, da ya call it? It mate for ruff times for mos farms in da area. Da German farmers vent to der kin to keep da damn banks from foreclosing. Ya see, in da '20s tings vas pretty goot. Banks lent money so da farmers coot get bicker and make more money. But da goot times din last, and den da Depression.

"Huntz vas making da money on da shine. Day say his vas da bess, and he know how to get a buck outa dem tight Svedes in Dakota. Vit his money, first he lent some to begging Germans who knew he hat da cash, but den he treat dem like his kits, no von borrow money. Huntz joost vait for dem banks to foreclose and bought da farms for cheap."

Flarehty said, "Now I know why the Germans hate him, too."

Wilson County was almost all Catholic, but the German, Polish, and Irish disliked each other so much that many of the small towns had two Catholic churches. At one end was a German church, while at the other end was a Polish or Irish church. The Italians, French, and Spanish were not represented well, if at all, in Wilson County. The few Scandinavian Lutherans were tolerated as long as their relatives stayed outside of the county.

"You said everybody in Crossing hated Huntz? Then how come no one turned him into the Feds about his stills. The Feds offered rewards."

Hildegaard, now perched on a big rock further down river, waited until the frustrated and winded Sheriff caught up. He explained that everyone was afraid of that man. He was short, only five feet eight inches, but his shoulders were as wide as a keg and his fists looked like the hams of his hogs. Many owed him money and were too afraid he would take their farms. Others figured if they squealed on him, he would squeal on them. Making money on the shine was better than getting Huntz.

Evidently, some still got word to the G-men, but when they went to search his pig barns, the stink from the pig shit was so bad they gave it up. The stink covered up the sweet smell of cooking shine. Huntz never cleaned any pig shit from that end of his pig run for over twenty years. Huntz knew when the Feds were coming and which pig barn they had a warrant to search. When they tore his pig barn to pieces, they only found enough pig shit to fertilize twenty acres."

Flarehty asked how Goering knew what was coming.

"Oh, some of da Feds are like you and da County Attorney. Day like money more den day like doing da yob," laughed Hildegard as he said it.

Hildegaard went on to tell him how Goering had worked his wife, Alice, so hard doing house and farm work and how he physically abused her. This contributed to her faltering health. He also told how Goering bought a new Packard, a Capone car. He was a superior mechanic and metal worker. He built his own stills and, rumor had it, that he modified his Packard, enabling him to haul gallons of moonshine on his many trips to North Dakota "ta visit da relatifs."

One of these trips to Dakota produced a blonde, teenage housekeeper; "ta help vith da sick old lady." Hildegaard said, "Da young blondt dislike her yob and Huntz in a few veeks."

Then, Huntz told the neighbors that Alice was so sick, "Dat I haf ta moof her to a sanitarium in Sioux Falls," Huntz and his Packard disappeared for four days. No one saw Alice leave with him. In fact, no one ever saw Alice again. But Huntz came home flashing more money.

Hildegaard went on to say that the pretty teenage housekeeper disappeared soon after. "She vent ta vork for udder relatifs in da Cities," Huntz told anyone who would listen. Stories of the young girl having had duties of not only making Huntz's bed, but also warming it, added to the rumors of her running away. Huntz's kids confirmed the bed warming rumors, even more reason why they hated him. Their sickly mother had to put up with all of this in the next bedroom.

By this time Axel Hildegaard seemed about ready to pack it in. He had two five gallon pails half full of crappies and figured he had delivered enough information to Flarehty to earn his stipend.

Sensing this, Flarehty went to his used LaSalle and freed up a crock jug from the wheel well of his trunk. He offered a swig to the Swede. It was the good stuff. After a few more slugs and the offer of the rest of the jug, the Swede found a new voice and continued with the story.

The story found Huntz with several more trips to the North Dakota relatives. Each trip produced a happier Huntz with more money and a new blonde, teenage girl. A few months after the arrival of a new girl, she too was nowhere to be seen. Huntz sent her to relatives in Chicago, he said. Another trip northwest and another shapely young blonde, she lasted nearly six months. "She hat lef for a yob in Dalute."

By this time, Hildegaard said, "I don't tink der is anyone vitin fifteen miles of Crossing dat don't hate old Huntz. Day all pray, even my vife, Bente, dat da goot Lort vill destroy dat dirty…"

"Okay, I get all that, but what about the shooting of Goering?" asked Flarehty.

Axel told the Sheriff that, after the demand, and the price, of moonshine had dropped, Polanski was having trouble making his bank payments on the farm. He was a terrific smear player. The man could talk to a deck of cards, and they seemed to talk back. He had a knack for the game and was lucky to boot. His luck in everything else was bad, but smear… He knew the German considered himself to be the best smear player in the county. Huntz could usually be found on Saturday night, now that Prohibition had ended, at the California Wine House in Crossing.

Most of the county bars, as was the case before 1919, had primarily an ethnic clientele, but the California Wine House was operated by a genial Hungarian and attracted all who could afford it. It offered the best and most expensive drinks, including the best hooch if you knew the code words in asking for it. It offered good food as well.

Hildegaard continued, "Da German vas der taking on all foolish a'nuff to tink day coot beat him at smear. Dis is how Polanski hope to make his nex payment."

The Swede went on, "The Pole valked into da Vine House on dat April Saturday night. He hollert ofer da noise of da crowd, 'Hey, Goering, I hear you tink you are da bess smear player in da county.'

"'You hert right, you dumb Polack.'

"'Vell, you hasn't play me,' challenged Polanski as he vaved his fist full of dollar bills. 'I haf twenney fife dollars. Vill dat be a'nuff to buy kraut for your hogs?'"

Huntz knocked all the bottles off his table and slapped a deck of cards on it, yelling, "Deal." Polanski was indeed good at his game, the Swede related. Within an hour he had fifty dollars of the German's money. Huntz was shocked, and by that time a little soberer. He had thought the Pole an easy mark. Polanski gathered his loot and got up to leave. Huntz Goering stood and screamed, "You lucky Polander, if ya are so goot, give me von more game for fifty dollars."

They sat down and began to play. At first Polanski thought his luck and skill had run out, but now he was sure Goering was cheating and accused him in front of all. The German jumped up, raised his fists and demanded that the Pole do the same. "I vill teach ya ta call me cheater."
The Wine House owner, baseball bat in hand, approached and told them, "Take it outside or you will feel the sting of my Louisville Slugger."

Goering, Polanski, and the majority of the crowd headed for the door. Huntz turned and commanded, "Any von who comes out dis door vill meet my fists nex." No one followed.

As the two ex-card players squared off in the street, Polanski realized that his small wiry frame was no match for this ham fisted Goliath. He quickly reached into the pocket of his barn coat. The pocket exploded with the shot from a .22 pistol that caught Goering in the gut. Polanski turned back into the Wine House, picked up all of the money, walked home, kissed his wife and went to bed. At least that was how Hildegaard put it.

The Swede went on with the story. As Goering had instructed, no one stepped out of the California Wine House to help him. No one in the entire town came to aid the bleeding German. Some say they heard prayers of thanks as Huntz Goering bled to death in the main street of Crossing.

Flarehty added, "The prayers must have been long and devout. The coroner said it must have taken close to half an hour to drain him."

Hildegaard said, "Time to go. I haf a'nuff fish for a Friday fish fry for all my Catlick frens."

A day after the fishing expedition, Flarehty sent deputies to arrest Leopold Polanski. The county attorney sent other deputies to obtain witnesses to testify in court. What they heard was, "Oh, yes, Polanski shot da German. I dint see it, but I know he dit it."

"Ya, dats vat happen. A guy tolt me, but I can't remember vat the guy's name vas."

"Yes, I heard that, too. I live in the place above, across from the California Wine House. I heard the shot, but I had the shutter pulled."

Variations of these stories repeated themselves over a dozen times, with many saying they knew Huntz cheated. The County Attorney said, "The murder was like Lady Godiva's ride through Coventry without a Peeping Tom, Pole or German who could see. They all saw "nutting.""

Wilson County could hold Polanski for a few days, but without witnesses the Pole would go free. The Polish were protecting their own. The Germans, while not admitting it, were thanking the angel or the devil that God sent to answer their prayers. Those who owed "The German" money would not have to pay, so why should they speak up? Friends of Huntz's wife, Alice, said, "He deserved worse." His kids were released from their serfdom and now each had a farm and 320 more acres to divide. All others in the area knew better than to disturb the new peace that descended in and around Crossing.

On a late May night, before Polanski had to be charged or released, the weather had taken a turn. The warm, sunny temperatures had turned into an electrically humid, cloud-churning day with stifling heat. Polanski baked in his jail cell which felt more like a room bordering the south side of hell. He began to fear he had already arrived in there as punishment for shooting

The German. Soon sheets of rain swept the jail. The low rumbling clouds and repeated walls of rain made visibility near impossible. Middleton street lights could not be seen. The electric lights in the jailhouse began to flicker and then died. Flashes of purple lighting captured the fear of jailers and prisoners alike. Then a sudden bolt of blinding light appeared in the northeast window of Polanski's cell. This was immediately followed by a booming blast that shook the foundation of the old building.

Following the flash of searing light, darkness filled the cell. Slowly a dim light was framed by the jail cell window. The light rapidly grew in size and brightness. The wind hollowed. The rain pounded. Flames now filled the window's frame. Polanski was sure he could hear the crackling fire of hell.

He demanded to know what was happening. The jailer, Jake Jablanski, told him, "It's the end of the world - Armageddon - the powers of good and evil are fighting for control of all creation." Jablanski may even have believed what he had just said.

On his knees, Leopold demanded to see a priest. Jablanski donned all the rain gear he could find and headed for the parish house of the Church of the Seraphim, two blocks to the northeast. He could see a towering inferno rising from the roof of the church and attacking the steeple. The blaze was caused by the lightning strike that had sent Polanski to his knees.

Jablanski found young Fr. John Denehry among those clustered near the church, gazing at the flaming steeple and roof. As the Middleton fire brigade raced toward the flames reaching to set fire to the low clouds, Fr. Denehry dutifully marched the other way to the jail to tend to Polanski's soul.

Polanski, still on his knees, praying, saw the good priest and barked out for all to hear, "Bless me Fodder, for I haf sin. I shot dat dirty bas- excuse me, Fodder, I kilt Huntz Goering. May da Lord safe my soul."

The priest replied, "Your sin is forgiven."

The confession of Leopold Polanski answered many prayers, but other new prayers still awaited heavenly responses. The county attorney now had witnesses: the over hearers of Polanski's confession. He could now go to trial, but wondered if he

could seat a jury that would convict. Maryls Polanski needed her husband home on the farm to meet the bank payments and provide for her and their three children. Flarehty worried that the fallout from the trial might affect his re-election campaign, both at the ballot box and in the re-election coffers that produced votes.
The still active moonshine practitioners needed protection from a closer look by all, especially from the Department of the Treasury and the FBI.

 A year before all of this began, a young Irish attorney hung his shingle in Middleton. He had a law degree from an ivied school back east. He had more brain power than most, and a way with words that held sway with any audience. He wanted to make a name for himself without the help of family and friends. Thus the shingle hanging, as they said back east, "In the land of the great unwashed backwoods barbarians." He had one more need, a big case to make his mark. He prayed for such.

 As the Polanski case headed for trial, finding an attorney to defend him was an issue. No one wanted the job, and the judge was reluctant to appoint a local. The young Irish attorney made it known that for the right fee he would defend Polanski and get him off with only "a little jail time."

 Even more numerous than all the new prayers, rumors continued to play a part. The rumors of continued moonshining, the rumors of a nasty end to the life of Alice Goering that had nothing to do with a faraway sanitarium, the rumors of the North Dakota housekeepers who may not have run away, the rumors of Polanski's buried coffee cans. The Irish lawyer talked much of rumors and a need to help Polanski. There were further rumors of Sunday collection baskets in the churches of the county. Polish, Germa, and even Irish appeared with donations for the defense. Other rumors of those who had the most to lose with a trial made donations. There were rumors that the prayers of Maryls Polanski were answered as she dug up more garden space so she could feed her children. This led her to uprooting a coffee can loaded with cash. The Irish bars were filled with rumors of an Irish leprechaun who planted the can at the end of her rainbow garden. The Irish lawyer seemed to be smiling.

But to be sure, the young Irish lawyer, with a pot full of money, began to make his mark in Wilson County. He marched into the Romanesque style Wilson County Courthouse and glibly explained to the county attorney how all would benefit from a lesser charge against Polanski. The plea bargain would have Polanski serve a year and a day in the state penitentiary, which just happened to be in Middleton. No G-men would be involved. Re-election bids for Sheriff and County Attorney would be enhanced. Maryls Polanski could visit her husband at "Grey Stone College." Unsaid but understood, a young lawyer could make his mark.

Just in case the county attorney would not accept the reduced charges and sentence, the young lawyer guaranteed Polanski would testify about Goering's stills. Further information from the young lawyer convinced the County Attorney to agree. Polanski would plead guilty and be allowed to testify about the contents of Goering's pig yard that might ease many minds concerning the disappearances of certain people.

The trial began just after the Fourth of July. Leopold Polanski pleaded guilty to involuntary manslaughter. The pistol that shot out the pocket of Polanski's barn coat and put a hole in Goering's gut went off "accidentally" as Polanski grabbed for it with the intent to scare Goering.

Polanski testified that for several years before the shooting, he had spied on "The German" late at night in an attempt to recover "certain items," that he was convinced Goering had stolen from him. "I vas vatching him one night, I seen him drag vat look like a body to da far swampy part ov his hog yard and pile on mutt and pig sh- sorry, your honor, pig manure. Da smell of dat yard vas ten times more den da smell of dos ol boots Huntz hat. Den he vent back to his pig barns and let dem damn big Spotted Pole in China's loose. As dem hogs began to root, fight and feast on da stuff he drag out der, he yelled, 'Ya got ta feet dem damn svine hounts.'"

The judge sentenced Leopold Polanski to a year and a day to include time served. He would be out in time to plant his oats and corn in the spring.

When deputies and a dozen or so curious volunteers donned knee boots and bandanas covering their noses, they unearthed parts of four sets of bones in the swampy end of Goering's hog yard. The University of Minnesota Medical School said they belonged to four different women: one about sixty years old and the others between the ages of sixteen and twenty-two.

The prayers of three North Dakota families were only partially answered; they now knew of the whereabouts of their daughters. The hatred of Goering's children for their father only deepened. They had a German priest say a Requiem Mass before their mother's burial.

Middleton County moonshiners bought more sugar and cooked more corn. They also donated to the Sunday collection baskets in prayers of thanksgiving.

Sheriff Flarehty celebrated his notoriety for having solved the Dakota women's disappearances, as well as confirming Goering's murder of his wife. He hoisted a jug of Minnesota 13 and passed it on to his financial supporters for re-election. The county attorney did as well for his backers.

The young Irish lawyer quietly gave thanks on every St. Patrick's Day and prayed for more. Those prayers were answered in the form of a judgeship many years later.

The old lady, having recovered her strength from her trek to St. Columba's, gave her thanks in Polish to the Blessed Lady in front of her shrine. "Hail Mary, thank you for helping Leopold find his way and repenting for his shooting that dirty Goering. Please see that Alice finds a place near you in heaven. Thank you for seeing that Marlys and her children have a husband and father returning soon. I will ask the priest at St. Sophie's to come here for a special Mass, again, dziękuję."

## Boxcars and Beer

"Gus, you have to call the game," Dick Jensen of the Middleton Umpires Association pleaded. "Nobody else will touch it except old Henry Schumann, and he is no good behind the plate. He agreed to take the bases. He said he worked with you before, and the two of you work well together."

I shot back, "Nobody else is dumb enough to take that set up. It has disaster written all over it."

If this was not a playoff game between two teams from different leagues, such a powder keg game would not be played. Thirty years ago, the small Wilson County towns of Deep Wells and Double Depot last met. The feud started when both town teams filed charges with the State Amateur Baseball Association about attempted umpire bribery.

Umpire Henry Terwey reported that he had received two hundred dollars cash in the mail with instructions to call the game in such a way to ensure Double Depot would win. If he did the job as instructed, three hundred more would follow. Deep Wells wanted Double Depot ousted from state amateur baseball. Double Depot retaliated, claiming Deep Wells had set up the whole scheme to get them banned; therefore, they wanted Deep Wells banned. Since no evidence of who did what, other than the typed letter and the money, was forthcoming, nothing became of the accusations. The game was not played, and the two towns never scheduled a game against each other after that. Since then each team played in a different classification. There was no chance of a playoff for a state tourney berth. That changed when the Double Depot Boxcars were moved up to Class B competition. They were slated to meet the Deep Wells Brewers in a playoff for a spot in the state tourney.

The feud was bitter. Deep Wells, as it's team name suggested, brewed one of the most popular beers in Minnesota. For thirty years no bar in Double Depot offered it for sale. The Double Depot bakery was the toast of the county. It's breads and famous Double Depot pastries were sold in most grocery stores in Wilson County, but they had not been available in Deep Wells since the feud began.

The pastries were called Boxcars. Think of a long john built like a flatbed train car, with sides of the same dough. The sided flat car had a thick layer of cheesecake at the bottom which in turn was covered by a blueberry, cherry, gooseberry, or chocolate filling. Which flavor would depend on which day you showed up to buy. You couldn't be sure which you would get, but you would be sure of the best pastry in the county. Boxcars sold by the trainload.

Double Depot got its name because the town had two different names. The Great Northern Railway workers had nailed the name Fen on the depot. The workers didn't like the swamp south of the rail line and left the town with the name. The name became unpopular with the townspeople when they learned that a fen was a swamp.

A few years later the Soo Line Railroad built its tracks from western Minnesota to Duluth to haul grain to the lakeport for shipping. Since the town had already been dubbed Fen, the Soo rail builders tagged Second City on the depot on the far west side of town.

The town council was not satisfied with either name. They voted to rename the town. Dozens of names were suggested and the ensuing campaign for a new name generated so much animosity the council put an end to all discussion. They directed the US Post Office to name the town Double Depot.

Ironically, the said freight depots were used less and less and finally closed. All that remains next to the old buildings on either track is a long siding spur adjacent to the main line.

Deep Wells naturally got its name from the deep, cold artesian wells that fed the brewhouse.

The two-town feud rekindled as a result of the state playoff. An agreement was struck with the help of the State Amateur Baseball Association, the Middleton Umpires Association, and the managers of the respective teams to play the game in Meeker, Minnesota some thirty miles from either town. Meeker had an active baseball association which agreed to host the game in their beautifully manicured ballpark. Its grandstand could easily seat 1500. The town fathers rented additional portable seating and expected a crowd of over 3000. Meeker bars and restaurants salivated when they thought of the game day crowd.

The only hurdle left was finding someone stupid enough to call balls and strikes. Willy Hiltz, the Brewer manager, asked for me. I had umpired high school and American Legion games for him. He liked my plate work. John Porter, the Boxcar manager, also found me acceptable. I had called Legion games for him. Since I taught with him, I did not do Double Depot high school games. Oddly enough, I had not had either team in a town game in the eight years I had been umpiring. Porter said he trusted me to call an unbiased game.

I refused. Every official at the meeting implored me to accept. "We will pay you double."

"Gentlemen, this is a no-win situation. The feud aside, I teach in Double Depot. I know almost all the team members. I play softball with some and half of them I have had in the classroom. On the other side Willy Hiltz and I are shirttail relatives. I have known him for 16 years and played baseball with and against him. No matter what I call someone will accuse me of favoritism. I will be afraid to check my mail in case I'm offered something worse than a bribe."

"Gus," countered Wally Harris of the State Amateur Baseball Association, "if you don't take the game, we have no alternative but to call a forfeit for each team. Neither will advance to the state tournament. When people from both towns find out why the game won't be played, you'll have to move out of Wilson County."

"If I do take it, I'll probably have to move out anyhow. What about umpires from the Twin Cities, Duluth, Marshall, anybody not from the area?" I asked.

"We already tried. The history of the two towns is a state legend. Nobody will take it. We tried."

"This is blackmail," I shouted.

Then both John Porter and Willy Hiltz begged me to accept. Both said they would tell all in their towns how good I was and how they trusted my judgement.

"Double pay for Harry Schumann and me."

"Agreed."

• • •

Game day arrived as did thunder, lightning and rain. The Saturday two o'clock start was suspended. Because of the volatility surrounding the game, the State Amateur Association was in charge. They wanted the game played. The Meeker town merchants wanted the game played. The 3000 plus fans huddled in their cars wanted the game played. Consultation with the U.S. Weather Bureau in Middleton suggested a 3:30 window. We waited.

With time to kill, most of the ticket holders went from their cars to the bars and restaurants. This hamlet could count at least five bars and a few more eateries. Truckloads of Deep Wells Special Brew were stacked to the ceiling in every bar. An equal number of cases of Hamm's Beer from "The Land of Skyblue Waters," the choice of the Double Depot imbibers, was stacked as high and as deep. By 3:30 the crowd was well oiled.

Herb Bruening, the crafty forty-some-year-old lefty, offered the first pitch at 4:02 for the Boxcars. It seemed like Bruening had been around forever. I know he had me by at least 15 years. Tom Zimmer, a flame throwing right hander, toed the mound for the Brewers. He grew up in Deep Wells and had pitched two years for Middleton State College. Scouts believed he would sign a professional contract before next spring. The Meeker baseball club had performed a near miracle to get the field in such good shape.

Both pitchers seemed to be totally in control. After four innings there was still no score. Zimmer surrendered one hit while Bruening gave up a weak single in each inning. The crowd seemed calm as not one hitter, pitcher, or catcher barked about a called ball or strike.

Things got a little dicey in the fifth. A Boxcar batter hit a towering pop-up to the right side of the infield. Although the rains had not returned, strong winds were now blowing in from left field. The gargantuan first basemen for the Brewers, 36-year-old Stan Heck, stared at the second basemen who ran toward the first baseline pointing toward the grandstand yelling, "The wind. The wind." The big oaf at first got his brain functioning, looked up and trundled as fast as he could, chasing the pop-up. His path flattened Harry Schumann, slowing the infielder enough to miss the foul ball.

Harry lay on the grass not moving. I ran to him as players from both teams gathered around. Over a minute passed before Harry opened an eye and said, "Did he catch it? I lost track." By this time Carol, his wife of forty-three years, was pushing her way onto the field. When she got to him she knelt and blurted out, "Harry, Harry talk to me."

"What's the matter? You need money for a hot dog?" winking Harry said. Then he looked at the big old first baseman and said, "I think you broke my collarbone."

By that time the Meeker volunteer fire department was on the field with the emergency van and the stretcher ready to move Harry off to the hospital 30 miles away.

Harry's wife looked at them and then at Harry. "Come on, Harry, I'll drive you myself in the car. I can smell the beer on these guys every time they exhale." Harry was helped to his feet by his good arm, and off the two went.

After consultation with both managers and every official they could dig up, a decision was made. They would continue the game with one umpire. What started out as a difficult task just went beyond difficult. I looked up at the rolling clouds and said, "Thanks, Lord. Just what I needed."

The next inning with the Boxcars batting, the lefty hitting center fielder chopped a ball down the first base line. Stan Heck, the annihilator of Harry Schumann, danced to the foul line, reached into foul territory and snatched the ball while tagging the bag. I swept my arm toward the stands indicating a foul ball. Stan went wild. I walked away while Willy Hiltz came out to quiet Stan down. He didn't want to lose a good hitter to an ejection.

Not to be a smart alec but to show I had no bias, between innings I pulled the rule book out of my pocket and walked over to the Brewers' dugout. "Stan, here, look at this. The rule states that the position of the ball, not the player, determines fair or foul." Stan threw the book to the ground, stomped on it and yelled, "The damn book is wrong."

In the seventh inning Double Depot got a runner on first with no out. A sacrifice bunt put him on second. The next batter lined a single to center. The runner from second tried to score. The throw beat him to the plate. Micky Legget, the catcher, applied the tag and, before I could think, I yelled and signaled "safe." Micky jumped up and screamed, "Gus, are you nuts. The throw easily beat him. He slid right into my mitt."

The heavily drinking crowd went wild. Popcorn boxes, plastic cups and beer cans flew from the stands. Willy Hiltz charged home plate.

I put my hands up to signal stop. "Before either of you say or do things you will regret, listen to me," I barked. They did.

"Micky, show me exactly what you did."

Micky got down on one knee, placed his catcher's mitt with the ball in it, covered with his free hand, and placed it in the middle of home plate. I told him not to move. "Now, Micky, look at your glove. What happens before the runner's foot touches your mitt?" Micky didn't answer. He just knelt there staring at his glove.

"The runner touches the plate before the tag," said Hiltz.

"Gus, technically you are right. But, oh, you are so wrong. What were you thinking in a game like this with a crowd like this?"

"Willy, I didn't think. I just called what I saw. He was safe. Now it's your turn to save this game. You better tell the crowd why the runner was safe."

After Hiltz addressed the crowd and settled them for the moment, the grounds crew cleared the field of debris. The game resumed, one-zero, Double Depot.

In the bottom of the inning Deep Wells tied the score on a double followed by a two-base throwing error. Tie game again.

In the ninth inning the crowd on both sides was getting more and more rowdy. With one out the runner at first, who had laid down a beautiful bunt single, stole second on a close play. I called the runner safe. The second basemen yelled, "He took his hand off the bag. I tagged him." John Porter ran out to protest.

"John, come over to home plate." He did. "John, I'm the only umpire in the game. How can I tell from here, the only place I can be to call balls and strikes properly, if the runner lifted his hand off the bag? He's out. End of story." John kicked the dirt on his way back to the dugout.

The next batter slapped the first pitch toward the hole between short and third. The runner broke on contact and should have been an easy out at third if only the shortstop made the play he had to make in a tie game in the bottom of the ninth. Instead of throwing to third, he fired across the infield to first. Bang, bang at first. Who could tell? It was that close. But I had to tell. "Safe." Porter again charged across the infield to where I was standing not very far from third base. "How can you call both of those plays against us? The crowd will kill you."

"Remember, I am the only umpire here. I was as far from first as I could get. Then I had to make the call at first base because your shortstop made the wrong throw. He had a sure out at third in a tie game. I was positioned to make that call. His poor judgement put me totally out of position for the call he forced me to make. You know damn well how close that play was. Now stand here for a few minutes and argue so that the fans will think that you're doing your job. Later, do your job by telling your shortstop he screwed up."

"Gus, I don't believe you're real. Look at the debris on the field."

"No matter how I call it the debris flies." Porter kicked more dirt as he returned to the dugout.

The old lefty, Herb Bruening, then got back on the mound and retired the next two batters on infield pop-ups.

The score stayed tied going into the twelfth inning. The rain had returned. Tom Zimmer of Deep Wells had fifteen strikeouts. Herb Bruening scattered ten hits. Each had yielded a lone run. The skies opened up. The rain came down in sheets. Micky Legget reminded me that we both could be somewhere else by now if I hadn't been so stupid as to call the runner at the plate safe. We both could have saved our legs from this. I halted the game before a pitch in the twelfth could be thrown.

While it rained, I found Wally Harris and suggested that if the game were to resume the beer sales at the park had to be stopped. Both managers agreed. The Meeker concessionaires erupted, but when threatened with the responsibility of having the game called a double forfeit, they relented. "We still can get rid of all that other junk to eat and drink. This is the season's end."

The end of beer sales message spread quickly. The crowd, which was now about half the size as at the start of the game, craved more beer. They set out for the town bars to wait out the rain.

The game had to have a winner to determine the state tourney entry. I was told we would wait at least two hours before the game could be called. One of the local bar owners learned by way of telephone that the weather to the southwest was clearing. Convinced that the game would resume, he made arrangements to set up a beer stand on his brother-in-law's lawn across from the ballpark. Quickly more beer stands magically appeared on other lawns. Beer flow resumed. After a two-hour delay, with the grounds crew working for thirty minutes to make the field somewhat playable, the game resumed.

The delay meant new pitchers. The styles were reversed. Hard throwing Zimmer was replaced by soft throwing, sore armed Brewer manager Willy Hiltz. Easy throwing Herb Bruening was replaced by hard throwing 20-year-old right hander, Dicky Mier. Even though neither team voiced issue before on ball and strike calls, every pitch now was greeted with wild protest from the fans. Debris followed. The Wilson County Sheriff's Department had sent reinforcements. After a few thrown bottles, several drunks were tossed into the back of a cruiser and were spirited away to Middleton. The crowd quieted some after that and refrained from throwing things in protest.

The rain clouds reappeared, and the field was getting darker by the top of the 16th inning of the tied game. Meeker's field had no lights and the clock was showing 8pm. By the bottom of the 16th mist had turned to rain. Double Depot was able to get a runner to second base. With two outs the Boxcar shortstop hit a shot to center field. The ball bounced, and the center fielder came up throwing. Too late. The Boxcars apparently had won the game. About half of the remaining 500 fans roared in approval.

However, Willy Hiltz, who must have been watching me or the runner, yelled, "Watch." He toed the rubber, stepped off and threw to third. The third baseman touched the bag.

"Out at third base. The runner missed the bag."

All hell broke loose. Fans stormed the field. I headed for the Boxcar dugout and grabbed the runner whom I had just called out. He stood there as I got the attention of his manager.

"Now," I said, "tell John that you did miss third base. Father, remember the 8th commandment."

Father Faust, popular Double Depot parish priest and star hitting left fielder sighed, hung his head, waited a long time and said, "I missed the bag."

"The 8th commandment?" snapped the puzzled Boxcar manager.

"Thou shalt not lie," I responded. "The good priest is a holy man, indeed."

There would be no 17th inning. The cloudburst continued. The rain, the dark and the lake on the field ended play for the day.

The State Association told the PA announcer to inform the crowd that the game had been called. As I headed for my car, I picked up a three-deputy escort. I didn't feel it was necessary, but the uniforms carried on like they were the bravest and most important three in the county. A flashbulb flared in front of my face. I jumped in shock. Then more flashes.

When I got to my '50 Chevy, the officers got into two county cars and led me out of town, one in front, one behind, full lights and siren. Two miles out of town lights, siren, and patrol cars vanished.

The next day The Middleton Times front page featured the face of "STUART AUGUST, TERRIFIED UMPIRE." They never explained in the story of the game that my terrified look came from unexpected flashes from Sylvania blue dots.

A midweek Times sports section headline read: DEEP WELLS AND DOUBLE DEPOT GRANTED STATE BERTHS. The story stated that at the suggestion of umpire Stuart August both teams deserved the entry.

Harry Schumann's shoulder healed. I got triple money for the game. Both Double Depot and Deep Wells lost out in the tourney. I umpired for a few more years, but not in either town.

Oh, yes, five years later Double Depot bars offered Deep Wells Special, and the people of Deep Wells could purchase the best of Double Depot Boxcars in their own stores.

The principal, Mr. Kennedy, had approached me in spring and asked how I thought we could get these fifteen seniors through the required speech class. A few of them had already tried and baled on the quarter class. Even though these special kids had been treated well by their classmates, these low achievers were too afraid to face a regular class. Now they were all in the same special speech class.

My name is Stewart August. I am a speech and English teacher. When I was growing up kids called me Stu, but early in my career a fellow teacher labeled me Gus and it stuck. I never wanted to be Stu or Gus, but I'm fine with either. What I wanted was to be a teacher. So many of my teachers did so much for me, convincing me to do something, to be something. In high school I was pushed into teaching some grade schoolers after the school day ended. It was a real class, six kids for ninety minutes once a week. I was given a free hand.

I enjoyed the teaching. Had I not been pushed into it, I would never have known that I could teach. I would not have discovered the joy of it.

Now, as a teache,r I am faced with the modern day craze of standardized tests: "Let's find new ways to quantify what students learn." I still think the greatest learning is unquantifiable. State legislatures want to reduce students, actual human beings, to lab rats or chemistry analysis byproducts. "If we can't quantify it, it is not important."

I often wonder who determined how and which teachers made me who I became. I don't remember who taught me how to write better or read better or do math. What I do remember is which ones made me do things I didn't think I could do. The self-confidence they gave me when I succeeded was the greatest gift I ever got from any teacher. I don't remember taking any tests that measured such gain or quantified an increased love of learning that came with the success the newly gained self-confidence produced.

Years later, as I neared a classroom door I heard, "Yeah, you think you can do any better? You dumb, shit. At least I didn't stand up there sayin' nutin'." I recognized the voice of Dennis. He was one of the fifteen special education students waiting in my room on the first day of their required public speaking class. These kids had low self-esteem and few academic skills accompanied by a great deal of timidity. A few strutted about with much roostering bravado to cover up their insecurity. They made noise and preyed upon the weaker. I was here to make them face one of the most dreaded phobias, performing in public.

I heard Larry say, "Yeah, we're all just a bunch of stupid losers, but I'll knock anyone here on his rear end if he says one word while I'm up there. I didn't stay in school this long not to graduate."

"Shut up, big mouth," Dennis shouted. Before it got worse I stepped through the door. Silence followed. I did have a reputation as a hard core disciplinarian.

Teaching is a challenge. I want the best for my kids. I want to help them be better at whatever they want to be, but most of all

I want them to believe, "They Can Be." But how do you know if you helped?

This group in particular needed more help than any other group. In school they achieved very little that was positive. Their only notoriety was of a negative nature. They were seniors. Each had enough D minuses, sprinkled with the occasional C and one A in art. Some classes they passed on merit, but many of the passing grades were gifts or obtained in a class where, if you showed up more often than not, you passed. The only obstacle in their path to graduation was a required speech class taught by Stewart August, a teacher who only gave a passing grade to those who did it the old fashioned way, "by earning it."

Last spring I suggested to Mr. Kennedy, "Let me get all of them in one class with no other students. I will do some modification, but basically, I will teach the same class, same number and types of speeches. However, they will be geared a little differently, and I will require little written work. I can adapt the material to their needs." He liked the idea and made the scheduling happen.

Before I could lead this class through what I had planned, I had to put out the brush fires that had already started. I had to douse an ingrained culture and rekindle a new one in the charred remains.

I stood before them silently. I knew what they were thinking, what they were waiting for. I had a reputation as a hard case: very strict, no personal attacks. They sensed that I had overheard at least some of the bullying a few minutes ago. Still, I stood there, saying nothing. The unease mounted. After a full minute I asked Emma to close the door. I began.

"What are other students in this school saying about this group?" I began moving among them, in and out between the tables as I spoke in a quiet, solemn voice. "What do they think of you?" I waited for a response. None. All eyes dropped, staring at the table in front of them, much uneasy shifting.

"What? No answer? Do I need to tell you?" A long pause, "You know. You all know they are saying 'what a bunch of stupid dolts.' 'They'll never be able to give a speech.' 'They couldn't find the words to ask for help if they were drowning.' 'What a bunch of idiots.' 'Losers. All of them.'"

Even more quietly, "Isn't that right? Isn't that what they are saying?" A few heads were shaking yes.

"And what about the teaching staff? Aren't they asking each other what a fool August is if he thinks he can teach them anything. He is a deluded ass. He thinks he's a magician." I waited for a response. Silence, no movement.

After the long silence I had them move the tables and chairs out of the way and invited them to sit in a circle on the floor where I was already sitting. They all silently obeyed except Jackie. She just stood staring at the floor in her mini skirt. I went over to my desk grabbed my sport coat off the back of my chair and threw it to her. She caught it and looked at me.

"Use it," I said. She started to put it on. The room erupted in laughter. Emma dashed over to her and whispered, "No, Jackie, cover your legs and sit down." We all heard Emma, but no one said a word as we sat in a circle, Jackie, legs covered, included. I guess that is what we needed. The class seemed to relax. They looked at me and waited.

"You know what? Those outside this room are wrong, dead wrong. You are not stupid. You are not worthless. You have brains. You have knowledge. You have skills. I know school has never been easy for any of you. Over and over you've been repeatedly told what you can't do. Let's hear about what you can do. You can all talk. I heard you outside the door before. I heard you in the hallways. I heard you at lunch time. All of you can speak.

"Skills and knowledge? We have a room full of it. Jack can fix most cars ever made. Emma, I understand you are the best babysitter in the area. You are known as a child whisperer. Parents want you if they are lucky enough to get you. Steve, you have a way with animals, especially horses. You are good. Maddy, the art teacher tells me you want to be a wood carver like your dad. She thinks you will become a good one. Larry, you're a trapper, still making money selling your furs today when few others do that. I hear you are learning how to tan hides. Harvey, you and your family raise rabbits for meat consumption, I bet you know more about those big rabbits than anyone else in the area outside of your family." I had done my homework. I found out as much as I could on each one of them.

The only one left for me to comment on was Zack. Zack had more problems than any of the others. His parents dumped him on elderly grandparents when he was three. The grandparents were in their seventies, farmers trying to keep up a small dairy operation in a changing farm culture. They were old school, still milking by hand and doing everything the way farmers did thirty years ago. The result was poverty and social isolation. Zack was in no way prepared academically or socially when he started school. His only relationship with others was with his grandparents, now well into their eighties with many health problems.

Zack's only claim to notoriety in school as a freshman was his bi-monthly toss into the showers by students, led by the male phy-ed teacher. Zack's home learning lacked totally in personal hygiene. His daily barn chores and limited clothes closet made him an odor to be avoided. Students asked not to sit near him. The school nurse and a county social worker labored hard to help Zack get his teeth brushed, clothes cleaned at least once a week, and an unforced personal shower in the boy's locker room. By his senior year Zack was more presentable but still socially inept.

Zack's preschool education was nonexistent and, with his lack of social skills, he started behind everyone in all phases of school activity. As the years progressed he continued to lag further and further behind. He was a good looking big-eyed kid with jet black hair who seldom spoke.
"Most of you may be surprised that Zack has the best handwriting of anyone in this school system. If Zack were Chinese, he would no doubt be the best calligrapher in the country. His skills would be celebrated. Zack, I hope you can put your artistic skills to work. If any of you need a graduation announcement done up, show Zack what you want. Give him a good pen and ink and you will have unique graduation announcements, the best in all the school. I am convinced Zack won't overcharge you." Zack came as close to a full smile as I had ever seen on him.

"Okay, can we now agree that the people in this room have skills and knowledge that other people lack? You are not worthless, you have skills and knowledge to contribute. Speak up, let me hear it. Let Me Hear It! We are not stupid… Let Me Hear It!"

Jackie's voice squeaked, "We are not stupid."

"Everybody, let me hear it."

A few more voices and then the whole class, "We are not stupid. We have skills and knowledge."

Then I stood, "Who in here wants to graduate?" A few hands went up. Then all hands followed. I asked them to reassemble in their chairs behind their tables. "We start on the road to your graduation today. You are going to give speeches in this class. You will give the same type and the same number of speeches that all of the other students give.

"First, we will learn the ground rules. NO ONE, I repeat, NO ONE will put down anyone in this classroom. No one will make fun of, laugh at, make faces at, or mock any speaker or speech. If anyone does, out the door with no return. Good bye to his or her diploma.

"Remember you are all good at something. Better at it than most people. Tomorrow you give your first speech."

All gasped while shifting in their chairs. Bodies tensed. Fear streamed from their eyes. "Yes, your first speech, but it will be done sitting in a circle on the floor." A few snickers followed. Jackie blushed. "I have drawn up a list of 8 pairs. I will read the list in a few minutes. In the remaining class time you will visit with your paired partner and interview each other. Ask questions about what you do for fun, or a hobby, or a part time job. Find out what the other is good at. Keep it clean. Remember where the door is and how it can lead away from graduation."

Jackie smiled and said, "A door to graduation?"

Ever ready, Emma whispered, again too loudly, "He means if we don't keep it clean, he will kick us out."

"Oh," frowned Jackie.

"After class today ask other kids and teachers what this person is good at. Pick whom you ask carefully. Ignore smart alec answers. Remember, no put-downs in this class

"Tomorrow we will share the good, positive things about our partner. Give examples of what you mean. Quote somebody about him or her if you can. Now write down the main points I suggested in your notebooks."

Jerry, who had been looking around, piped up, "Is this everyone who will be in this class?" I nodded yes. "Then you got a math problem, Mr. August. How do you divide fifteen into pairs? Unless we cut one of us in half and throw the rest away. I suggest-."

"STOP. Remember, no put downs of anyone. No cracks about appearance, clothes, habits, race, religion. NONE. Remember where the door is."

"Okay. Okay."

"Now, Jerry, if you have fifteen and add one, you get?"

"Sixteen."

"Divide by two."

"Eight."

"Okay. Eight pairs. The first pair will be you and me. Now here are the other pairs," I read them off. "Scatter about the room and interview each other." Jerry and I sat near my desk. Just before the bell rang, I said, "Tomorrow each will give a one to two-minute speech on his or her partner. You are here to learn how to be better speakers. Tomorrow is a start, not a polished finish. If we goof up, we get back up and try again. It's like learning to ride a bicycle. It will work. See you tomorrow."

The next day began with me talking about Jerry. I told of his interest in fishing and hunting, how he shot his first deer at the age of twelve. Even though he didn't want me to, I talked about how he helped his mother plant her garden. He said I liked to travel and he mentioned a few of the places I've been. He said I liked baseball and saw twenty or more Twin's games a year and that I umpired baseball and refereed football.

Surprisingly, the entire class showed up. Too afraid not to, I guess. The whole class got through the hour without too much of a struggle except for Zack. He just sat there. I asked him questions about his partner, Emma. Zack said, "She likes kids. She babysits. She is nice to me even outside of class." Mission accomplished.

I told them the next day we would again sit on the floor in a circle and each would tell us of a dream or a nightmare they once had. "Keep it clean. Remember I'm not entirely stupid and was once a teenager, also. You won't be able to slip in the off color things you might think you can plead innocence of."

"What if you can't remember any or don't dream?" Misty asked.

"Then dream tonight or make up something you would like to dream."

The next day went well. Even Zack was quick to tell us all about the deer he saw in their meadow.

"How about that, class? In less than one week of the quarter you all gave two speeches. Well done. The key is to talk about something you know. Be prepared, know what you are going to say. Practice the speech. Give it to your dog, cat, horse, or a tree stump. Give it to yourself aloud. Give it to a brother, sister, parakeet, grandparents, a friend, or the moon.

"Next week I'll show you how to organize a speech. I will give you a few examples. The week after that you will give a speech about a place you would like to visit, or a place you have already visited. You will tell us three things about this place. First, tell us where it is and how we could get there. Second, tell us what interests you so much about this place, what there is to see and do there. Finally, tell us how you found out about this place. Spend time this week finding out as much as you can about the place. Ask people about it, read about it. On Thursday we will go to the media center so you can look for information." I made sure that all of this was written into their notebooks. This took the rest of the period. During the preparation week I gave them example speeches about Hibbing, Minnesota, Pike Place Market in Seattle, and Machu Picchu. I illustrated how I introduced each speech, made my three points clear, and how I concluded each speech.

As the quarter progressed the speeches came slowly. Each round the speaking was a little smoother, more natural, and a little more developed. Confidence began to creep into the speeches delivered.

The highlight of the quarter came with the demonstration speeches. The students had to use visual aids and were to show us how to do or understand something. I spent a week showing them how to use visual aids: what to do, what not to do, how to make them big enough for all to see, or use other methods to compensate for that. Again, I stressed picking a topic they knew. All speech topics had to be cleared with me. This is where the fun began. The first topic I had to approve was wood carving. Maddy wanted to demonstrate how a wood carver carves. This involved scalpel-sharp knives. I went to Mr. Kennedy for permission for Maddy to bring the knives to school and use them in the classroom. He got big eyed and said he couldn't allow it. "Your career and mine will be over with one slip of a special-ed student's knife."

"Mr. Kennedy, you wanted a way to get these students to legitimately pass public speaking and graduate. I convinced them that speaking is easy if you talk about things you know best. Maddy's dad is the best wood carver in the state. She has been working with him. She has problems with academic work in school, but she has shown me pieces she has carved. She's good. She even earned an A in art."

"But, Gus, the risk."

"I spoke with her dad on the phone. He said, 'She is good, and she is careful. She knows that working with knives can be dangerous. She has seen my hands with the scars and a partially missing finger. She is so excited about doing this. She wants to show the kids she can actually do something worthwhile. This is the first time she has been excited about school except for an art class.'

"Mr. Kennedy, she needs to do this. Her dad gave his approval." Kennedy's face grimaced, but he nodded yes.

"Now that we have that one out of the way, here is a list of other approvals needed for some of the speeches: a horse, a wood splitter, a French Lop rabbit, and a chainsaw."

"Gus, I have never been so conned by one of my teachers in my life. Why do I put up with you? Why do I always have your back?"

"Because you are a saint who has taken the devil's job of principal in a high school."

The next week Mr. Kennedy attended every speech class of my special group. Maddy brought her knives, a block of pine, and a duck in two stages of being carved. She showed us how she was working on the second stage to make it a complete duck. Her nimble fingers expertly worked the blades to remove pieces of pine that weren't duck. Her big smile showed us how much she enjoyed her work and being able to tell us about it. We learned about wood, sharp steel, and feathers.

Mr. Kennedy then handed Zack his hammer, nails and a saw. Zack showed us his milking stool. He sawed a board and nailed it to another to show us how it was done. As instructed he had a piece of canvas on the floor to catch the sawdust.

Misty, who was determined to become a makeup artist, showed us how girls apply facial makeup. She hoped to show the girls present how to become more beautiful, and to show the boys what their dates go through for them. Of course, Jackie was her demonstration model and loved every minute of her demonstration speech. Jackie's speech was how to shorten a skirt by hem stitching.

Harvey brought in a French Lop in a cage. Big and strong, he was able to hold the forty-pound rabbit. He showed us the big ears and the powerful hind legs. He passed out recipes for rabbit stew and gave us a sample from the crock pot his mother sent with him. I had escargot in a classroom before when no one else would help a suffering speaker, why not rabbit stew?

Steve, an accomplished barrel racer, brought in his horse in a trailer behind his pick-up. He had constructed a roped off corral outside the classroom emergency door. He promised to repair any lawn divots. On his horse he pointed out the barrels and then rode around each one. The second time he did this he walked his horse through, explaining what he and the horse were doing. His friends from study hall acted as crowd control so no one could get near the horse.

Toby followed this outdoor speech with one of his own. He demonstrated his engine-powered wood splitter, which was put in place by Toby's father. I almost went crazy as clumsy Toby placed blocks of oak in front of the powerful wedged piston that split the wood. To my way of thinking his hands were entirely too close to becoming part of the splitting. He then told us how we could save money by cutting, splitting and burning oak.

After that class Mr. Kennedy said, "Never again, Gus, never again."

"So far, no fingers lost, no rabbits loose, but don't relax too much. We have another two days to go."

The next two days passed without disaster. Harry was the last speaker. Mr. Kennedy brought Harry's Husqvarna chainsaw with him from the office, where it had been left that morning, and passed it off to Harry.

Harry was a sight to behold. Most of the time he could be seen in the halls with his old, faded, stained, and smudged DeKalb baseball cap. In my classroom, no caps. Harry stood about 5' 7", 175 pounds. He had a good sized paunch. His thin, straw-colored, stringy hair hung down to his shoulders. It was combed forward to cover his high balding forehead. The hair was too thin to hide the shiny scalp. His feet exhibited well-worn tan work boots. His grey work pants were held up by red suspenders over a yellow and black plaid flannel shirt. He was seventeen going on fifty-seven.

Harry walked to the front of the room and placed the saw on the table, which he had covered with a protective piece of canvas. He removed a lead pencil from his shirt pocket, picked up the chainsaw by its upper handle, and held it out to his left side, blade pointed toward the side wall. He told us that if you used a chainsaw you had to know how it worked and how to clean it. Using the pencil as a pointer Harry lectured us on the parts of a saw: handles, top and back, engine, oil and gas ports, blade, and chain, which rotated along the blade. He put the saw down and removed an extra chain from his toolbox which was next to the table. He showed us the cleat like teeth that did the cutting. He explained the two cycle engine. He picked up the saw and broke it into pieces and explained the function of each one and how to clean it. He reassembled the machine. Then he set it on the table, anchored the saw with his left hand, pointed the blade up at a forty-five-degree angle from the table, and pulled the starter cord with his right hand. The engine roared into life. Harry picked up his Husqvarna, pointed it towards the wall and pulled the trigger, gunning the chain into action moving rapidly along the sword-like blade. Another rev of the engine and he switched it off. After the chain stopped rotating, Harry stepped forward and took a bow, holding his precious baby in front of him.

The class clapped for over a minute. Harry beamed during the long applause. Time of the speech? Twenty two minutes, no notes, a smooth professional demonstration worthy of Husqvarna's best sales rep.

After class Mr. Kennedy smiled, "Gus, that made risking our jobs worthwhile. I haven't felt this good in a classroom in a long time."

The class final was to be a persuasive speech. We discussed how TV commercials try to get us to buy a product. I showed a dozen or more ads and public service announcements. Then we looked at what they did to make us want to buy or donate money. Answers ranged from saving money to it's a better product. We talked about happiness, guilt, and of course, sex. Someone brought up that they wanted you to like their company because, "They are good guys."

I told them about the use of logic and how it is used to get us to buy. I told them how companies use emotion to get us to buy. I finished by telling them how companies want us to think that we can trust them in order to get us to buy.

The final speech was to sell something of their own. Bring it from home and actually offer it for sale. They had to hand me a sheet of paper indicating what method of selling they were using based on the ads and PSAs we had watched. They had to bring a signed permission slip from home okaying the offering of the item for sale.

The last few days of class were filled with sales pitches, the introductions of the product, the reasons we should want to buy it, proof of those reasons, and a concluding statement.

We were offered cassette tapes, a tie, baseball cards, a dozen homemade brownies, a Barbie doll, a hunting knife (parental and principal permission in hand), a bag of peanut butter cups, a baseball glove, and more. Perhaps two of the most memorable sale pitches were delivered by Jackie and Zack. Jackie came to class dressed in a short skirt and a tight sweater. She offered her best pair of fishnet stockings for sale. I was about to stop the show when she looked at me and said, "We said sex sells."She had me there. I guess someone did pay attention. She got nine dollars from Larry for the prize. I later learned that the stockings had belonged to her older sister, who was unaware of her contribution to the class.

The last speaker was Zack, the young man of few words and fewer friends. When Zack's name was called he got up, went to the front of the room and stood there, stern, sad faced, looking at us. He stood, the class quietly waited. They seemed to be afraid to breathe. Zack stood in place for over a minute. The class began to shift in their seats but remained quiet.

"Zack," I said, "why are you up there?"

"To sell something." He stood expressionless without moving.

"Zack, what are you selling?"

He reached into his pocket and took out a ballpoint pen and held it at arm's length in front of him between his thumb and forefinger. He stood there and stared at the pen.

"Zack, what is it?"

He brought the pen closer to his face and slowly turned it from side to side, rolling it in his fingers and then held it again at arm's length for us to see, and said, "It's a pen."

We waited. Zack, arm extended, stood still. The seconds stretched longer and longer. The class- church quiet.

"Zack, why should we buy it?"

Again Zack reeled in the pen, looked at it, end over end, up and down. Then he extended his arm again offering us a view of the pen. As time ever so slowly ticked away Zack finally spoke, "It has ink in it." Again he stood silent.

Harry, of chainsaw fame, jumped up and ran towards Zack yelling, "I'll buy it, I'll buy it. Here's a quarter." He grabbed the pen and gave Zack the quarter and said, "You're done."

He then put his arm over Zack's shoulder and led him back to his seat. The class applauded. They had passed any exam I could devise by that rescue and applause.

That year they all graduated.

Years later a speaker in my humanities class, Professor Holmer, told us that, as people, we acquire knowledge, learn theories and skills, and develop capacities. He said that learning capacities is what makes us human. His list of capacities included such things as appreciation, compassion, courage, justice, kindness, love, pity, and understanding. He said, "We need to become capacitated rather than being incapacitated."

I look back on that special class and I feel somehow, in some way, most of those students, maybe only through osmosis, learned compassion and a few other capacities. Standardized tests will never quantify this. I think those kids learned something of special value.

You Can't Scare Me Away

As I sat on the couch with an arm around Whinny, I could see the caps of four bullets in the handgun of the kid standing beside me. He couldn't have been more than sixteen years old. We had been told to put all of our valuables on coffee and end tables in the living room of this large, newly built house on the far northern outskirts of São Paulo, Brazil near Interlagos. We were told that if any of the six gang members found anything we held back, we would be shot.

   This I believed. During my two years of teaching at Escola Aparecida I heard numerous accounts of home invasions. Some of them ended in bloody slaughter for all but the home invaders. Some ended in bloody shootouts with the military police. The shootouts were like the Wild West movies of the 1950s. They accounted for loss of life in all three factions: the invaders, the police, and the invaded. However, most ended with all safe minus valued possessions.

I looked at my messy pile of cruzeiros on the table next to me. When I arrived in São Paulo two years earlier, I was told I would be robbed. Always carry some money, not too little or risk being shot by an angry, disappointed thief. Not too much because you will be held up at some point. Other advice included not to wear any jewelry that you couldn't afford to lose, not to wear anything like an earring. Thieves would rip jewelry off the body, hence you didn't want it attached. That was not a problem for me. I never wore any jewelry, not even a watch. Well, nothing other than a wedding ring, but after my divorce I was no longer attached to that.

Lucky for me my friends had watches, rings, clip-on earrings and more cash than I carried. All of this was sitting on the various tables in the room, being collected by another young member of the gang. His pistol was tucked into his belt as he filled a pillowcase with the loot.

I have heard people say that when they found themselves in possible life or death situations the world slowed down, akin to watching in slow motion. I can attest to that. I felt as if I was watching a scene in a movie. I was there, but I was not a part of it. I wondered if I was already dead and viewing the scene from the beyond. I recalled a kidnapping story about some Aparecida students of two wealthy families who were kidnapped and held for several million dollars in ransom. This would have been ten or twelve years ago, in the early 1970s, before I arrived. The storyteller said that, usually in such cases, the children were returned unharmed after the ransom was paid. This one had not gone off exactly as designed. Panic set in, and the children were shot.

This sad affair was related to me after I had scoffed at hearing some of our students say they had never ridden a São Paulo city bus or taxi. I thought they were too snobbish to ride public transportation. The kidnap story helped me understand the overprotective parents. Still, I could not get used to students being picked up in limos by their armed drivers. Our school was a gated enclosure. We had kids from 37 different countries. Some were children of foreign counsels in São Paulo; some were children of businessmen representing international corporations from the U.S., Canada, Japan, Korea, and most of Europe and South America. Some students were born in Brazil of expatriate parents, and a number of the students were from some of São Paulo's wealthiest families. I never could get used to hearing a second grader stomp her foot and say, "Where's my driver? He's late again."

The reality of possible violence was ever present during my stay in São Paulo, but in most of the stories of robberies and kidnappings no one was hurt. The grandfather of one of our senior girls from Argentina was kidnapped. His ransom was paid twice for two separate kidnappings. The last one was said to be at that time the largest South American ransom ever paid. He was returned safe and sound both times. Marina was never alone off of school grounds or away from the family mansion in nearby Chácara Flora.

My mind jumped from Marina back to the scene at hand. Whinny, sitting next to me on the couch, began her second panic attack, shaking and moaning. The gunman told her in Portuguese to shut up and sit still or be shot. One of the few native Brazilians in our group, Ricardo, told the gunman that the woman didn't speak Portuguese. Could he tell her in English what was just said? Permission granted. The result, Whinny shook even more. I pulled her closer to me and began to hum a soothing tune. The gunman stared at me, but as Whinny began to settle down, he let it go. I hummed on.

Maybe Whinny had been thinking about an episode outside of her and Grace's apartment a few months before. They had heard sirens and tires screeching. They looked out the front window and saw a military VW Fusca (in the U.S. we call them Beetles) with a cop leaning out of the window on each side, waving a pistol. Sirens blared as they passed out of sight, but the sound of gunfire could be heard from down the block.

What a going away party this was turning out to be. The host house was a newly constructed fancy abode belonging to one of our teachers and her Australian husband, who made more money in a year than all the teachers assembled for this party. I guess the make of the cars and the size of the place in the luxurious housing tract caught the eyes of this roving band of pistol packing marauders. The construction of the twelve foot, barbed wire topped fence that would enclose the structure had not yet been completed. No armed guard had been hired. Most of the neighboring mansions had one. Three of the group, me included, were leaving Brazil as our two year contracts expired. I had almost completed my tour without having been robbed.

Another of our honored departees, Angelo, was not so lucky. This was his third go round. He was a bandit magnet. The first was on a beach in Rio. Angelo liked the sun and his sleep and made a poor choice of sunning on the beach while grabbing a nap. He awoke minus his watch and wallet. A few months later, a block from his apartment, a lone gunman relieved him of his cash.

Our invader hosts were not very happy to find so little cash and so little inexpensive jewelry. They didn't realize we were teachers rather than wealthy friends of the host. They made a few of us stand while they searched us for more treasure. Again, threats in Portuguese were made. The translation, "Take anything you have not yet put out for us on the tables, and you will live. If we find anything more we will kill all of you." Home invaders were known to shoot if they did not get cooperation.

The bandits demanded that I stand up to be searched; they patted me down and made me take off my shoes. They found nothing and moved on to another high school teacher, Ralph. The same happened to him. Again they found nothing. Ralph sat down and put his shoes back on. This time he was luckier than last time. Ralph was a long distance runner and often ran 3 miles to school in the morning. He would shower in the gym and change clothes before class. One morning a lone opportunist, gun in hand, relieved him of his wallet, watch, backpack and expensive running shoes.

After a few more fruitless searches the invaders switched tactics. They asked for the lady of the house. Annie identified herself and they took her on a tour of the house, opening drawers, cupboards, and closets. They collected some jewelry and several bottles of Scotch and gin. They carried two TVs, a VCR, and a stereo unit to the front door.

They repeatedly asked her and her husband where the safe was. They were told there was no safe. Again, there were repeated threats, "If we find a safe, we will kill you all."

While the two youngest gun toters remained with us in the living room, the other four re-combed the house, turning up carpets, looking behind wall hangings, and tossing all things out of the closets. The search revealed no safe.

Finally, they gave up the quest. All of us were ordered into the bathroom. Fifteen of us, including Jean who was eight and a half months pregnant, huddled body to body. Jean and a couple others were standing in the bathtub.

As the door was slammed shut, we heard, "Yoo hoo, I'm here. Sorry I'm late. I brought my three bean salad." Relieved of her culinary gift, Ursula, another teacher was hustled into an already cozy bathroom. Annie asked in Portuguese if our jailers would be so kind as to turn off the oven before they left. They did. We later found that they ate most of the four pork loins that were to be a part of our feast. Before the bathroom door was again shut, we were told to stay in there an hour before leaving. They said they would leave one shooter behind to see we complied. We heard what sounded like the movement of furniture. The noise outside the bathroom door suggested that we were being barricaded in.

About a half hour later we heard the opening of the front door. I guessed that the thieves were leaving and beginning to cart their collection out the door. Then all hell broke loose: gunfire, shot after shot, the sound of breaking glass and splintering wood. We all dropped to the floor as best we could. Some of us supported others prone above us. Two others helped Jean sit down in the tub.

Ricardo said, "Some neighbor must have called the police. They must have noticed what was happening. The damn fools. Military police love to shoot it out."

"Don't I know it," said Laim Shaw. My slow motion mind triggered a Laim Shaw story. Two months ago, while walking home from the bus stop to his apartment, he saw a VW cop car chasing an old, beat up wreck. Another cop car came from the opposite direction, and the junker being chased stopped. Three guys got out and put their hands in the air. The uniformed policemen exited their cars and opened fire on the three. Laim said he was scared to death and didn't want to be next. He stayed hidden behind some trees until they left. The cops tossed the bodies in the car that was chased and drove off.

More shots rang out hitting the house. Perhaps the heightened fear boosted my adrenaline and my slow motion mind brought another scene into view. One Sunday at the Hippie Fair in downtown São Paulo I was checking out the art and handicraft booths. I saw the police trying to remove two beggars from the fair area. The Hippie Fair was one of São Paulo's largest tourist attractions. Beggars among the tourists did not present a good image. When the beggars resisted, the cops began to kick and beat on them with batons. I guess I am a coward. I walked away. I couldn't watch. On the other hand, what could I do? Interfere, lose my work visa and be sent back to the States? The beatings would still go on.

Still more shooting and my escapist mind now drifted to another scene. My friend Jay, from the other American school in São Paulo, told me that he lived next door to a police precinct and had to move. He couldn't stand the yelling that often came from the cop shop as prisoners were beaten.

Shots continued, sometimes in volleys followed by silence and then another blast, more glass breaking. A few bullets pierced the wall of the bathroom, fortunately above our heads.

After several minutes of silence we heard footsteps and then voices from within the house. The cops unbarricaded the bathroom door and our sardined group unpacked, with Jean still pregnant and all intact. The cops talked to the homeowner and Ricardo, who was the only native speaker of Portuguese. Both were told to report to the police precinct on Monday for formal statements. The cops, after seeing to the removal of the six dead bandits, left. No crime scene investigation in São Paulo in those days.

Most of our hyper group paced about, sat down, got up and paced some more, constantly talking about how they thought they were going to die. White faced, a few just sat in chairs staring straight ahead.

Darla, a twenty-four-year-old elementary teacher, paced about while raking her fingers through her hair. She stopped in front of me and turned. Her rear end was at eye level. I was about to yell, but I controlled my shock and merely asked, "Darla, what is that in the back pocket of your jeans?"

Her right hand slipped into her pocket and removed a half

karat diamond engagement ring. In a shocking voice and nervously holding the ring, she said, "They weren't going to get this baby."

Ricardo shouted, "Darla, if they had found that on you, we would all be dead." Darla burst into tears.

If they had asked Darla to stand to be searched, the ring would have been noticed. Darla was a tall brunette in tight jeans with a rear end that demanded attention. She just sat down and buried her face in her hands and wept. No one approached her for at least twenty minutes.

When most everyone's adrenaline levels dropped to near normal, the crashed party broke up without our having had pork loin or three bean salad. Ricardo and Jean stayed with Annie and Ian. The rest of us left.

Oscar drove his Fusca with Angelo, Grace, and me as passengers. The fifteen mile trip back to our Borba Gato neighborhood was pretty silent. Finally, Grace asked, "What time is it?"

Oscar raised his left hand from the steering wheel as his sweater sleeve fell back and looked at his watch and said, "Five thirty."

"Oh, Oscar," Grace yelled, "What did you do?"

His face turned red. "I must have forgotten I even had it on. I was so scared." For thirty seconds we all remained speechless. Then, almost as if on cue, all of us except for Oscar burst out laughing. A bizarre end to an almost disastrous day.

After a year of graduate school back home, I returned to Escola Aparecida on another two year contract.

Six inches of snow had me thinking twice about making it to the Gophers' basketball game. The Gophers were playing highly ranked Purdue and had a chance of winning. I wanted to see the game. I thought about parking, snow emergency plowing restrictions and wading through the stuff. A city bus was the answer to my dilemma.

By the time I got to nearby Brookdale Mall, plows had already cleared the parking lot. In five minutes I was on a #14 bus headed for downtown. My wait was short. 16A buses ran every fifteen minutes. I soon stepped off the 16A at Oak and Washington and hiked one block to William's Arena.

The evening was good. The Gophers won in double overtime. I walked out of William's Arena into a starry but cold January Minnesota winter. The 16A arrived quickly. It was indeed a good evening.

Once downtown things took a turn for the worse. I couldn't remember which 14 bus I needed to get back to my car. As usual after a heavy snowfall the thermometer quickly dropped. The bank clock on 7th and Nicollet read a minus six. After 10 pm most buses ran every forty-five or sixty minutes. Along with a dozen others waiting for a variety of numbered buses, I paced the sidewalk and tried to stomp cold from my feet.

By ten forty-five a 14 bus pulled up to the old Donaldson's bus stop. As I walked up, the door opened. I stepped up inside and asked the driver if this bus stopped at Brookdale. "No," he said. "This is a 14h, you need a 14g. One should be along in about fifteen minutes." As I headed back into the cold, the door shut. Instead of pulling away the bus sat there for several minutes. The door reopened, and the bus driver stuck his head out.

"Hey, mister," the driver shouted, "Come on. I'll drop you off at the mall on my way to the bus garage. This is my last run." I got on the bus. There was only one passenger, a young girl who looked somewhat familiar. "The girl said you were her teacher a few years ago, and she really wanted to talk to you. She's a nice kid who takes my last run about three times a week. So what the heck. I like her. Let's go." The good evening returned.

I looked at the girl again. She took off her scarf and big, knit, cold weather cap. Her hair fell over her shoulders. Then a voice emerged from the unwrapped bundle. "It's Zenith. I had you for creative writing for twelve weeks."

The voice and now visible smiling face shocked my frozen synapses into firing. I did remember. "Yes, Zenith, I remember you, the girl who didn't think she could write, the girl who wrote horror stories about her life, the girl who needed to learn punctuation, grammar and spelling. Yes, Zenith, I remember a most talented student."

Zenith was a foster child who was placed in our school six weeks into the year. Child Services said she would only be there for four to eight weeks. She was placed in my creative writing class because the counselor thought that would be the easiest class to slip in and out of.

As the bus rambled out of downtown and up the unplowed residential streets, Zenith gushed. "I was so scared of you. The first day I heard some kids say 'I hope the new girl is ready for this. I bet she doesn't know how strict and demanding this guy is.' I think they wanted to scare me. They knew I was a foster kid. But you made me comfortable. You told me to write about what I knew, to tell the stories I knew. That's where all the ugly family baggage came from. I wrote what I had lived."

"Zenith, what are you doing now? And why do you ride this bus three times a week?"

"Oh, Mr. August, I have so much to tell you. Things are so much better now than when I was in your class. I got pulled out of your school after only twelve weeks. That was the longest I had been in any school for over a year. My dad kept moving and had me switching schools. Then I got sent to foster parents who liked me. I still live with them. I'm going to Metropolitan University in downtown Minneapolis. I take the bus there and back. I have a part-time job in south Minneapolis. That's why I ride this bus. I work four to ten, three days a week at St. Joseph Children's home. I get paid. Oh, I have so much more to tell you."

"Sorry, folks," the driver said. We had pulled up to a bus stop on West Broadway in Robbinsdale. "I would like to give you two more time and hear more of the story, but this is the end of my shift."

I turned to Zenith and said, "How about I take you to lunch or supper. You pick the day, and I can hear all about you." She said she was free Saturday and she told me where and when I could pick her up.

As the bus headed for the mall, the driver said, "I wondered why she took this route regularly. She's always reading. Such a polite and smiling kid. She really seemed desperate to talk to you. Twelve weeks, you must have made an impression." As I got off the bus, I thanked the driver for giving me the opportunity to see Zenith again.

Saturday, I picked up Zenith at the address she gave me. We went to a Mexican restaurant in Robbinsdale. Zenith filled me in on the details of her life since she was in my class. After a longer stay than was expected at our school, she was placed with an elderly couple who had taken in foster children for years. Getting on in age, they no longer had any kids living with them. The social worker who had supervised Frank and Terry asked them to meet Zenith and take on one last teenager. "Frank and Terry, they asked me to call them that from the beginning, seemed to like me right away, and I just fell in love with them. I lived in their basement for a year and a half. I was a junior in high school, and with their help my grades got better and better. You helped, too. You convinced me I could write. You asked me to use my brain and learn the basics. I never thought I was smart. I still don't, but I will continue to fake it. You told me that, if I didn't think I was smart, to fake it; no one would ever know. I guess I am still fooling them."

"Zenith, you are fooling no one. You are smart and talented."

"Anyhow, when I got to the end of my senior year I began to panic. In June I would turn eighteen, and after I had my high school diploma, Child Services would no longer have a place for me. One day Terry found me crying and asked what the problem was. I told her I was scared-- where was I to go, what was I to do?

"Terry gave me a big hug and said, 'Zenith, I guess Frank and I waited too long to tell you. If you want, you can stay here in the basement. As long as you stay in school, you will pay no rent and can eat with us. We will help you to get scholarships, loans and part-time work.' They are such wonderful people."

"Zenith, are you still writing, keeping a journal?"

"Yes. You told me to write what I know, so I wrote all those stories and poems about my life. I continue to do so. Last Mother's Day I wrote a poem about my mom. I wish she was still alive so I could read it to her. I wish I had written it before she died. She saved me. She protected me from my deadbeat dad as much as she could, she ended up taking beatings that were meant for me. Without her my dad would have made my life even more of a hell."

"Yes, I remember the stories you wrote. I always wanted to ask, and I didn't think I should. Do you really think he tried to put you in all of those dangerous situations you wrote about so he could collect on the life insurance policy he had taken out on you? You had several close calls."

"All that is true. The last was the clincher. He ran the car into a tree after he told me to unfasten my seat belt and get his box of snuff off the backseat. Stupid me, I should've known better. After I unbuckled and reached back, he drove off the road into a tree at sixty miles an hour. He had his seat belt on and was unhurt. The EMTs said they couldn't believe I escaped with so few injuries. That was the summer after my sophomore year. In the fall I came to your class.

"Because of that crash and all the other dangerous situations, Child Services wanted him arrested for child endangerment. They never could get enough evidence for a trial, but they succeeded in taking me away from him. That's how I got into the system.

"I had been writing all that negative stuff, but now I write about Frank and Terry, and I just wrote about you and that nice bus driver. I hope I live to have more good things to write about."

"Tell me about college."

"I am a junior and I'm majoring in Sociology. I went to North Hennepin Community College for two years, and now I'm at Metro U. I want to work with kids like me. I want to be a parole officer or a social worker and help foster kids. My adviser got me the job at St. Joseph's. All the kids there are without family or have non-supportive families. I was coming from there when I met you on the bus. I am trying to get the kids to write about their lives. It was good therapy for me. Maybe it will be for them."

• • •

For the next year and a half I had an occasional meal with Zenith. She told me of her classes and work and how happy she was. After she graduated she got a major grant to pursue her master's degree in social work at a university in Texas. Over the years we exchanged Christmas cards. The last several years I had heard little from her.

Then I received a written invitation. On another cold, snowy night I looked into the window of a bookstore in St. Paul. A large poster advertised "January 19th only- Meet best-selling author, Zenith Bahr. Hear her read from her book, From Hell to Foster Haven."

I sat in the back row of chairs next to an elderly couple. Soon the proprietor introduced us to, "Zenith Bahr, best-selling author, social worker and pioneer in programs for foster children."

Zenith mounted the small platform and began. "Thank you," she said to the man who introduced her. "Before I begin with the reading, which will be followed by a question and answer period, I want to give two mighty thank yous. First, to my last and most wonderful foster family, Frank and Terry Engstrom, who are seated in the back row." The couple next to me waved to her and blushed. The crowd applauded. "I also want to thank the white-haired polar bear sitting next to them, Stuart August, who convinced me I could write. I know he succeeded because I see most of you have a book in your hands that I wrote."

"Tall and tan and young and lovely," the girl went walking by, from the front of the bus all the way back. She sashayed the entire aisle, looking straight ahead, not a smile on her face. As she passed, the sound of "aaahs" could be heard, mostly from the male passengers. Shaking his head, the bus driver smiled. We had been waiting five minutes for the girl from the Ipanema Hotel, just a few blocks from Rio de Janeiro's famous Ipanema Beach. I wondered if Astrud Gilberto was watching.

The bus passengers consisted of teachers of writing. We were attending a conference sponsored by the Association of American Schools, researching for more expertise in how to teach children, K-12, to become better writers.

The girl demanded all our attention, if not for seemingly being deliberately late, then for the exceptionally short blue and white sundress she wore. The shortness of her dress emphasized her long, tan and lovely legs. The rest of the dress revealed more tan around lovely curves. Indeed, she was, "tall and tan and young and lovely / The girl from Ipanema."

When we arrived at the conference site, the American School of Rio de Janeiro, we exited the bus, gathering around and waiting for the main attraction to show off her legs as she descended the stairs of the bus with a samba sway. Even the women seemed captivated. As she continued her sway, the passengers parted to allow her a red carpet path. The "aaahs" audibly returned. She moved ahead and disappeared up and into the school.

The school was mounted on the side of one of the many steep hills, or mountains, as the "Cariocas" called them. The white classroom building with blue trim was stacked on four levels up the steep cliff side. Each level was stacked in such a way as to support a white and blue terraced step that could not entirely scale the purple and green stone façade. The steep hillside was dotted with trees in full spring bloom of October. An occasional small monkey lazily swung from limb to limb.

We were directed to a third floor classroom. Each of the four levels of the school were accessible only by an outside stairway that connected to a walkway with a railing.

Forty or so of us found seats. Turning heads could not locate the "Girl from Ipanema." Then, again, she made a grand entrance, walking straight ahead without a glance or a smile. She found an empty desk in the front. The "aaahs" followed her swaying hips, I noted all of this from a desk in the back of the room.

The classroom architecture reflected Rio's climate. Overhead, long bladed fans stirred the steamy air. The accordion style outer walls were opened to the side of the mountain, allowing a breeze to sweep the room.

The Association of American Schools, along with the Atlanta-based Southern Association of Secondary Education, was responsible for accrediting South American high schools. These schools granted American high school diplomas. Conferences in teaching writing, history, math, and science were made available yearly. The conferences rotated among various major South American cities.

We were in the classroom to hear a noted New Hampshire prep school expert enlighten us on the best methods of producing better writers. Eighteen schools from six different countries were represented.

The noted expert lectured us on his philosophy of teaching writing. His approach was hardly new. "Have students write, write, write, write." "Have them show you, not tell you." However, he presented us with several good methods of "showing." While he lectured, his attention was directed to his right to a front row seat. I had no doubt that someone was sitting in a manner to display her long, tan and lovely legs. Without a smile she stared straight ahead.

To break up the lectures we were placed in groups to write examples of the showing methods introduced. We then exchanged comments of the strengths of the examples. I was shocked to note that the Girl from Ipanema's group had only one female.

At noon we had to travel the stairways down and then up into another building that held the cafeteria, auditorium, gym and administrative offices. The cafeteria was on the top floor. I had heard about the American School of Rio's food service. Its reputation kept me from going there. I had brought my own bottle of water, trail mix and other snacks. I had been told that one Rio teacher in his first year there lost twenty-five pounds because of the unsavory food. I tend to think miles of stairways had much more to do with that than bad lunches.

Instead of following the others, I sat on the bench on the veranda outside the classroom enjoying the breeze, the view of the purple and green cliff side, and the monkeys swinging from tree to tree. About ten minutes into my trail mix I noted the long and tan legs of a samba dancer in front of me. "Hi, can I join you and borrow some of that for my lunch? I couldn't eat what they were serving. My name is La Donna."

"Yes, sit down. Have some nuts, dry fruit, and cereal. I see you have your own water. I am Gus. I teach in the high school at Escola Aparecida."

"I teach high school English at the International School of Porto Alegre." After a long pause she said, "It wasn't the food over there, I just had to get away from all those guys. They followed me, and each one asked me to join them for lunch. I don't know why they do that."

Smiling, I said, "I can't imagine," thinking to myself, 'No lady, you didn't get to the head of the line to climb those stairs because you wanted to be sure there was an empty seat off by yourself.' However, I didn't mind that the alpha female had chosen my table for lunch. I don't really think so, but perhaps I did hear a single "aaah."

"Gus, when we take the bus back to the hotel could I sit with you? I don't want to have to put up with those others, and I just get cool stares from the women."

What could I say? On the bus she asked me if I would mind accompanying her later on a walk; she had some errands to run. I accompanied her into shops that catered to the Ipanema beach crowd. She purchased postcards, stamps and some personal items. Her street samba produced the familiar "aaahs" that she relished, in spite of her straight-ahead stare. The presence of an escort kept "aaah-ers" at bay.

The next day at the conference, a routine of the day before repeated: La Donna front row, a clamor to be in her group, a lunch of trail mix on the veranda with me, and a shared seat on the bus. This time the bus deposited us at the intercity seaside airport in Rio. Goodbyes, and a scamper to flights that would scatter better writing teachers, brought smiles to all. Several males, those "who would give their heart gladly," were still awaiting a smile from the Girl from Ipanema. All they received were shattered dreams.

That was September. Back at Aparecida, an April day found me ambling down the hall towards a teachers lounge. At the far end of the shadowy hall near the principal's office a vision emerged, a rhythmic figure floated my way. I knew that shape, that syncopated walk. Soon the straight ahead stare became that of La Donna.

"Hi, Gus, how are you?"

"La Donna, what are you doing here? You're a long way from Porto Alegre."

A smile, a shift of her hips and a melodic voice, "Oh, I moved to São Paulo. I am enrolling my two kids here."

My puzzled look changed her flirting smile to a sheepish grin. "I guess I forgot to tell you I am married. My husband, he's German, works for a Frankfort Agri-research firm. They are working 150 miles south of Porto Alegre trying to develop genetically engineered apples to grow in a climate where the temperature doesn't drop below freezing. Apples need freezing weather to germinate."

"Your husband has been transferred to São Paulo?"

"No, he is still at the research facility. He stays at the compound there; I rarely get to see him. I got bored. I quit my teaching job and moved up here with my friend, Erika. Her husband works at the same place as mine. I convinced her she was bored and would find São Paulo much less boring."

"But won't you get bored here," I replied, "With no teaching job?"

"Oh, I'll have plenty to do. I make friends easily. I also teach dance, jazz and other free and modern forms. I have been thinking of taking up yoga."

She flashed out a leg, did a pirouette, and bent her leg back out and up almost to her head. This in her short shorts rather than a short sundress. "Besides, I have you to show me São Paulo."

She took me by the arm and asked me to walk her to her car. "Why don't we get started on seeing the city by going to dinner this evening? Meet me at my newly rented house." She gave me an address and a general idea of where that was.

With my trusty São Paulo map book and a patient cab driver, I found La Donna's house. The maid, who spoke only German, answered the bell at the outer gate. I was rescued by a boy of ten or eleven who spoke English and German. He was La Donna's son, Wilhelm. "Are you Gus? My mom called and said she would be late, come in and wait."

I did as bid. For an hour and a half, we waited, I met Sonia, Wilhelm's sister who was about six years old. They were both blue eyed blondes, unlike their dark haired mother. Sonia was trying to learn to write the alphabet. Rather odd I thought; by six she should be a year or two beyond that. Then I saw the problem. I recognized most of the letters, but the order and several of the letters had me confused until I realized that some of the letters themselves were backwards. An "E" looked like the number three. For an hour, Wilhelm and I struggled to reverse her "C, B, As."

Following La Donna's late grand entrance, the two of us set off to Kitzpiel, an Austrian restaurant whose décor represented the Alps. I listened for the "Sound of Music," but I heard only samba tunes. I learned La Donna was of Italian descent, born and raised in Tampa, Florida. Her mother was divorced and remarried a German citizen and moved with her ten-year-old daughter to Wiesbaden, Germany. La Donna graduated high school at an international school with an American diploma. Then it was back to Florida for college where she earned a degree in English with an education in endorsement. Then it was back to Germany.

"I got teaching jobs at American international schools in Germany. While teaching in Frankfort I met Gerhardt. We had Wilhelm and Sonia. It was never a good marriage but I tried to make the best of it. When his work took him to southern Brazil, I thought things would improve, but I couldn't live in the research compound miles and miles from what resembled a city. I talked my friend, Erika, into moving to Porto Alegre, a city of about a million. There I was able to teach English at the International school. We have been in Brazil for almost 3 years now. Porto Alegre was almost as boring as the research compound. So I talked Erika into coming to São Paulo with me. She had 2 children but they go to University in Germany. She is older. Her husband is all wrapped up in apple research. She likes São Paulo better. She can spend her husband's money more freely here. There are so many more stores and more expensive things to buy. She has already discovered the shops on Avenida Polista."

Apparently, Gerhardt had a long extended weekend once a month and was expected soon. But when he wasn't around, she told me my company would be appreciated. She was interviewing for dance instructor positions and had already met some nice people. "São Paulo is so refreshing."

So went the rest of the school year: occasional dinners at restaurants, some at La Donna's, including a dinner party with all her new São Paulo friends. In her three years in the country she learned Portuguese well. The majority of her new friends, mostly male, were from the two studios where she taught various dance lessons. No doubt her long, tan legs looked good in her instructor leotards.

For me the school year ended in the middle of June and I flew back to the States for seven weeks, returning to São Paulo in the second week of August. American and international schools in South America kept a schedule resembling that of North American and Europe. Thus, we had a long break in June and July. We also had five weeks or more over the Christmas and New Year holidays. La Donna phoned and I learned she was now a substitute teacher at Escola Aparecida.

I saw La Donna at school a day or two a week. In addition to eating out, we went to see plays at the British club or the other major American high school in São Paulo. We also took in movies, often the two children were a part of the movies. This developed into occasionally being asked to babysit on Sundays, the maid's day off. La Donna had "various activities to attend to."

Sundays at La Donna's with the kids involved helping Sonia with her flexible alphabet and her reading. La Donna convinced Sonia that Scrabble was a good game for her to play. Playing Scrabble with Sonia was a new adventure. She liked to win. This exceptionally bright young type soon taught me that the rules of Scrabble did not prevent her from spelling words in reverse. "Read the rules. See, it doesn't say you can't." She was very good at this version of elbbarcS.

Sometime early in the semester La Donna got serious over a meal at an Italian restaurant. São Paulo has outstanding restaurants that feature almost any ethnic cuisine design. After the antipasto, La Donna leaned closer and quietly said, "You know I told you that Gerhardt and I are not getting along. Since the move to Brazil I have become frigid. After the birth of Sonia I began losing interest, and now I am totally unable to have sex. Gerhardt is so macho that he can't deal with that very well. That is why he so seldom comes to São Paulo, even when he has the time.

"Now you understand my behavior towards you. We can only be friends, but you are the best friend I have in São Paulo, you and Erika."

So life continued. We ate out. I babysat. She bestowed upon me an occasional gift of a nice shirt, linen, a nice tie, silk, and other items designed to improve my image. These were followed by a smile, a thank you, and a hug.

In October, the three American schools in São Paulo hosted another Association of American Schools' Conference. This one featured the teaching of math. By this time La Donna was a regular at Escola Aparecida, she was popular with both students and staff. She was a rare commodity, a sub who could actually teach. Since volunteers were needed for the conference, La Donna was highly visible for this new round of admirers. Her movements were well noted. Some eyes were delighted to follow her graceful prances where other eyes seemed to offer a stare and a scowl. The "aaahs" were still audible, but the groans were growing louder. One of the math teachers from Porto Alegre stopped me toward the end of the first day, asking for directions to the restroom. I didn't think he actually needed my help; his need for assistance became clear when he asked if I knew La Donna. "I do," I said. He rolled his eyes and said, "If you would like to hear a story, lets meet for dinner." I like stories. Arrangements were made to eat at a German restaurant near the conference hotel.

Harvey Killian of Cedar Rapids, Iowa said he enjoyed the spätzle he had just finished. As he began to sip on his schnapps, he asked what La Donna was doing at Aparecida. "Subbing," I replied.

"Do you know why she was fired at Porto Alegre?"

"FIRED? I thought she quit. She said she was bored with Cowboy Brazil."

"She likes to be admired by any male over fifteen. She had an affair with one of her students, an eighteen-year-old senior from Texas. He was a wild cat who walked out on his divorced, rich father. The father worked for a Texas Agri-business conglomerate. The dad was more concerned with making money and chasing mulatto skirts than he was with the kid. La Donna filled the father's void with, at first, motherly love when he left his dad's fancy apartment and moved in with her kids. The student received far more than motherly affection. It was two weeks before the father even knew he was no longer at home.

"By this time the boy's deductive powers led him to believe that if La Donna's husband was out of the picture he, La Donna, and the 2 kids could be one happy family. Perhaps La Donna contributed to his deducing. The boy went back to his father's apartment when the father was at work and borrowed the keys to a car and found his father's handgun. He headed for the German apple research project near the Argentine border.

"Student gossip could not be corralled, and soon the entire school knew. Mickey Worth was on his way to snuff Gerhardt Lutz. The boy was stopped 20 miles from the research compounds." Harvey went on, "Money talks. Rich daddy and the conglomerate Agri-business influence in both the Brazilian and American state department provided enough juice to get La Donna fired, Mickey sent off to a U.S. military academy, and the entire affair hushed."

"What about La Donna's apple tree geneticist?"

"Geneticist? He's the head of security for the German science firm. Lutz's father is a wealthy tycoon who owns a dozen enterprises, including the security firm and the genetic fruit research company. Gerhardt is the black sheep of the family. By sending him across the Atlantic and 150 miles into the middle of nowhere, the father hoped his no good son would finally stay out of trouble."

I did indeed hear an interesting story that evening. How many more La Donna stories were yet to come?

The American School's conference sure had an interesting sidebar featuring the Girl from Ipanema. The conference adjourned and life returned to normal at Aparecida. La Donna continued subbing and working to attract attention from the male staff. However, the American School conference opened a new chapter in the La Donna story. The conference leaders had advertised their endorsement of a masters in education degree offered in Brasilia during the Christmas break. By taking courses for 14 days at the American school for two Christmas sessions and two sessions in late June, the degree could be had. This was easy advancement on the pay scale without having to do much work. The degree was offered by a Boston Aryan university. The professors loved their January term in sunny, exotic Brazil. Two weeks in Brazil made for opportunities in Rio or the Brazilian northeast coast or, even more exciting, the Amazon. This was mostly paid for by someone else.

When second semester classes commenced at Aparecida the last week of January, I learned that, while I had traveled through Argentina and Chile, La Donna had traveled to Brasilia and towards a masters degree. Several of our faculty members were in the program. The newcomer to the group was our new biology teacher, Derek Bergen, the surfer like blonde Adonis from California. Jo Jo, his wife who taught in our elementary school, was visiting her parents in the states while Derek was apparently practicing biology in Brasilia.

La Donna and Derek's adventure was grist for the Aparecida gossip mill. Apparently, La Donna had dumped me for Derek. This was a shock for me for I never knew I was in a position from which I could be dumped. She was now having an affair with the blonde biology teacher. Of course the two of them, often having lunch together at school, fed the gossip.

Jo Jo's ears caught all of this as well. As La Donna and Derek were happily dining on a school lunch in a cafeteria filled with a dozen faculty members and a few hundred students, Jo Jo, having been told of the lunch tryst, marched into the cafeteria armed with a glass bottle of water. She stepped in behind La Donna and tried to deliver a message. Derek deftly intercepted the message by deflecting the bottle before it met with La Donna's head.

Jo Jo and Derek both missed school for a week. With the shortage of available subs, La Donna, claiming innocence in all of it, taught Derek's classes.

Things calmed down at Aparecida after that. Interestingly enough, Derek was said to disappear for a few long weekends and then for an entire week. During his week-long absence, La Donna was not available to sub. This prompted Jo Jo to call me and ask if I knew where Derek was, or if I was going to see La Donna. Her calls were made after having sought refuge in a product of the Brazilian vineyards. "Gus, why did he do this to me. I know she's tall and tan and lovely, but I've got more than that woman. What is she that I am not?" Jo Jo was indeed a looker with more curves than La Donna. I guess the answer was in the area of "forbidden fruit," but for Jo Jo, I had no answers.

I didn't tell her that on some of those weekends I was asked to entertain La Donna's kids with a movie, McDonald's, and games of Scrabble backwards and forwards. These were the weekends Derek was out of town.

Rumor turned to reality three weeks before the school year ended. The ringing of my house phone awakened me at 1:00 am on Sunday. The zelador, twelve floors below, rattled on in high pitched and excited Portuguese, which only told me that something or someone had him on the brink of hysteria. Finally, after hearing some commotion, I heard La Donna's voice in the background. As best I could, I told the zelador to send her up.

I opened the door to a blood smeared La Donna. Her face and hands were streaked red. She was barefoot and appeared to be clothed only in a man's white dress shirt. The view on the cool Brazilian night confirmed the lack of underwear. No wonder the zelador was losing his mind: tall, tan, lovely, bloody and practically naked. I am sure he didn't know if he was lucky or should be terrified.

La Donna pushed me aside and cried, "He's going to shoot Derek, he's going to kill Derek. He has a gun. He knows where Derek lives. He has a gun and is on his way."

After I got La Donna calmed down a bit and the blood cleaned off her face and hands, she told me that Gerhardt was in São Paulo for the weekend. He had been drinking and accused her of having an affair. She denied it but, with more drinking and more accusing, he told her he had his father's security firm follow her and had proof of her affair. He knew where Derek lived and had already found the place. He had rented a car for the weekend and now was on his way to shoot Derek.

Her hysteria returned. "Do something, do something, do something," she shouted.

"What can I do? I don't even know where Derek lives. I am no commando who takes on drunks with a gun. I don't think I can protect him with prayer."

Suddenly she jumped up, "Call Derek. Warn him."

I got the Aparecida handbook for Derek's phone number. After six or eight rings Jo Jo answered. "Jo Jo this is Gus. I need to speak with Derek."

"Gus? Do you know what time it is?" A long pause…
"What do you want with him?" A longer pause, "Gus, answer me."

Finally, "Gus, this is Derek, what's the problem?"

113

"Derek, we have a mutual friend."

"Okay, I understand. What is it?"

"Our mutual friend has a husband. The husband has a gun. He's drunk and on his way to your apartment. He says he is on his way to pay you what you are due. He knows how to handle a pistol."

"I'll take care of it." He hung up.

After more talk, I got La Donna to settle into the second bedroom of my apartment.

Sunday morning at 8:30 I rubbed the sleep out of my eyes and went to prepare some breakfast for my bloody guest. Before I got to the kitchen I found the other bedroom door wide open, the slept-in bed empty and no trace of La Donna in the apartment. The shirt she arrived in, the t-shirt I gave her, the blanket, and La Donna were gone. Repeated phone calls to both La Donna and Derek went unanswered.

Monday at school I sought out the principal, Laim Shaw. The genial Irishman laughed when he saw me, "at least you didn't get shot. Come into my office. I'll tell you a story."

In his office he told me, "Apparently La Donna's husband was shot early Sunday morning near Derek Bergen's apartment. The story being told is an armed security guard at the complex shot him thinking he was an intruder. The military police said that Gerhardt Lutz had a gun and was stinking drunk.

"Derek Bergen has not reported for work and Jo Jo says she does not know where he is. She says he left their apartment after you called."

During the last weeks of school both Derek and Jo Jo resigned. Derek's resignation was mailed from the U.S. Jo Jo hand delivered hers two days before school let out.

La Donna was not available to sub. Apparently she, along with her kids, had left the country for Germany to deal with the unexpected death of her husband. I guess money still did the talking. Nothing more was said in São Paulo about the death of a German apartment intruder. The story should have ended there.

However, two years later, 1989, I was back in Minnesota teaching. On a February weekend I journeyed to the University of

Northern Iowa's overseas teaching fair. I wasn't looking for employment; I went in search of friends I had made during my four years in São Paulo. The overseas teaching circuit is a small world, with many people chasing new dreams and following old school directors to yet another part of the world. I must have exchanged stories with a dozen people. Some were searching for employment in such places as Taipei, Singapore, Chennai, Karachi, Munich, and Stavanger. Others, just like me, came to visit.

On Sunday I was walking down a hallway in the Education Center when I heard, "Hey, Gus." I turned and who did I see walking toward me, hand in hand with big smiles on their faces? Derek and Jo Jo. In unison they said, "Gus, good to see you."

They smiled lovingly at each other. They said that after a year of rest in Hawaii they just signed on to teach in the South Pacific. We chatted and said our farewells. They strode off hand in hand. Oh wonder of wonders.

• • •

Ten years later I took advantage of spring break and fed my baseball passion by going to Fort Myers, Florida to see the Minnesota Twins in spring training. For me the joy of spring training games is about seeing the prospects, the future. I saw two games and, while the Twins crossed over to the Atlantic side of Florida for a few games, I ventured to Sanibel Island. The beaches reminded me of my time in Brazil. But, as beautiful as the Sanibel beaches were, they were not Rio or Florianopolis. As I sat on the sand I concluded that the bikinis of Sanibel do not compare to the tongas of Rio. My textile inspection had me watching a young, tall, tan stroller pass to and fro, "Looking straight ahead but looking not at me." She seemed to step out of a song. "When she walks she's like a samba that swings so cool and sways so gently." I thought I heard the "aaahs" of the song. I could not see the girl's hair which was hidden under her wide brimmed floppy hat. A voice from behind said, "Does she remind you of someone? Perhaps me?" I turned and looked to see tall, tan, and lovely legs. As I raised my eyes I saw a face that was as lovely as ever.

"La Donna."

"Yes, Gus."

"How did you find me here?"

"I didn't. It appears you found me."

She smiled and said, "I did. I saw you earlier up the beach. I wasn't so sure it was you, so I watched and remembered until I was sure. Come, let's find the beach bar and talk."

We did. La Donna had left São Paulo the June after the shooting of Gerhardt. She said the Lutz Estate provided a sizable trust for Wilhelm and Sonia. The trust allowed the children to live well and attend the very best of schools. Wilhelm was now fulfilling his grandfather's dream as a geneticist studying apples and other fruit trees, learning the business and eventually is expected to take over the entire conglomerate. "He is now twenty-two and living in Germany."

"What about Sonia?"

Smiling, La Donna said, "Oh, she's around when she's not at St. Ann's, a girl's prep school in Fort Myers. I maintain her home and manage her trust."

"And you? What are you up to when you're not managing a trust?"

"Oh, I still teach some dance, do a little writing and volunteer some."

"I see that you still maintain that stunning Girl from Ipanema look."

"I won't admit to anyone but you that I'll never see forty-five again, but I still have no trouble finding handsome men, like you, to keep me company."

"Yes, handsome like me, but not so handsome as to get me shot at."

"I do feel bad about how I used you, but like you said, you were never in any danger and I made you look good by being seen with me. You will be happy to know I am finally beginning to see the light. I have my eye on a handsome and filthy rich widower who thinks I can make his dreams come true."

"When?"

Instead of a straight ahead stare, a smile, "When Sonia graduates from St. Ann's and turns eighteen and I am no longer the manager of her trust."

Just then the girl from Sanibel beach that had captivated me before La Donna made her presence known sashayed over to our table.

"Remember me?" She smiled and took off her floppy hat. Long, straight blonde hair tumbled out and covered her shoulders. Up close she was even more stunning.

"I do remember you, the cheating Scrabble player with a twist on the alphabet."

"I still win the prizes I want."

La Donna piped in telling me how proud she was of Sonia. Sonia beamed as La Donna gushed about how Sonia had overcome her handicap, had a 4.0 GPA at St. Ann's, and was already accepted at several highly regarded universities.

"Which will you choose?" I asked.

"The one that has the most challenging and handsome male faculty. I still like to have an edge when I play.

"Mama was sure she recognized you. I remember how nice you were to Wilhelm and me, how you played Scrabble with me and asked Wilhelm about his reading. I remember the movies, too. I owe you my thanks. But now I must run. I told my friends I would go swim with them. We found a group of good looking college boys. They look ripe for torture. So much luring and tempting to be done. So many hearts to break."

As she got up, she bumped into me, held her body close and slipped a folded piece of paper into my hand.

La Donna said she had people to meet, perhaps we could have dinner in Fort Myers the next evening? I agreed. La Donna swayed away.

After La Donna left, I thought about those last two most interesting years in São Paulo, then I unfolded Sonia's paper gift and read:

*Sug,*

*Evah dluohs amam tahw uoy evig ll'I dna thginot enin ta sllehS*
*aeS ehT ta em teem. Eavh dluohs ehs ekil uoy detaert reven amam.*

*Ainos*

After a moment of confusion, I remembered Sonia's version of elbbarcS and reread the note backwards.

"But, Mr. August, you gotta pass me. Mr. Gordon told me I have enough English credits to graduate. He said I have twelve solid quarters of English, and I had passed all my requirements. I didn't need this credit.

"Then two days ago he called me in and said he goofed. I was one quarter shy of graduation. I still needed a class as an elective credit. So just give me a D- and I'll be out of your hair."

"Donny, all you need to do is turn in all your written work that you ignored this quarter. The answer is always the same: if you want credit for the course, you need to run all the way to the finish line. To get the same credit other students get you need to do the work they do."

"I bet you're just doing this to get even with me, Mr. August, because of what I wrote on the paper my friends turned in for me last year. You just want revenge and waited till now."

Last year the paper I thought Donny had turned in said in part, "Mr. August is a big fat slob and a damn poor teacher." He had written the paper and showed it to his friends. They dared him to turn it in that way. He backed down from the dare because he told them he needed the required writing credit and wasn't going to take the class again. Unfortunately for him, one of his friends slipped the paper into the inbox on my desk. Donny, being Donny, was late in getting his rewritten version turned in.

I read his original paper. I pointed out that he had not done sufficient research. I wrote on his paper, "Donny, you got half of it correct. I am fat, but I am a damn good teacher. Be certain you have the evidence for what you say." Donny received a D- on the paper.

"Donny, if I may remind you, you passed that class. I didn't get revenge then, and I am not getting it now." Donny just sat there hanging his head.

"Donny, why did you ever take another class from me when you didn't have to? You know I require you to do all the work or no credit."

"I took it because you have several group projects in that class."

"Oh, so you like group work and cannot get enough of it?"

"No. Diana, Virginia, Cheryel and Polly were taking it." Donny smiled.

Those girls were four of the most attractive girls in the school. "So, Donny Casanova, you figured to get into their group each time."

"I did every time. We got good grades on the projects. I showed those babes Donny Welker had brains if he wanted to use them. Just from those projects I should have enough points to pass."

"Yes, Mr. Casanova, you do. However, you failed to do anything else. Not one other thing. You know I don't give credit for a race unless you run the entire distance."

"But, Mr. August, I didn't think I needed the credit. Old Goody told me I was all set."

"Then your issue is with Mr. Gordon. However, when you turn in the rest of your work you will get your credit."

"That will take me a month. I haven't even read the book.

How can I write those papers? I could go to summer school in that time, not do any work and still get a D-."

"Be my guest. Less hassle for me." Donny stalked out of the room.

The next day, the day before graduation, I was grading final papers and tests. I got called to the office. Mr. Kennedy, the principal, told me that Donny Welker's parents were coming in at four o'clock to speak with me. "You know Mr. Welker is the president of the school board. He asked me to change Donny's grade to a D- so he could pass and get his diploma the next day. He said he didn't want to be handing his own son an empty sheepskin. I told him, 'I don't interfere with the grades my teachers submit unless someone can show me why I need to step in.' I told him if he wants Donny's grade changed, he'll have to deal with you. He and his wife will be here at four."

Pete Welker was a smart, hardworking businessman whose wealth contributed more in taxes than anyone else in the school district. Donny was their youngest child and the "apple of his mother's eye." Unlike his older siblings, Donny chose a smiling personality and charm over hard work. He knew how to manipulate, and he was the idol of many a young girl, and of course his mother. No wonder he was able to weasel his way into the groups with all of the "babes."

Janette Welker enjoyed her social status in the community. She bought and handsomely wore the finest, most expensive clothes that Nordstrom's had to offer. She reveled in the eye catching glances she garnered over most of her fifty years. She did not understand the word "no." Donny must have learned much from his mother.

At four o'clock Mr. Kennedy ushered the Welker's into my room and said, "I'll leave the three of you to work things out."

Pete Welker presented his organized argument:

Donny was told that he had the required credits.

Donny earned enough points to get a D-.

Did I have a need to humiliate the Welker family in front of relatives and the community?

Did I think I was God and could stop Donny from graduating?

"No, Mr. Welker. I am not keeping Donny from graduating. I did not keep him from doing his work. I didn't force him to take this class. He can receive an empty diploma and complete the work. Then his diploma can be mailed to him. Or, he can go to summer school and get his diploma that way."

Then Mrs. Welker got up from her chair, marched a few steps away, turned and pointed her finger sharply and said, "That will take several weeks. His friends know all about this and are already laughing. Relatives and the community will be asking why he is in summer school. We have a family fishing trip to Canada already booked for the rest of June. We have already paid for his graduation party this weekend. We can't cancel, and all who attend will talk behind our backs about Donny's empty diploma."

Variations on these themes went on for another hour and a half. I had visions of the three of us doing this dance until tomorrow's graduation. All arguments for common sense, logic, responsibility, and mercy had run their course many times over. Finally, at six o'clock, I stood up and stated emphatically, "You win!" Smiling, I said, "I will give Donald Welker a passing grade." I marched out the door and skipped down the hall. The Welker's rushed out into the hall and in unison screamed, "WAIT!" The skipping must have done the trick. "Wait, what are you going to change his incomplete to? You'll give him a D-, right?"

I stopped, slowly turned, smiled and said, "I am changing it to an A+."

Both rushed up, and Mr. Welker said, "An A+? Just give him a D-."

Mrs. Welker said, "His friends will laugh. Everyone knows you never gave an A+ in your life. People will find out. They will laugh at us. They know he doesn't deserve an A+."

"Mrs. Welker, he doesn't deserve a D- either. When I give something away, I only give the best. I don't want to be known as cheap. An A+ it is." I turned and walked toward the office.

Mrs. Welker's high pitched voice screeched, "DON'T."

Mr. Welker quietly said, "He'll go to summer school."

# Sideways to and from the Falklands

"Gus, there is someone here from the U.S. Embassy in Brasilia to see you," said Laim Shaw, my principal at Escola Aparecida, an American school in São Paulo, Brazil. "He's waiting in my office."

As I entered Mr. Shaw's office, a middle aged man in a blue tropical suit with a toucan tie rose from a chair and extended his hand, "Mr. Stuart August, I presume. I'm Tim King, U.S. Cultural Attaché. Sit down and let's talk."

He closed the door and took the chair opposite me. "The British Embassy has requested an interview with you."

"Why would the Brits want to speak with me? I liked the British pantomime I saw at their club," I replied jokingly.

"You did travel to the Falkland Islands in January of 1982, did you not?"

"Yes."

"It seems that the British Foreign Office wishes to speak with a few travelers who visited there before the war. They have asked us to assist them in an interview with you. According to them, they are trying to establish the atmosphere of the place prior to the war. They say they have no interest in you other than just hearing about Port Stanley and the people, just a friendly chat.

"If you decide to cooperate, entirely up to you, I'll accompany you to see that your rights are protected. They wish to do this at ten o'clock Saturday morning at the British Council here in São Paulo. Take a day or two to consider. I will call you here at school for your answer. Our embassy hopes you will cooperate; however, we are not pressuring you to do so.

"If you decide to go, I will have a car pick you up at your apartment at eight-thirty a.m."

After King left, Laim Shaw asked me what that was all about. I told him.

"What in the hell ever possessed you to go to the Falkland Islands?"

"Laim," I laughed, "I think it all started when I was a kid. I had a board game I loved called Cargoes. The board was a map of the world. The game tokens were little cast iron ships that moved across the cargo lanes of the world. A pair of dice propelled the vessels from port to port where they picked up varied dollars worth of merchandise while trying to avoid costly sea hazards and duty taxes. I cruised the world picking up wool in Perth, diamonds in Durham, machinery in Liverpool, and turtles in the Galapagos. I guess the game wasn't entirely accurate in its depiction of world commerce. There are no ports in the Galapagos, or export of turtles. But, I found my way to Hong Kong, Singapore, Calcutta, Port Said, and New York. The Falklands were on the map, but not on any of the trade routes. I loved playing. I guess I had to make my life extend beyond the board game."

"So, you had to go there?"

I told Laim that, as it started out, the Falklands were not on my mind. Oscar Swift, a good friend and history teacher at Aparecida, and I had planned on going to Uruguay and Argentina over Christmas break. From the beginning the trip seemed to go sideways.

First Daffy Drake, one of our elementary teachers, heard about our adventure and asked if she could join us. Twenty-eight years old and younger than both Oscar and I, Daffy was not the most popular person on our staff. She tended to think quite highly of herself, and seemed to look down upon the rest of us who were not sophisticated Californians. Her clothes were highly fashionable, and she tried every method she could to enhance her appearance. She was not unattractive but saw herself as a show stopper. However, once she opened her mouth, potential admirers turned away. A sense of snobbishness gave way to a steady whine about most everything she encountered in São Paulo. I knew Oscar would not be happy to have her along. I left the decision to him. I could ignore her complaining, but I knew Oscar would not cope well with her. Oscar was too nice a guy to say no so Daffy became part of the group.

Two unhip men as traveling companions was not what Daffy wanted. She asked and even begged other females to join us. As I said, she was not real popular; thus, no takers.

She finally convinced Helen Yarbrough, an elementary teacher from the other major American school in São Paulo, to join us. Helen was as southern as southern could be. Her Georgia drawl was her trademark as much as her tan and a glass in her hand. Helen was a sun and whiskey worshipper. She was the most tanned woman I ever met. Her fifty years on any beach she could find had cured her wrinkled skin to the texture of old leather. Helen was not a drunk as such, but she was never far away from a day brightener.

The gang of four met with a travel agent who came highly recommended by other staff members. He was an Argentine with a British wife who had worked for years in São Paulo. They sent their children to the British school. He outlined a ten day junket to Montevideo, Buenos Aires, and on to Mar del Plata in Argentina. That left us another ten days. "Where else can I book you?" No one said a thing for a while.

To lighten the mood I said, "How about Port Stanley?"

"Port what?" winced Daffy.

"It's in the Falkland Islands, a British Colony in the deep south Atlantic. I booked a couple into a nice boarding house there last year."

Daffy perked up and asked if many tourists went there. When she heard that it was a remote destination, she smiled and said, "Then I could tell everyone about a place none of them had ever been. I want to go."

Helen asked if she could find Beefeaters gin there. The travel agent smiled, and said, "I don't know for sure, but it's British and they have pubs there."

"Honey, count me in," drawled Helen.

Oscar rolled his eyes and finally said okay. The travel agent was a salesman and closed the deal, the Falkland Islands.

The junket only continued to go sideways. A week before we were to leave Daffy said she couldn't make the original departure date of December 22nd. She had just heard that a relative of hers would be in Rio over Christmas. "I just have to be with family on Christmas Eve."

Then Oscar decided he would never have his final tests corrected and grades in by the 22nd. He would join us in Montevideo on the 26th.

The travel agent said he might be able to cancel two of the tickets, but he had to keep two of us to maintain the special rates he had gotten us for the entire trip. Hence, the morning of the 22nd at 7 a.m. I met Helen at the airport. I was off to spend four days in Montevideo with a woman I hardly knew. That was to be some Christmas, sharing a room with Georgia southerner.

On the plane, I told Laim, she said her friends asked her, "What in the hell are you doing going on a vacation with a man you don't know who doesn't even drink and is a far cry from your party style life?" She said she didn't bother to add we'd then be joined by whiny Daffy Duck and highly professional Oscar Swift.

I asked, "How did you reply?"

She said, "Damned if I know, but bring it on."

Helen and I had a good four days in Montevideo. We toured the nineteenth century Opera House, a most elegant display of dark hardwoods, lush seats, velvet curtains, and opera boxes framing the second tier balcony. We learned the history of Spanish speaking countries of the southern part of the continent at the San Martín Museum. We both truly enjoyed the education given to us in paintings, displays, and artifacts. The capitol building was colossal and beautiful. Magnificent stone, colorful mosaics, grand staircases, and woven tapestries told the history of Uruguay. We stopped to admire the inventory of the many rock shops. Uruguay has some of the finest and largest agates on earth. The finely cut and polished stones featured reds, blues, greens, and even oranges. I was amazed. As a boy I had collected agates, but I had never seen anything to match these.

Helen said that she was enjoying the trip. She especially liked it that I was in total agreement with her that every couple of hours we would stop at a little bar to rest. Helen soon learned that the local Spanish for whiskey was wicky. She ordered her "wicky sour." I was happy to order a soft drink they called Pomelo Sip, similar to a can of Squirt. In São Paulo I could find no such flavor; Brazilians don't like anything sour. I couldn't even find a grapefruit at the weekly fara. Grapefruit was for export only. Helen toasted me, "Gus, you know how to travel."

The best part of the first two days was a fine supper. I was told we couldn't miss the Old Port area. One of the biggest warehouses had been converted into an indoor eating mall. A dozen restaurants could be found inside. If you like seafood, it was there. But for me was the A-framed wood fire grills. The iron grills were at least ten yards long and perhaps three yards wide on each side. Under the arch, wood embers glowed and crackled. Decorating the grill was every type of sausage and cut of meat that Uruguay could produce. The aroma of the wood fire and the sizzle of the meats was heavenly.

Part of the pageantry was watching the grill masters with oversized meat forks moving the cuts from the lower portion of the grill to the upper where they would be kept warm. Then someone from the other side of the grill would get a specific order from a customer. The customers were seated at a bar fronting the grill on each side. The grill master would poke a fork into a steak and toss it over the A-frame to be picked out of the air by another fork and placed on an eager eater's plate.

Since Helen worshiped the sun, she wanted to go to the beach on Christmas Eve and Christmas Day, which was fine by me. I walked to the zoo and both animal and people watched. Later I walked to the beach to meet Helen at a restaurant for our Christmas

Eve dinner. Helen loved men almost as much as the sun and her drink. She introduced me to two American basketball players she met on the beach. They played professionally in South America. On Christmas Day Helen headed back to the beach. I found a Catholic church for Mass and later that morning walked through the residential neighborhoods to the sounds of family and Christmas dinners. I trekked to the casino near the beach but did not have the proper attire, coat and tie, nor the proper bankroll, too small.

Oscar and Daffy made their way to our hotel on the 26th. The next day we crossed the Rio de la Plata Estuary, over 200 miles to Buenos Aires, on a hovercraft. After several days of touring Buenos Aires, Oscar, who apparently had enough of Daffy's moaning and Helen's frequent requests for a wicky stop, decided that he had too much work to do to get ready for next semester. He headed back to São Paulo.

Daffy, Helen and I flew to Mar del Plata, Argentina's most popular beach. We found out that our travel agent had booked us into a jet set resort up the coast with a private beach, nightly stage show, and a four star restaurant. This was not in our budget, so, it was back to the city beaches.

In Mar del Plata our *South America on Twenty-five Dollars a Day* helped us find a friendly, family run place off the beaten path in our price range. Daffy didn't complain about the price, but never stopped finding fault with our accommodations. The three beds in one room allowed for a one foot aisle between each bed and perhaps two feet between walls that the headboards did not abut. She screamed that the shower did not have enough water pressure, "How can I rinse my hair?" She also found fault with the lack of a shower stall. The small bathroom, stool and sink included, served as a shower stall. She wailed when she realized that, unless towels were placed under the door, the shower water flooded the bedroom.

Helen just smiled, "Let's hit the beach."

She and Daffy did for three days. I walked the city while they tanned and boy watched. I people watched and read from one of the many books I always travel with. Each evening I'd meet them at the beach. I walked among the sun worshippers who were lying in rows ten deep along the shore. There was a five foot travel path between each row. I strolled, investigating the bikinis, until I heard the distinct Georgia drawl, "Y'all, over here."

Every evening we tried to find a restaurant. For the most part that was easy. South Americans eat dinner at 9 o'clock or after. I say for the most part because one of those evenings was New Year's Eve. Our cab driver told us it was useless to try and find a place that was not reserved for the entire night. Helen and Daffy, adorned in their classiest apparel, heels and all, had the driver take us to every place he could think of. After an hour and a half we gave up and he dumped us at a cheap pizzeria near our accommodations. After a meal of pepperoni on cardboard we toasted in the New Year with cans of Pepsi Cola. Helen laughed. Daffy bitched. I ate lousy pizza.

A few of the single males in the pizzeria invited Daffy to a party. She blew her stack because neither Helen nor I would accompany her. "Daffy, we don't know these people," barked Helen. Daffy sulked on the walk back to The Hovel Ritz.

Things had to get better, so onto the Falklands. We flew to Comodoro Rivadavia. The people there wished for more notoriety than being the jumping off place to the Ilhas Malvinas, formerly of Argentine rule. The Comodoros were now banking on an offshore oil bonanza. For some strange reason the Argentine Air Force operated a small commercial airline that offered the only flights to the Falklands.

I told Laim that another complication to visiting the islands was the duration of stay. We would arrive around noon and leave that evening between six and eight. Only after our arrival would we be given the departure time, or we could stay for eight days and leave between six and eight. "Laim, I tell you the only direction we moved on that entire adventure was sideways."

• • •

At 8:30 Saturday morning a car from the U.S. Council picked me up. Tim King met me at the British Council and introduced me to Nigel Smythe. Smythe had a military cut to him, lean yet muscular, jacket, no tie, khaki pants, highly shined black shoes and close cut hair. He said he was a Cultural Attaché posted to Brasilia. I began to feel like I was being attached to death.

"Gus, may I call you Gus? I am told that all of your friends call you Gus."

"Yes, Nigel." He seemed to wince at my use of his first name.

"Well then, the British Home Office is conducting a few informal, let us say surveys, concerning the atmosphere in the Falklands before the war. Just to, sort of, get a complete picture as part of the before, during, and after wrap-up to what transpired. According to our immigration records you arrived in Port Stanley on 3, January, 1982. Is that correct?"

"It could be. I know that we were in Mar del Plata for New Year's."

"Yes. The "we" you refer to consisted of Daphne Drake, Helen Yarbrough, and you."

"Will you be interviewing them?"

"Perhaps, perhaps not. Will you tell us what you saw, did, and with whom while you were there? I hear you're quite the storyteller so just sit back and spin the yarn for me."

I sat back in the most comfortable chair in the room, a recliner. Smythe remained rigid on his straight backed chair. King sat forward, looking as if he might jump to my rescue at any moment. I wondered what was at stake here. All settled in, I told my story as best as I could recall it.

• • •

We were met at the airstrip by several Land Rovers. One of them had the name "Baxter House" decaled on both sides. That was the name of the boarding house we had been booked into. Before we could get to it, we were accosted by a man who had been riding in another Land Rover with another decal on it, "Falkland Islands Immigration". Both sets of decals appeared to be detachable. They herded the entire passenger contingent into a cinder block building. One by one each of us had to enter separate rooms, one for females one for males. There was an armed male soldier in each room. The process took an hour. Of the fifteen of us, only four were staying for the eight days. I was surprised that so many flew in only to be there six to eight hours. One was from South Africa. On the plane he said he just wanted to say he'd been there. The others had bird books and binoculars, or sales catalogs.

Back outside we heard, "Would Daphne, Helen, Stuart, and Carlos please come with us?"

Helen frowned, "Stuart?"

"Yes," I said, "Stuart August, Gus."

Carlos introduced himself as Carlos Olgiata, an Argentine newly graduated from college off on a lark before settling down to work for his wealthy father's firm. Carlos appeared to be in his early twenties, about 5'10", 170 pounds. He seemed in good shape with a trim haircut. He wore hiking boots, denim jeans and a wool button down shirt, Pendleton perhaps. He spoke excellent English. The two Baxter girls introduced themselves as Sophie and Emma. Emma appeared to be about fifteen. She was a tiny girl, who in spite of having a face that reminded me of "a wee slickity mouse," was strangely pretty. Sophie, perhaps eighteen, was broader and taller. She too was attractive but in a somewhat unusual manner. They said they were sisters; however, they didn't resemble each other. They both wore jeans and sweatshirts.

At the boarding house, daughters Sophie and Emma introduced us to a portly matron, Mrs. Baxter. She gave us the house rules, "No smoking or drinking, no vulgar or blasphemous language, and quiet after ten p.m. Breakfast at 7:30, lunch at noon, tea at four o'clock, and dinner at seven. If you are not going to be in attendance, would you please inform the household the evening before concerning breakfast and for the remainder of the day. There is no Mr. Baxter." She paused for a few seconds. "No more questions? Good." She marched off.

Sophie showed Daffy and Helen to their rooms on the main floor. Emma led Carlos and me up narrow stairs to two separate attic rooms. Mine was small with a risk for my head from the slanted roof, but overall it was roomier than our accommodation at The Hovel Ritz.

The three of us used the time before dinner to explore Port Stanley on foot. It was a functioning port with a freighter docked at its pier. According to our guidebook fish, mutton, wool, and scrap iron were the only real exports. The scrap iron was collected over the years from abandoned machinery and shipwreck salvage. Since there was an almost total lack of industry, other than sheep, on the islands, and no significant agriculture beyond family gardens, just about everything had to be imported.

The most dominant buildings were governmental. The columned, stately Colony House was large and contained the many offices bureaucracy needed to govern some 2,000 people. A smaller white wooden building housed the post office.

On a small hill just west of the village were fancy houses occupied by the governing bureaucrats. At times families were present but often not for long periods. There was an elementary school, K-6. Education beyond that, if not homeschooled, was to be had at the British school in Montevideo, or back in Britain. If we wished to shop there was a good sized general store for non-perishable groceries, clothing, shoes, hardware and a few other sundry products. You could order furniture and other larger items from a catalog, with a two month wait for delivery. There was a small chemist shop. Near it was a small building that housed a doctor's surgery. Major health issues had to be addressed in South America or Europe. A small veterinary clinic was also near the chemist's.

There were two pubs, a law office, and what passed for a beauty salon which was open only by appointment. The island had telephone service. It's building consisted of an office and repair shop.

There was no hotel. Government VIPs stayed in fancy housing near the administration buildings. If you didn't qualify as a government official or VIP, you had to make do in one of several boarding houses. There were about 500 humble family dwellings in Port Stanley.

Few cars or pickup trucks were on the streets, all gravel except for the High Street that ran east and west parallel to the waterfront. The most popular vehicle was the Land Rover. There was little need for automotive transportation because there were few miles of road in all of the Falklands and nowhere to go. The Land Rovers were popular because they functioned well without a road. Those who owned them, at times, rented them out to the locals, thus the removable decals we saw on arrival. Bicycles and motor scooters provided the major means of mobility other than walking.

Our town tour only lasted a few hours. The only thing we didn't see was the military installation located a few miles behind the administrative mansions. A few RAF fighter jets, with accompanying support staff and a small infantry company were stationed there, in all, a few hundred military personnel. The jets were hangered on the base and reached the airport runway via its own taxi lane. Such an arrangement suggested to me that the British never really thought they would have to defend the islands. They were spending hundreds of thousands of pounds to make the locals feel safe.

Back at the Baxter house we were discouraged from sight-seeing in the military area. "They don't want anyone to see that they have nothing to do," smirked Emma.

"Good information, but did you get out of Port Stanley?" Nigel interrupted.

I went on to tell him that the next day we asked about where we could go and what we could do while there. Mrs. Baxter said that it was almost impossible for any tourist to rent a vehicle. The owners feared they would be mistreated, and they couldn't afford the waiting time for parts and repairs. Once in a while, if the weather cooperated, tourists could hire a local pilot to take them up. Mrs. Baxter said, "Most visitors here are bird watchers and hikers. I suggest you do the same."

By this time Carlos had joined us for dinner, roast mutton, peas, and potatoes. I didn't know what he had done while we explored the town. He replied to Mrs. Baxter, "That will be fine.

I expected to go birding. I have cameras and notebooks to record what I see."

Daffy huffed, "Dammit, why did I ever agree to come here if that is all there is to do? I'll die of boredom." Mrs. Baxter melted her with an evil eye.

The next morning, after our toast and scrambled eggs fried in sheep fat, Daffy claimed to be ill and decided not to venture out. Helen and I ventured into the misty, windswept lanes of Port Stanley. The climate was said to be oceanic and never varied to any degree. At that latitude temperatures hovered between forty and sixty degrees Fahrenheit with an occasional five to ten degree extreme. The wind was ever present and harsh at times.

At the far east end of the village we found Port Stanley's version of a Seven Eleven. A garrulous old codger owned the place. He asked who we were and what brought us to Humble House. We introduced ourselves and told him our story. "I call this place Humble House because it is the home office of my entire business enterprise, and I call it Humble because this shambles of a store, and my entire stock of merchandise, are nothing about which to brag."

The shelves of his Quonset style building were stocked with beer, soda, bags of chips, candy, small cans of foodstuffs and any other small item that could be found in a convenience store. Helen combed the shelves and asked, "My Lord, where can I buy a real drink in this berg?"

"Lady Helen, you need not call me Lord, Stan will do. My legal name is Stanley Fawks. I guild myself with Lord Stanley to try and remind me that I am a proud member of the British Commonwealth. I need to do that since the Brits themselves tend to forget about us. I only hope that they wake up to protect us when the Argentines invade, and they will. Every week I go up to the state house and remind them that they are coming.

"As for your drink, love, there are two pubs and their hours are twelve to two and five to seven."

"What an uncivilized place," Helen drawled. "A Southern Belle needs a libation every so often to keep her peach blossom charm about her."

Lord Stanley winked and asked Helen to bring her reticule with her. He led her behind a curtain. Ten minutes later they reappeared, both with wide smiles. The old codger told us that we might hike to the airstrip and invade the privacy of the mother penguins on the east Atlantic shore.

Helen and I went back to the Baxter House only to find a reluctant Daffy. However, Carlos had returned from his trek about town and asked to join us. Helen was delighted. Daffy frowned, perhaps regretting her decision to remain indoors. It seemed Carlos was now a prize to vie for in the eyes of my female companions.

As we headed for the airstrip with cheese sandwiches for our lunch, Helen rattled her journey pack and showed Carlos and me ten bottles of mini drinks that she had paid a lord's ransom for at Humble House. Stan had gotten his hands on smuggled hard liquor bottles that airlines served on their flights. Helen said, "He told me that since Argentina was about to invade, he would risk selling me some of his illegal stash."

Carlos smiled and said, "The only Argentine invasion has been and will be the scrappers who keep looting the sea wrecks off the western coast of the Malvinas."

At the mention of Carlos, Nigel seemed to perk up and said, "Carry on, old chap, carry on."

After we crossed the airstrip, we found the sand banked shore of the Atlantic. As Stan had told us, the place was flopping with Rockhopper penguins, less than two feet high. There were hundreds of them up and down the coast. As we moved closer, they scattered. We did find nests in the embankment. Holes about a foot in diameter were scattered about. Little black and white heads with darting eyes poked out and then disappeared. "Madre pengui-no does not like us. She retreats to her nest to protect her niños," laughed Carlos.

The scene was beautiful. For several hours we mingled with these magnificent flightless creatures as they scurried in and out of the salt water and in and out of their cavern nests. Then we sat down on an unoccupied dune and dined on English cheddar between savory slices of wheaty, homemade bread. Helen broke out small bottles of Beefeaters gin and offered us one. Carlos preferred whatever he had in his canteen, and I opened a can of Tab for which I had overpaid at Humble House. Helen was not offended and proceeded to down two bottles before we continued our dance with the penguins.

I really enjoyed the weather. The bristling wind and cool mist were a welcome change from the summer heat of São Paulo. Hugging warm cotton and wool clothing to my body felt good. There seemed to be a comfort in such warmth. As we trekked about the beach dunes and through the grass and weeds of the fields we peeled off some of our clothing, letting a stiff breeze cool our sweating bodies. Some of life's greatest pleasures are the simplest. During our scenic ramble Carlos took pictures. He said he enjoyed bird watching and keeping a notebook of what he saw. The Falklands were known for their many species of birds. They were plentiful but not as colorful as those in Brazil. Carlos continued to snap away with his two cameras and various lenses, including a telephoto. Helen and I paid little attention. She had given up trying to capture birds on the wing. But she used two rolls of film on the penguins.

When Helen asked Carlos how he could afford such fancy photo gear, he laughed, "Señor Olgiata has money enough. He encourages my photography. He will even look at such dull pictures as those of the airstrip. But do not think of me as ungrateful. I do not waste his pesos on drugs and liquor. I will soon join his enterprises and give return to his investment in me."

After our dinner of fried fish and potatoes with fresh raspberries for dessert, I was ready for bed. The day's walking, wind, and mist had tired me. It was still light as I climbed to my attic retreat at 9:30. At that latitude summer days were long, 3:30 a.m to 11 p.m. I slept fairly well, only waking up once to the sound of a mouse clicking across the linoleum floor. But exhaustion came to the rescue, and sleep returned until the rooster greeted the sunrise just before 3:30. I should've known that all those eggs and promise of Sunday chicken dinner required a hen house and boss of the yard. I managed to stay abed until 6:30.

At breakfast I reported the mouse nuisance. Carlos and Helen heard no such clatter and Daffy squealed, "God no, not mice."

After another evil eye aimed at Daffy, Mrs. Baxter smiled and instructed Emma and Sophie to do the usual.

That morning it was bird watching sans penguins for all four of us. I must admit that I was amazed at the number of birds one could see just sitting on a grassy slope. In and out, high and low, flew every color and shade of black, brown, gray, and white I could imagine. As we moved from lower berms to higher berms, Carlos kept clicking. Helen asked to stop for a wicky break every now and then, and Daffy complained of dust allergies. I sat back and thought, oh what a wacky mismatched menagerie this group is.

We ate our sandwiches and napped on the leeward side of a hill. Carlos lent us his binoculars to follow the birds and cloud formations. We could see for miles from the highest hill. There were no trees to speak of on the islands. Many varieties of grasses and shrubs decorated the areas around buildings. Attempts at growing trees failed. Most only got to be three or four feet high. Those were always bent away from the wind. Like old men, they arched closer and closer to the ground as they aged. That day's venture had taken us due south at least five miles out. All the way back Daffy let us know how much her legs ached and, "Could we rest?" Helen always agreed and reached for her bag.

That evening dinner seemed to have an abundance of carrots and potatoes in our mutton stew. The islanders depended heavily on their gardens in which root crops flourished. Carlos suggested that tomorrow we could try and locate a sheep herd. He was told not to miss seeing a sheep dog work. Mrs. Baxter suggested we walk out toward the military base. There are always sheep in the area she said.

Daffy by this time was soaking her feet as we played Clue. She said she would sit out tomorrow's walk and write some letters and read. She wanted her friends to get mail postmarked in the Falkland Islands with Falkland stamps. The post office did a booming business with stamp collectors.

At ten the next morning we headed southwest out of Port Stanley. As Mrs. Baxter predicted, we soon encountered sheep. The shepherd was moving a flock of several hundred. He had a border collie to help him. The sheep did not seem in a cooperative mood. The shepherd was forever whistling. A piercing sound carried across the landscape, and the dog responded by snapping at the heels of the sheep moving them in one direction. Then a different whistled pitch had the canine shepherd change the vector of the flock again. We sat on the hillside watching. We would hear a whistle and the dog responded by driving the sheep yet at another slight vector change. Occasionally, a really shrill whistle would call the collie's attention to a straying lamb. She ran around the little critter back and forth, bringing the lost lamb back to the flock.

    The shepherd must have been aware of his audience. He soon had the dog moving the sheep in all sorts of directions, few of which seemed productive to us. The dog appeared to be getting frustrated. I guess the shepherd had to show off. I'm sure he rarely had an audience in the stands.

    After two hours, with the sheep now about two miles away, we moved on after a lunch of scones and cheese. Helen must have paid more ransom to Lord Stanley that morning, as she had a new supply. Today's treats featured Scotch whisky. She offered. Again, both Carlos and I declined, he for his canteen and me for my Tab. We followed more birds and soon found ourselves heading in the direction of the military base. Carlos continued his picture and note taking.

    This produced a response from Nigel. "Did Carlos suggest heading for the base?"

    "No, we were following Mrs. Baxter's advice, and Helen was dying to see the young soldiers, so we trudged on."
We got about a hundred yards from a twelve foot chain linked fence with razor wire on top. Then a jeep came sweeping down from over a rise with a driver and two armed soldiers. The sergeant asked who we were and what we were doing. "Just tourists in search of the soul of the Falkland Islands," Helen offered in her Georgia drawl. Then she offered them a taste of her Scotch collection or "perhaps a nip of gin."

    We had to produce our passports. After inspecting them and us, they asked a few more questions of Carlos. He told them of his rich father rewarding his son, the college student, with a leisurely trip.

"Didn't they ask Carlos about his cameras?" Nigel asked.

"Come to think of it, Carlos must have put his cameras in his backpack. I don't remember seeing them then. Helen had given up trying to capture flying birds on film and had left her camera in her room. I didn't have a camera. They did ask to see Carlo's binoculars and then returned them to him."

The sergeant told us that this was a restricted area, and we should move on. The jeep didn't move until we had gotten a quarter of a mile away.

"Well, at least I got to see some soldier boys. The young one with the rifle was a hunk. I guess I need to locate the pub and maybe I'll find the RAF," purred Georgia Southern in her best Belle of the Ball tone.

The next day we went in search of a Land Rover to rent. Since there was a lack of roads to anywhere, few Land Rovers were to be found. The sheep ranchers, town merchants and craftsmen all had them, but they were needed for business. The plumber and the carpenter who worked from their shops behind their houses needed them to get tools and materials to job sites. The vet needed his almost every day. Lord Stanley, after another behind the curtain negotiation with Helen, suggested we try the owner of the general store. "He's a tight Scotsman, that old bastard, but if you up the price a notch or two, he won't be able to resist."

Before we got to the general store, Carlos said that Señor Olgiata could afford it. He would pay the bill, but suggested that Helen use her charms and do the negotiating. Sure enough Lord Stanley nailed it. Finally, the Scotsman caved in. We could rent his vehicle.

We had cancelled lunch at the boarding house in favor of a pub lunch. Bangers and mash was the daily special. When we got there, I realized why Daffy had insisted we go to the Rose and Thorn for lunch. They were showing the video of Princess Diana's wedding. Now I realized the purpose of her morning absence. Daffy had gone to get in line two hours earlier just to get us tickets to get in. Emma or Sophie must have told her that it would be crowded. I had always heard that British royalty was a revered symbol of the Empire. The place was packed, mostly with women. In lieu of an admission charge, a collection basket borrowed from the church was passed. During the entire viewing not a peep was heard other than the oohs and aahs.

After the ceremony, dozens of small discussions featured Di's dress. Daffy was thrilled to have waited two hours to get us tickets. None of it much mattered to me.

That evening made it a complete pub day. Instead of dinner at the Baxter's we headed for The Albatross, the pub halfway between the village and the military base. Military personnel were discouraged from visiting the village pub we had been to earlier in the day. The relationship between the military and the locals was dicey. Think of town and gown in a small U.S. college burg. The situation in the Falklands, however, had an added twist. Young people growing up in the Falklands seemed to have the same goal: "I gotta get out of here." This was not an easy task, but it was much easier for a male. He could always join the military or perhaps get an education off the island. Males always had more educational opportunities. Although not easy, the best chance of leaving the island for a female was marriage. Finding someone to marry who was bound to leave the island was limited primarily to the military.

"Look, Nigel, are you sure this is the stuff you're looking for?"

"How did you get your information on the people of the Falklands?" Nigel asked.

"Some from guide books, mostly from what Carlos told us. He said he had written a sociology paper on the people of Port Stanley."

"This might be a good time to nosh," replied Nigel. "Our cafeteria offers a fine menu of both English and Brazilian foods."

Tim King treated me to lunch, and an hour later I was returned to what had become my recliner. I was offered a cold can of Tab by Nigel. How nice of the Brit to indulge a Yankee with a cold drink. He requested I go on with what Carlos had said about the people.

I went on to say that since young women might escape the island by way of the military, many of them frequented the out of town pub. They walked or rode bicycles there. As I looked around, I thought I caught a glimpse of Sophie Baxter, but whoever it was darted out of my line of sight. Carlos said that the soldier boys were much like many of the Falklanders, bored. There just wasn't much to do. So the Brits welcomed the local ladies. Occasionally there were a few marriages, mostly of the shotgun variety, but at least an escape for a few of the former maidens. However, most of the marriages failed. The divorcees, usually because of economics, were forced to return to Port Stanley.

Because of the resentment of the local men toward the soldiers cherry picking the local available women, fights in the pub were common. That is why the military didn't want their boys going to the village pub, because there the situation would have been even more volatile.

Carlos said that his research found that marriages in Port Stanley and the rural outposts were a shambles. Drinking from boredom and escapism was an issue for both sexes. Most adults in the Falklands had been divorced at least once. Friends remarried husbands and wives of friends or former friends. In some cases, after several divorces, the original couples remarried. Children were totally messed up. Youngsters were often confused as to which adult in the household was the actual parent.

Inbreeding was another issue according to Carlos. The gene pool was small, and the almost total lack of immigration didn't help. Perhaps the children left behind as a result of the pleasure-seeking military was in some way a genetic boon to the population. As a result of the inbreeding, the mental and physical makeup of the islanders was filled with extremes, a few positive but mostly negative. I recall seeing some of the most hauntingly attractive people there. Emma Baxter was one such exotic beauty. Come to think of it, perhaps Carlos' information explained why Emma and Sophie did not resemble each other physically. The gene pool might also explain some of the eerily strange people I saw there.

The pub night was interesting. I got some pub grub that was a contrast to what we were getting at the Baxter house. Helen found some good ale and several RAF pilots to buy it for her. Daffy, likewise, got plenty of attention from many of the Brits, but her table had a constant changeover. Her whine quickly countered her batting eyelashes and skimpy tank top.

The next day was a windy, rainy day. The three of us stayed inside and played board games. From time to time Emma or Sophie joined us between their list of chores. Daffy refused to play Scrabble with them. "They cheat." The girls denied it.

"Yes, you do," replied Daffy. "You try to get by using spellings like 'centre' and 'cheque.' You try to use a Q in anything to get a bigger word score."

Carlos chose not to play and slipped out in raingear and a backpack. He came back before dinner, saying he had a good day of meeting new people and had a lead on getting a pilot to fly us over the islands. But most of all he confirmed our Land Rover for the next day. He paid the fee, obtained petrol along with lunch and drink provisions for us. Helen said that, to be sure all bases were covered, she would see Lord Stanley the next morning and pay the price for visiting his back room by listening to his rant about, "The Argentines are coming," and of course meet his ransom for the release of his little bottles.

The next morning, with Carlos at the wheel on the right hand side, we were off to find if East Falkland Island had a yellow brick road for us to follow. East Falkland is the larger of the two main islands. There were several dozen more islands in the archipelago, some only a pile of rocks populated by penguins.

"Nigel, you must already know this. By the way, I never truly understood what you Brits were doing there. What do you want with a place that, until 1764 was unpopulated. The French, Spanish and the Argentines tried settlements there and gave up. Only you Brits claimed and stayed. What is there that you want? Are you hoping to find oil? Is it to keep a claim in on Antarctica for its future recovery of minerals and oil there?" By this time I was tired of the whole thing.

Nigel gave no answer. He only asked me to continue.

The gravel road out of the village took us across acres and acres of grassland with only sheep and birds to see. Occasionally we would see a sheep ranch: a main house, shepherd barracks, a barn and outbuildings, all looking old and in need of paint. A few children and fewer women occupied these places. The males outnumbered the females by at least ten to one. We visited a little, but we didn't feel welcome at most places. Once we were invited in to chat and given water to drink. The matron offered us lunch which Daffy quickly turned down.

We drove across the grassy weeds along the south coast of East Falkland. The shores were rocky and sandy. We spotted an occasional wreck off the coast. I asked Helen if she wanted to bask on the beach and take in some sun. She smiled, reached into her bag and took out a bottle of Smirnoff, uncapped it and tossed it down. "I'm fine," she replied. We stopped and, using Carlos' binoculars, surveyed a few of the offshore wrecks. Carlos said the wrecks dated from the whaling days when this was a prime area. Today the fishing is mostly north of the Falklands. The many rocks we could see no doubt had hundreds of cousins we couldn't see, hence, the wrecks. Carlos told us the Argentine scrappers were forever entering the Falkland's sovereign waters to salvage. The British mostly warned them off, but the scrappers themselves at times ran aground and were arrested.

Nigel asked me if we were taking pictures. Again, I said, "Only Carlos. Nigel, I don't think you'll find this tour featured in Baedekers, but it was a fun day filled with junk food, snacks supplemented with tepid cans of Tab for me, Lord Stanley's supply for Helen, and much whining from Daffy who emptied a bottle of Chablis. Carlos seemed at peace."

That evening Emma and Sophie proudly displayed the trophy mice they had captured in my room. Five furry, claw clacking, creatures were laid out. The girls displayed their "super trap," a pail half filled with water, topped with a paper cover featuring a hole in the middle. The hole's rim merrily smeared with peanut butter. Happy mice attracted to the smell of the peanut butter climbed the stairway made of old books to the top of the pail only to realize they were not endurance swimmers. I rewarded the girls each with a nice, crisp U.S. Hamilton note.

The next morning was shopping day. With only a few days left on the island, we raided the general store. I stocked up on paperback books in English, as I needed a resupply to last me until

June. Among others I found a Penguin copy of Herman Hesse short stories, which I prized. I also stocked up on postcards, pennants, and a Falkland t-shirt, but the best was a wonderful tightly knitted wool sweater. The storekeeper assured me it was made with genuine Falkland wool that was exported to Glasgow and returned as the most beautiful sweater American dollars could buy.

Carlos found us and said he had good news, bad news, and bad-good news. "The good news is I have rented us an airplane to tour both East and West Falkland and the rocky penguin colonies off the coast.

"The bad news is the pilot who flies supplies to the sheep ranchers can only take three of us."

Daffy smiled and said, "Good, I get airsick in small planes. I'll read a few romance novels I just bought."

"You said you had some bad-good news?" I said.

"Yes. The bad news is the pilot is charging us mucho pesos. He knows we've been asking to fly out to see the Emperor penguins, and he thinks he can rob us. The good news is my patron will cover it all."

• • •

We trudged across the airstrip and climbed into a four passenger Cessna. I felt lucky in small aircraft, having survived one small plane crash without a scratch on me. Our Falklands flight was enjoyable. We saw thousands of sheep and stopped to drop off dry goods at six sheep ranches on East Falkland and three more on West Falkland. West Falkland was separated from East and was about a third of the size. The terrain of West Falkland, sheep and all, looked the same as East Falkland. Three more stops, and it was on to the Emperor penguins.

During the trip we asked the pilot to get down low, so we could see a herd of sheep, a flock of penguins or an occasional coastal wreck. Carlos flexed the shutter attached to his telephoto lens. Helen flirted with the pilot and kept offering a sample bottle of bourbon or vodka. Luckily, he had sense enough to refuse the booze, but seemed to like the flirting made richer by Georgia Southern's long, drawn out vowels. I relaxed and enjoyed the peacefulness of land, sea, and sky. The place had a serenity to it.

We were lucky. The weather was the best we had the entire stay, little wind and bright sun. We were told that if we were lucky we might even catch a glimpse of sea lions. The sea lions loved the rocky home of the Emperor penguins. The penguins made good snacks.

On the second pass, low and close to one of the islands, we saw a huge sea lion grasp the head of a four foot penguin, raise up on its behind and snap its head back and forth. On the third snap the outer skin of the penguin flew off. The sea lion sat down to eat his dinner.

Nature can provide a violent reality. Even Carlos gasped as Helen screamed. I just stared in awe. We had witnessed what few tourists ever see. The pilot told us we got our money's worth.

At the Baxter House Helen repeatedly described the sea lion incident over and over. Daffy said she knew she made the right decision not to go. She had returned to the pub to see a Princess Di rerun.

We were to leave the next day. A call to the boarding house that evening was another step sideways. The next day's plane would be held over because of Falkland and Argentine negotiations about the future of such flights.

The next morning Lord Stanley ranted about how this was just another prelude to the Argentine invasion. He told Helen that if she wanted to fuel up for the next day's flight, she had to get it now as he had a letter to write, this time directly to Margaret Thatcher herself. "I'll warn those block-headed politicians again."

That evening as we headed back to the pub in town, we encountered several men who looked like fishermen. They came out of Stan's Seven Eleven, speaking a Slavic sounding language. I asked them if they spoke English. One did. They were fishermen off a Polish fishing vessel, part of a whole fleet, factory ship included. They were happy to stock up at Stan's on the things that were not available in Poland. Happy, now they were off to the pub for more forbidden fruit. As we walked along with them I learned the meaning of some of the Polish words and sentences my grandma used to utter. Some were as nice as, "How are you?" Others I was surprised to learn she used.

Nigel popped in here. "If you please, did the Polish fishermen talk to Carlos?"

"No, Carlos was not with us."

The next morning we said goodbye to Mrs. Baxter and thanked her for her hospitality. Emma and Sophie drove the four of us to the airstrip in a borrowed Land Rover. We hugged the girls, and said goodbye, giving each a good sized tip for all their help. Boarding the plane I was happy our overextended trip had ended.

The happiness ended at the air terminal in Comodoro Rivadavia. Because of our one day delay, we had missed our connection to Buenos Aires. Perhaps tomorrow. "I can't stand it. I need to get out of this godforsaken part of the world," Daffy screamed. All in the small terminal looked at us in fear. "I demand to see the terminal manager." The yelling continued until armed soldiers led her away. Carlos seemed to have melted into the scenery and disappeared forever.

Helen and I figured jail for Daffy and a longer stay for us. Two hours later Daffy, unescorted, gave us a big grin and waved three tickets under our noses. We left on the next flight out and spent the night in a fine Buenos Aires hotel. As we sat in the hotel bar listening to Daffy tell us how marvelous she was at getting us out of that "hell hole," Helen just sipped on her Chartreuse, a green liquor. She said it was time to go back to being a "gentile lady of the South."

"And that," I told Nigel Smythe, "is the last of the tale. Lord Stanley was right all along."

Nigel said thank you for assisting Her Majesty's government. He didn't think further services would be required.

Tim King walked me to the consulate car and said, "Thanks, you did a nice job. I looked for it, but I don't think they recorded any of that, but you never know."

When I got back to my apartment, I called Laim Shaw. I told him to cancel Monday's sub as I was not under arrest. We met for dinner, fantastic Brazilian pork loin and plenty of pão de queijo. We talked about having watched the news clips of the war. The Iron Maiden, Margaret Thatcher, responded contrary to Argentine thinking. She came to the rescue of the under-defended Falklanders. The Argentine military was no match for the British Navy and Air Force. The war featured the exotic looking Harrier Jump Jets taking off from the British fleet. They resembled hummingbirds as they ascended vertically and darted off on a line to wreak havoc on the Argentine occupation. The bombardment and shelling spared Port Stanley itself, but I told Laim that I had feared for the safety of Emma, Sophie, Mrs. Baxter, and Lord Stanley. I was worried about the toll the Argentine military had on all the sheep and penguins. Argentina planted thousands of mines on East Falkland. After the war the poor wandering penguins and roaming sheep found more mines than the British minesweeping teams.

Laim asked, "Why did Argentina invade? What did they hope to gain?"

I reminded him of the political cartoon from the Herald Tribune that depicted two bald men fighting over a comb. One forehead was labeled Argentina the other Great Britain. "Laim," I told him, "the Argentine government was facing much unrest throughout the country because of its financial situation, corruption, and the disappearance of the many dissenters. To get the people's minds off the issues and to rally support, the government gambled by rekindling an old slogan, 'The Malvinas are ours.' They thought their chance for success was overwhelming and that would rally the people."

I repeated the words of our Argentine travel agent when, after the war, we asked him why. He said, "Growing up in Argentina there were three things pounded into our heads: one, the Pope is right, two, Communism is bad, three, the Malvinas are ours."

"Laim, I guess they underestimated the Iron Maiden. She showed the British, and the World, no one can push the Empire around.

"So the bald Brit got the comb."

"Is that sour grapes Irish in you coming out?"

• • •

Two months later I walked into Laim Shaw's office and showed him an article from the Herald Tribune. The headline stated, "Great Britain Arrests Spy." I recognized the man in the picture.

"How do you feel now?" Laim asked.

"I feel bad for Carlos. He was a nice guy. But when adults play games, nice people, sheep, and penguins get hurt."

Laim sighed and said, "Next time visit Iceland. I don't think Denmark wants it back."

## What's a Penny Worth?

Walking out of my empty classroom, I found Penny Logan sitting on the floor crying. "What's the trouble?" I asked. She just sat there looking at the floor, sniffling. I told her that she might do a little better by sitting in my room for a while. I offered her a hand and helped her into a desk. I sat in a desk next to her and waited.

A few minutes later she picked up her head and through the tears said, "I don't know what else to do. I can't get anyone to help me."

"You feel hopeless," I echoed.

"Yes, Ms. Robins does nothing. She said she didn't witness any of it. Mr. Thompkins, some principal he is, keeps saying 'Don't worry. I'll take care of it,' but nothing changes." Her head went back down and the sobbing got louder.

I waited some more and finally asked, "What would you like to see changed?"

Her head popped back up and through the tears, she spewed, "Make Darcy stop bullying everyone and stalking me."

"Tell me about it, Penny."

"You know Darcy, the new girl this year? They said she got kicked out of her last school for terrorizing kids. Well, she does the same thing here. She especially picks on little Caitlyn Gruber. She calls her "Grubby" and "Smitten Kitten." She yells at her and tells her she's stupid and worthless. One day in Ms. Robins' class she took two girls out in the hall to talk to them. As soon as the door shut, Darcy immediately jumped over an empty desk and started in on Caitlyn. I stood up and shouted across the room, 'Darcy, leave her alone. She has done nothing to you. If you need to pick on someone, pick on me.' Then Ms. Robins and the two girls came back in. Darcy stared at me, then went back to her seat. After the bell, as we were walking out of the room, Darcy came up behind me and picked at my sweater over and over saying, 'Okay, bitch, the picking begins. I'll be picking, picking on you.' That started it."

Penny went on to tell me that, since that day, Darcy had haunted her, followed her all over and called her names. Whenever Penny went to the bathroom, Darcy was there. Darcy taunted her by calling her "Dirty Penny," "Measly Red Cent," "Lousy Copper," and any and everything else to mock Penny's red hair.

"Penny, did you tell anyone about this?"

"I told Ms. Robins and Mr. Thompkins. I already told you what they said. I told my parents. My dad said you can't fight money and power, that Darcy's parents have both. That's why she's in our school. In order to kick a kid out of school that school has to pay tuition to the next school. My dad says she's here because the school district wants the tuition money. He says other school districts wouldn't take her.

"You know that new driveway and that new electronic sign with the flashing messages out front? The school board says it was an anonymous gift. Well, guess what? That all happened this summer after the school board agreed to let Darcy come here. All the kids know it, too. 'Money talks,' my dad says.

"My mom tells me just to last out the year and graduate. Then it will all be over.

"Mr. August, I'll never make it. What can I do?"

I advised Penny to start recording every time Darcy harassed her, to rite down the exact words she uses. I told her to go back to the principal and let him know the problem still exists. I told her to document that, too, time and date on everything.

Two weeks later I found Penny again outside of my classroom crying. I asked her to come in and sit down. She blurted out, "Mr. August, it has to stop. I can't stand it. I can't sleep and I'm scared to come to school or to go anywhere. It has gotten worse. Now she is following me outside of school. Saturday, she tailed me and my friends for two hours at the mall. Then we went to a movie, and when we came out there was Darcy and her posse from her old school. Darcy, as she strutted by us, said, 'Here, Henny Penny, here, Henny Penny, you worthless piece of copper.' Then she threw a handful of pennies at me. I love my red hair, but I think I'm going to dye it some other color."

"Penny, leave your hair as it is. It's beautiful. You need to tell Mr. Thompkins that Darcy's behavior has escalated. Tell him, if he can't stop her, your family will go to the police. Document all of this."

The next week I saw Penny. She said she did as I advised. Mr. Thompkins said he would speak with Darcy. "She has stayed away from me all week."

The next week Penny was back in my room with more tears. "Mr. August, Darcy told me," as she sniffled, "that Mr. Thompkins told her not to talk to me. So she said she would now stop talking. But do you know what? Everywhere I go, there she is. In the hallway, the bathroom, at lunch. She is there just staring at me." Penny sniffled and wiped her runny nose.

"Last Sunday at the mall, there she was. If I went to a teen clothing store, her face would pop out from between the tops or the skirts. She just scowled. In the food court she sat at the next table and glowered. After ten minutes my friends and I left.

"When we got to the parking lot, we found my car with four flat tires. There was a note on the windshield under the wiper. In block print it said, I HAVEN'T SAID A WORD."

"Did you call the police or tell Mr. Thompkins?"

"My dad said no cops. I did tell Mr. Thompkins and showed him the note. He grabbed the note, said he would take care of it and walked away.

"Yesterday Darcy came up to me at my locker and just stood there grinning. As she walked away, she flashed the block printed note so I could read it. It looked like the same one that was on my car. She walked away singing, 'I haven't said a word.'"

"Did you go back to Mr. Thompkins?"

"What good is that? All he tells me is that he will talk to Darcy. But she doesn't stop." Penny burst into louder sobs and bigger tears rolled down her freckled cheeks. She slumped to the floor of my room saying, "What is going to happen to me?"

I, too, had had enough. I told Penny to wait in my room while I marched to the superintendent's office. If the principal wouldn't help, maybe going over his head would. This had to stop. No job was more important than the safety of a terrorized teenager. I walked into Mr. Maris' office and asked the receptionist if I could see him. She said he was in a meeting. I took a deep gulp of air and told her to interrupt and tell him I needed to see him right now. So she did.

Mr. Maris came out of the conference room with a stern look and pointed to his office. After he shut the door, he looked directly at me, "Mr. August, what is so important to you?"

"Mr. Maris, you can fire me, I don't care, but something has to be done about a terrorized student, and it must be done immediately." He asked me to explain, and I did.

"Where is she now?"

"In my room crying."

"Take me to her, please."

When we reached my room, I introduced him to Penny. I told Penny to tell him her entire story and to show him the documentation in her notebook. I left the two of them and went to the teacher's lounge to try and reverse the direction of my blood pressure.

The next day I was summoned to the superintendent's office. "Mr. August, thank you for what you did for Penny. What made you think I should fire you?" He smiled. "I understand your frustration, and I'm glad you had the gumption to act. Now I need to take measures to move some people to act on this. I also need to have a motivational chat with someone who should have brought this to my attention sooner."

A week later Penny, without a sob or tear in evidence, came to my room. She told me Darcy was not in our school anymore. Mr. Maris told her mom and dad that if Darcy comes within one hundred yards of Penny, the police will arrest Darcy. She thanked me for helping her. Then she added, "You know I didn't work very hard in your class. I didn't like you. But I needed help, and I knew no one else was doing anything. I knew you would, so it was not an accident I sat in the hall next to your door.

"Maybe I can repay you. I know you keep telling us to go on to school. I'm going to work hard the rest of the year and try to get into a community college. I'm going to get my grades up and get a four year degree. That can be my thanks."

I gave her a hug and said, "That would be a good thank you for both of us."

154

Billy and Bobby: Or What They Found

Billy and Bobby rode the tour bus through St. Paul. The guide regaled them with mobster stories of the 1920s and '30s: the tales of Ma Barker and her boys, the Hamm Brewery family kidnapping. Then there was the history of the shootout at the Lindon Court Apartments with John Dillinger and Homer Van Meter, and how FBI Agent Wallace Jamie first used wiretapping to sway a grand jury. They loved the bootlegging tales that featured the limestone caves along the Mississippi River. Most of all they were fascinated by Nina Clifford and her house of ill repute right across the street from the county morgue. St. Paul was a safe haven for mobsters then.

On the fifty-mile drive back to the small town of Geneva, the boys talked about the tour and how much fun it would be to investigate like the FBI guy and the newspaper reporter who blew the lid off of St. Paul in the 1930s.

Billy said, "I sure am glad you talked me into taking Mr. August's summer school class on Minnesota History and Authors.

Who would've thought they had an ice palace or winter carnival then?"

"Sure," Bobby added, "I liked Larry Millet's story, *Sherlock Holmes and the Red Demon,* about James J. Hill's railroad and the Hinckley fire. I wish I had been Holmes."

"Ya, Bobby, but *The Scarlet Plume* by Frederick Manfred about the Sioux uprising and all the hangings in Mankato, we don't hear about that stuff in our usual history classes," Billy said.

Both agreed that *Main Street* was just okay, but Steve Thayer's *St. Mudd*, which told about ridding St. Paul of gangsters, was the best of all. That's what prompted their shelling out the cash for the St. Paul Gangster Tour.

Bobby said, "The only bad part of this day is that the Twins are out of town; we could have taken in a game. Do ya think they will win another World Series like last year when they beat the Cardinals? Boy, 1987 was some year."

After a lull in the conversation, Bobby popped up. "You know what? We could be investigators. Let's investigate Sally Sea. You know, the old lady all the kids call a witch. She shoots at people who go near her place."

"Geez, Billy, she shot at those kids who went out to harass her on Halloween. She didn't hit anybody, she was just trying to scare them. But you're right, she lives alone near Lake Maria State Park. Her shack backs up to the ravine and woods that abut the park. We could investigate who she is and write it up for an English class next year."

"Okay, Bobby, 'the game is afoot,'" Billy said in his best attempt at being Sherlock Holmes, "but I don't want to get shot. How would we even get close enough to talk to her?"

"Remember in class when we discussed how historians worked, how they gathered information before interviewing people? They gathered information from others, looked for angles to get a foot in the door. Then they used that information to prepare questions for the interview."

"I remember. So, you are saying we need to find a way in that won't get us shot. We need to talk to people who live near her."

The next day, after working at their summer jobs, the junior detectives drove to the farms near Sally's isolated shack. They heard, "No, we don't talk to her." or "Who wants to get shot at?" At the last farm their luck changed. A teenage boy, who went to a neighboring high school, said that his parents talked to Sally and sometimes bought groceries she needed; coffee, sugar, vinegar, and so on. Sometimes he delivered her the goods. No, she didn't shoot at him. He said she likes bananas. The boys thanked the kid and headed home.

Billy and Bobby were at the grocery store the next day buying five pounds of bananas. That evening they returned to the farm where they had found the kid who had visited Sally without getting shot. They asked the kid, Ike, if he would ride with them to Sally's and give her the bananas. He said, "I called some friends of mine, and they said they knew you two from baseball and that you're okay. So, yes, I'll go along."

Billy and Bobby told him they wanted to interview Sally. They told Ike they didn't believe the stories about her being a witch. "Tell her we think she is just a private lady who wants to be left alone, but we still want to get her story to convince others not to bother her. The bananas are hers even if she doesn't talk to us."

As they crept up her half-mile dirt driveway, they noticed vast gardens on either side of the road. Behind the gardens were fruit trees. Ike told them to stop about two hundred yards short of the shack. "Maybe it would be better if you waited here."

He took the bananas and approached the old house. The door slowly opened and the barrel of a gun emerged. Ike stopped, spoke toward the barrel and then the barrel waved him forward. He spoke to the gun barrel as the holder of it was not visible to Billy and Bobby. After five minutes of conversation, Ike handed the bananas through the door. The door closed.

Back in the car Ike said, "I told her what you told me. I said that I had talked to my friends who know you and that they and I both trust you. I told her the bananas were hers. She wants the two of you to walk up to the door and stand there for three minutes. Then you are to leave and come back tomorrow at 6:30. By then she will have made up her mind."

The boys did as instructed. The three minutes, timed on Bobby's watch, seemed like an hour. The boys noted a seasoned wood pile next to the door. They noted an old DeSoto that didn't look like it had been driven for years sitting next to a weathered shed. Weeds had grown up in front of double doors. The boys noticed that the curtains on the front window seemed to move a couple of times; both figured they best not stare. After their three minutes of purgatory, they left.

The following evening at exactly 6:30 the boys parked where they had the day before. They slowly walked to the door. This time they had no bananas. Instead they had brought a huge bucket of Kentucky Fried Chicken along. Again, the door opened a bit, a gun barrel came out. The voice inside said, "Wait there while I decide." The aroma of the fried chicken, not worried about any gun barrel, wafted in uninvited. The aroma, the boy's angelic faces, or the woman's better nature gained the boys entry.

The boys entered a small porch that led into an old farm house kitchen. An old, neatly varnished pine table was the center piece. The six by ten-foot table was girded by six wooden bow back chairs as finely finished as the table. A Calico tablecloth adorned the top. An iron kitchen range was on the far side of the table opposite the door. Thick oven mitts hung on wooden wall pegs. The stove pipe from the range's center rose four feet above the stove and elbowed into the field stone chimney behind. A cast iron sink with a long counter and cupboard doors was on each side of the sink. To the right of the sink was a short-handled water pump. A window with curtains matching the tablecloth was above the sink. An open door showed the many shelves of a pantry. Other than the overhead lights, an old Coronado refrigerator was the only concession to the twentieth century.

Sally wore a long out of style dress that looked like it was made of expensive material. She wore heavy work boots, and her hair was nicely combed and held in place by what looked like pearl shell barrettes. She motioned for the boys to sit and join her in eating the aromatic chicken. Glasses of cold well water from the pump were placed on the table, along with cloth napkins.

She told them she wasn't ready to answer questions yet. She wanted to know what made them want to brave the shotgun to interview her. Stories from class, *St. Mudd,* and the gangster tour flowed eagerly as they told her of their desire to be investigators. She seemed quite interested in it all, especially the gangster tour. She asked what part of the tour they liked best. Both gushed, "Nina Clifford and the cat house." They told her if they had been around back then they would have checked it out- if they could've afforded it. Sally appeared to smile at all this.

Before the boys left, they learned Sally was a gardener and preserver of what she grew. They could see the filled Mason jars on the pantry shelves. She hunted, dressed and cooked her own game. She chopped and split her own firewood, but as she got older, she said, her aching bones made that chore almost too much. She seldom left the property since her brother died five years back. It seemed Sally's reluctance to answer questions had dissolved.

Two weeks later the boys returned with a pickup load of seasoned oak. Even though the gun barrel again greeted them, they drove up to the house, unloaded and stacked the split wood. By the time they had finished, a savory aroma, this time from inside the house, wafted outside. That and Sally's invitation brought Billy and Bobby into the kitchen. Sally was outfitted again in a nice, long, old fashioned, attractive dress. Warming on the stove were several pots, one of which turned out to be canned venison. Sally fed them all venison au jus, cooked garden-fresh carrots and peas, with fresh bread which she had baked that morning. With a meal prepared using the old kitchen wood stove, the boys were happy to have contributed to Sally's wood pile, perhaps in hope of future offerings. The food was as good as they ever ate.

Sally told them she was an avid reader. She was interested in all the books and short stories they had read for their summer course. She did a lot reading in the winter when she couldn't be out much. The boys promised to bring her the books.

During the fall months Billy and Bobby returned with more wood. Sally's latest serving for them consisted of roasted ruffed grouse which Sally had shot and dressed. Roasted potatoes and chopped cabbage, all from Sally's garden, accompanied the wild grouse. The boys had brought bananas and chocolate ice cream for dessert. By that time, they had banked on having a meal.

Sally talked about how she and her brother had come into some money years ago. They were tired of living in the mountain west. Since her brother had spent much of his thirties and forties living in rural areas, he had honed his skills in hunting, fishing, and had become a rather good gardener and orchard man. So, when the money came, they found this place and moved. Sally said she always wanted to return to Minnesota after having grown up in St. Paul. Now she was even a rabid Twins fan and loved listening to Herb Carneal on the radio. WCCO was a Clear Channel station she could pick up even after dark.

Every few weeks until the December snows the boys visited Sally. More wood arrived. They ate Sally's cooking and talked baseball and books. The boys told her of school and how they had decided to tell few people about Sally. They wanted to respect her need for privacy. Or, perhaps they wanted to keep their secret friend to themselves. They had told their parents, of course, and their parents agreed that little would be gained by telling about the "good witch Sally." The parents even helped the boys find the wood they gave her.

On Christmas Billy and Bobby came out to Sally's with presents. They gave her a pair of woolen mittens and a big old woolen coat that looked like something out of a Dickens novel. They found the coat and mittens at a thrift shop. The gifts included several Dickens' novels, including a copy of *A Christmas Carol*. And to top it all off they showed her a bottle of spiked eggnog they lifted from a Christmas party one of their parents had. They roasted the hot dogs they had brought over the open fire in the kitchen stove. "Just like a campfire," Bobby said. New Year's Eve was celebrated in the same manner.

As the snow piled up, the visits became more infrequent. The boys would show up with a plow on the pickup truck and keep Sally's road open. In winter they gathered closer to the big kitchen stove. They stacked wood inside the small porch so Sally wouldn't have to slog through the snow for it. Billy said the wood burning kitchen stove reminded him of the one his grandmother used for canning in the late summer and fall. Sally said she was beginning to worry. Her body couldn't put up with all the work it took to garden, feed the stove, and hunt like she used to. She also told stories of her youth: the St. Paul street cars, the Como Park Zoo, views of the State Capital and St. Paul's Cathedral. She enjoyed growing up there. But after she would get into her old St. Paul stories, she tended to shut down and seemed rather sad.

As the winter months dragged, Sally seemed to lose some zest. She told the boys she didn't feel much like cooking and visiting. Just a touch of the flu, maybe. The boys visited less often. When they did they brought tacos or sloppy joes they cooked up. They told her of their plans to till her garden. She said she hoped she had the energy to plant. They said they would help her.

In late April Billy and Bobby tilled her garden. They came out on Good Friday, raked the whole acre and a half and helped Sally plant potatoes. Bobby said his grandmother always insisted that the potatoes had to be planted on Good Friday. Sally again lacked energy and sat on a stool and watched after planting a few hills herself.

The next time the boys came out, instead of Sally's gun barrel at the door, they found a card taped to it. It read:

*Aloyocious T. Cabernack, Esq. of the law firm, Winston Slone and Carbernack.*

There was a St. Paul address and telephone number. A handwritten note read: "Billy and Bobby, please call."

The resulting phone call set up a meeting at Sally's with Aloyocious T. for the following Saturday. When Billy and Bobby arrived, they saw a BMW and a distinguished looking, graying man in a three-piece, tweed suit in the door that used to frame Sally and her gun barrel. "As you likely surmised, Sally has passed on. I was her attorney and am the executor of her estate."

"Estate?" Billy questioned, "You mean this old house?"

"No, young man, Sally was much more than a kind, elderly lady you befriended. Her name was not Sally Sea but Stacy Clifford. She was not the pauper she allowed you and others to believe. She was a wealthy woman. The brother she told you and others of was not her brother. He was her general factotum, bodyguard, and oh so much more than that. Come, let us look at the rest of Sally's house, which she told me you boys have not yet seen.

"The past two weeks Sally has been in hospice in St. Paul. The day after she planted potatoes with you, she called and said it was time. Sally has had cancer for some time. She refused treatment. As she said, 'It's time.' She was eighty-two."

The lawyer led the boys back into the rest of what they thought was just an old shack. The rooms behind the kitchen were much bigger than expected. This side of the field stone chimney had a fireplace and a large oak slab mantle. The room had a large T.V. set and an extensive stereo set up. She had all of the most modern forms of media and communication. Shelves of books lined one wall. The south side of the room was windows overlooking the wooded ravine that bordered the state park. A meandering stream snaked through the bottom of the ravine. The far side was wooded maple. There was a second room, a modern kitchen with all the appliances. A stairway led the boys and lawyer down one flight to several other rooms, including Sally's bedroom. The canopied four poster bed drew the boys' eyes. Soon their eyes noted the photos of a younger, risqué looking Sally. One portrait was of an elderly woman who may have been Sally, but a closer look revealed it wasn't. Mr. Cabernack said it was Sally's mother.

"Yes, Billy and Bobby, Stacy Clifford's mother was the infamous St. Paul Madam, Nina Clifford."

The boys were dumb struck and just stood there for several moments.

A sliding door off this series of rooms led to a flagstone patio complete with a large outdoor fireplace, tables, and chairs. Aloyocious invited the boys out to sit. He continued to tell Stacy Clifford's story. She and Clement, no longer the erstwhile brother, moved here twenty-five years ago. Clement was very handy and loved the outdoors, teaching Stacy all he knew about hunting, fishing, gardening, canning, and fruit trees.

Stacy had inherited her mother's business in St. Paul, but after the town was cleaned up, business was never the same. She and Clement left in 1936, moving to Denver.

Bobby quivered and squeaked out, "You mean Sally was a... a... a..."

"Let's just say Stacy was a good business woman who learned her trade at her mother's knee. Stacy took the girls and Clement to Denver and elevated her trade to that of a high-class escort service, catering to both wealthy males and females. She became a wealthy woman who, advised by me from St. Paul, invested in blue chip stocks such as AT&T, IBM, and 3M. She got in on the ground floor with Nike and Microsoft."

The lawyer went on to say that Stacy had become unhappy over the years with the changing situation in Denver as the powerful gangs tried to shut her out of the business. She made a deal with the FBI and local police to testify against the others in Denver who controlled prostitution. They lured younger and younger women into the trade, mostly run-away teens, hooked them on drugs and tossed them aside when they were used up. Stacy never treated her women and her few men that way.

"The deal allowed her to leave the business and the state. I helped her buy this property. Stacy had the money to add onto the old house. Most of it was replaced. All that is left of the original is the old kitchen which she loved and used in spring and fall. When you two entered her life, she used the old kitchen in winter when she knew you were coming or likely to come. She expected you on Christmas and New Year's Eve. You didn't disappoint her.

"Stacy had a beautiful old Mercedes Benz. It is still here in the garage. She and Clement took it out only after dark. They bought groceries late into the night at all-night supermarkets in the Twin Cities. They left here for weekends and entire weeks to visit St. Paul, Duluth, or Kansas City. They liked movies, plays, concerts. Stacy loved the Guthrie Theater, The Minnesota Orchestra, and the State Fair. She enjoyed the North Shore in fall.
"Since Clement's death Stacy lost much ambition and energy. But when you boys came into her life, she began to live again. The glow came back. She said that now she wished she had consented to treatment. But it was far too late.

"Boys, I have Stacy's will here. She's leaving most of her estate to a foundation that helps young women in Minnesota get out of prostitution, and helps run-aways from ending up in prostitution. I am setting it up and will see to its operation.

"She is leaving the wood pile next to her door, and everything in it, to you boys. In addition, she had me set up a college fund for you two. It will pay tuition, books, room, and board for four years at any college or vocational school of your choice. I already have your names and addresses."

"But, why?" Bobby asked. "She hardly knew us, at least not for very long."

"Boys, when Stacy was young and working for her mother she became pregnant. The wealthy businessman's father insisted she get an abortion, quite illegal and poorly performed in those days. She was told she had aborted twin boys and that she would never be able to have children.

"Billy and Bobby, she saw in you two what she had lost so many years ago. More importantly, you brought joy back into her life. Something she had not had since Clement died. You gave her reason to live. You don't know how excited she was about your visits. I heard every detail from her when I came out to see her every two weeks, after dark, of course."

He told the boys that after they removed the wood, he would contact them about the school details.

Two weeks later the boys came out to claim their inherited wood pile, the one near the door. On top of the wood pile was a gunny sack full of potatoes. Along with the wood, which they threw into the pickup truck's bed, they found a well-worn, but well cared for, leather satchel. They threw it in the cab, gave the place a tearful last look, and left.

As they headed down the driveway Billy opened the satchel and found a note. Bobby stopped the truck. Billy read the note:

> *Thanks, Billy and Bobby,*
> *for giving me back a part of*
> *me that had gotten lost.*
> *You two are the best.*
> *Stacy Clifford.*

The boys also found that the bag contained $20,000, some of it in silver certificates.

Billy and Bobby got out of the truck. They sat on the bumper of the pickup, remaining silent and staring toward the old shack they first saw nine months ago.

Finally, Billy said, "Ya know, Bobby, we started this as a game of detective, just having some fun. We came looking to find the wicked witch. Instead we found a crusty, lonely old lady. As the crust came off, we found an enjoyable, kind friend, many enjoyable visits and meals."

And then, Bobby said, "It turns out we had really found a fairy godmother. I guess that's a good thing for us, but you know, I would have been satisfied with friendship, the meals, potatoes and a wood pile."

After a long pause came a, "Me too."

In the dark Rollie and I crawled through the weeds toward The Hurd House. We had planned all spring how we would wait until after dark, duck out of our respective bedroom windows, and break into the abandoned house. The house stood on a triangular block on the northwest side of town, a few blocks from where we lived. It was the last house on 13th Avenue with nothing to the west but empty fields.

We approached the house from the field, crawling the last 200 yards. Rollie said, "We have to rip a board or two from a window, get inside. We gotta get into Jodi and Joni's bedroom. I bet we could find a souvenir bra or two. Man, those girls were something. Remember, we watched them in their swimsuits while they weeded the garden? We gotta get in there."

As we crawled closer, we noticed a cop car coming up 12th Avenue, moving slowly, flashing a spotlight across the weedy unkept yard around The Hurd House. Then the light made its way across the north side of the house, focusing on the boarded windows. The car moved on, then over and back down 13th Avenue. "I guess we don't try this tonight," I nervously said.

The next day, as we fled our sixth-grade classroom, Rollie and I talked about The Hurd House. Two years ago, Jodi, seventeen, and Joni, fifteen, disappeared. One day they were outside arguing with their mom and raising hell about how sick they were of living in that old run-down dump, and how sick they were of trying to grow anything in that rocky, sandy garden. The next day they were gone.

For weeks the Middleton police, the county sheriff's office, and even the FBI searched and investigated. Everybody in the neighborhood was questioned, even Rollie and me. Every field, quarry hole, lake, river and sandpit were dragged. Organized searchers, dogs, and divers failed to find a trace of the girls. A month later Mrs. Hurd moved out. There never seemed to be a father present.

We heard neighborhood men and customers at Strang's Greenery say that the Hurd girls' disappearance reminded them of the Lake Park twins who disappeared from a nearby town. Mary Pat and Mary Margaret O'Brien were last seen walking along a township road going to a neighbor's farm. "Those two were some lookers."

"Yeah, their picture in the paper, wow, you'd have thought they were twenty-five years old."

"Remember a few years ago there were the sisters from St. Ann? They were thirteen and fourteen."

"Maybe, but everybody said they looked to be twenty. All those girls had some bodies, and all those girls are gone."

"The first two were blondes and the O'Briens were redheads. The Hurd girls had coal black hair."

As the comments were tossed about by the northside males, we eavesdropped. We never got more details. As we moved in closer, we were always spotted and told to scram or the conversations turned to weather and sports.

Now for sure Rollie and I were going to figure a way into The Hurd House. Besides the thrill of the girl's bedroom, maybe we could find something the cops missed. Maybe we could solve a mystery. Besides, in the summer of 1956 there was little else to do after hours of weeding gardens, mowing lawns, playing baseball, and trying to avoid babysitting. We didn't dare hang around our houses.

The next time we got even closer to The Hurd House. It was a week after school let out. This time it wasn't the cops who scared us away; it was an old, dark green Packard with spot lights that repeated the maneuver of the cop car from a few weeks back.

The next day Rollie and I decided to ask Gramps Strang about The Hurd House. Gramps lived behind The Greenery. His one room house, we called it a shack, was behind the greenhouses and office in the middle of The Greenery's fields of flowers and vegetables. The Hurd House was the only place west of his. Beyond The Hurd House was 600 acres of open field with a ravine in the middle.

Gramps seemed ancient. He was probably only in his seventies or early eighties. He lived in that one room building as long as we had known him, all of our lives. He worked as a handyman for the Strang family, two brothers and their wives, who owned and operated the garden-flower shop. They called him Uncle Strang. Because he seemed so old, all the neighborhood referred to him as Gramps Strang. We kids just called him Gramps. He seemed to like us, and we visited him often. He worked in the greenhouses and the gardens. Sometimes he made deliveries and picked up supplies.

Since Gramps often spun yarn about the "good ol' days," we knew he was our best source on The Hurd girls. When we told Gramps about our adventures trying to get into The Hurd House, he told us that fooling around that house was not a good idea.

Rather than tell us about the house, the girls, and their parents, he told us about the ravine and the fields beyond The Hurd House. We knew about the ravine. We had explored it, summer and winter. In spring and early summer, it was filled with water. Frogs, lizards, occasional muskrats, and fox were to be found. In winter, rabbits, a mink or two, and what some of the older kids referred to as an ermine, but my dad said was most likely a weasel, kept us occupied—if it wasn't too cold or the snow too deep.

Gramps said that the ravine was actually the bed of a shallow lake that covered most of the center of the 600-acre span of open field. "When I was a kid we used to row boats and canoes on the lake. Each year when the spring waters were really high, the creek arm of the Mississippi that drained the ravine backed up and made the lake even deeper. Along with the water came bass, sunfish, and crappies that got trapped in the lake when the water receded. Because the lake was so shallow, the fish froze out in winter.

"That ol' lake and later, lakebed, made us young guys a bit of pocket money. We trapped muskrats; they used to build their mud huts there. We snared rabbits, even jack rabbits then. Once in a while we would get rich if we trapped a mink or a fox. Great pocket money."

"What was the lake called?" Rollie asked.

"Of course, it was Strang's Lake. We lived here for a long time."

I never could find anyone who ever heard of Strang's Lake. Years later I did confirm that the old ravine, now a modern housing development with leaky basements, was once a lakebed.

"Gramps, what happened to the lake?" I asked.

"Oh, it wasn't much of a lake, not deep enough. More and more murky weeds grew and sucked up much of the water. We tried to build a dam on the creek, but the city dug it up. Then that sand, gravel and cement outfit bought the land north of there and dug all those sandpits. They eroded and ended up cutting off the water from the creek. So, no spring water backed up from the river."

"Yeah," Rollie blurted out, "but the ravine is still there and has water in it much of the year. We caught tadpoles and lizards and put them in tubs in Billy's basement, but his mom put a stop to that."

I jumped in, "We trapped pocket gophers in the field near the ravine, and Rollie's dad found a muskrat in their basement window well. So, you see Gramps, we still do what you used to do out there."

"Yes, boys, stick to exploring the ravine and the fields between here and the river. Forget about The Hurd House."

Gramps sat there for a while looking far away. "You know,"

he said, "that marley, peaty dirt on the southeast side of the ravine makes great potting soil. Before that land was sold to a local bigshot, I used to dig that stuff out and use it here in the greenhouses. I wish I still had access to that stuff."

The next day, always thinking, always looking for a way to pick up extra pocket change for baseball cards, Nut Goodies, or ice cream, Rollie and I formed a plan. With a couple of shovels and a pick ax we headed out for the ravine. We found the marshy southeast side reluctant to give up it's wet, spongy dirt. But two days of chopping and digging gave us a good pile. After a few more days of hot, dry weather we were ready. We commandeered a wide flatbed dolly and loaded it on two wagons from our playdays a few years ago and rigged a tandem truck to carry the dolly to the ravine. We piled the dirt on the dolly and tugged on the twin handles of the wagons under it. It took two hours to get the load of dirt to the side of Gramp Strang's shack where we tipped the load onto the ground.

As he ambled home to his mansion after his day in The Greenery, he broke out laughing when he saw our loot, then smiled and said he would give us each a dime for the pile. A dime, that meant two five cent packs of baseball cards, 12 cards in all and enough pink, dried out sheets of bubble gum for at least two weeks.

In spite of the hard work, I thought a dime a piece would draw Rollie into another raid on the ravine to purloin another pile of peat. "Stu, you're nuts. It's too much work for a dime. Besides, I don't need any more baseball cards."

"Okay, fine, but couldn't you use it to go to Fern's Drug and get a cherry coke from that waitress you think is such a cutie."

That sealed the deal for Rollie. We needed four days to dump another load at Gramps'. As Gramps handed over our dimes, I picked a tin disk out of the pile. It was a small pie pan. "Hey, Gramps, look at this." Gramps took the tin from me and sat down on his old, oak, court house chair in the shade on the east side of his house. He looked scared and older as he sat there staring at the dirt pile and then at the pie tin.

Finally, Gramp's spoke, "Boys, you know all that dirt is actually stolen property. You don't own it, and neither do I. I sure wouldn't want you guys to get in trouble. Then I'd be in trouble too for buying stolen property.

"If you boys don't hang around the ravine and dig up anymore of this stuff, I'll cover for you if the cops come around. I sure would hate to see you picked up by the law." Then he stared some more at the pie tin and dirt and mumbled something that sounded like, "Or even worse."

"What did you say, Gramps?" I asked.

"Nothing, boys, nothing. Why don't you take your bikes for a ride? Find a new adventure."

The next day Rollie and I finished our chores in the morning. Baseball practice wasn't until 5:30, so we rode our bikes around town. We ended up just off downtown on the other side of the huge rail yard that separated our neighborhood from the rest of the town. The rail yard was eight to sixteen tracks wide. The widest part of the four-mile stretch was in the middle and included a round house. The round house was a big circular building that had a lazy susan like wheel that was used to turn the train engines around and served as a repair shop for the railroad. On the downtown side of the rail yard a commercial and industrial expanse lined the street that ran parallel to the yard. The train depot, hotels, boarding houses, and bars and restaurants were once quite prosperous, but now were in decline and on the seedy side. Train travel was not as popular as it once was, and much of the freight business was now centered on another line on the east side of town.

The factories and rail houses in the area also had deteriorated. Some appeared to be abandoned. One of those buildings always intrigued me. It was three stories, yellow brick with a long-faded sign hanging down across the front doors. The sign could still be read, but just barely: Gumwalt Broom Factory. The building was boarded up like The Hurd House. We rode across the gravel parking lot that seemed to have had more traffic than an unused building justified.

We followed the path and found a backdoor to the building. The door was new, made of slick steel with a shiny padlock on it. "Hey, you kids get out of there. You don't belong here. Next thing you know you'll get hurt. Scram before I call the cops."

We did as told. We rode as fast as we could down to the far end of the yard, crossed the tracks and headed home.

That evening after baseball practice we asked Gramps about the broom factory. "How could anyone make a living making brooms? Who buys brooms?" bellowed Rollie.

Gramps laughed, "Before wall to wall carpeting and the vacuum cleaner, the broom market was good. That place closed down about four years ago. At one time they had over twenty people working there. They shipped brooms all over the Midwest. That whole area used to be booming. There used to be a fancy nightclub nearby, big money. During prohibition it was a hot spot. Slicks, gangsters, and money moguls used to come in by train from St. Paul, Chicago and K.C. to live it up. Middleton was off the beaten track and noted to have a controllable law enforcement. The nightclub would use the broom factory parking lot."

Rollie burst out, "I bet they had hookers, too."

Gramps smiled, "You little devil. Rollie, at your age you shouldn't even know about that stuff."

Rollie grinned and said, "But, I do, and I bet they did."

"Yes, they did. There were many red-light houses there."

"Why did the nightclub go out of business?" I asked.

"Well, like I said, the passenger train traffic and most of the freight traffic shifted to the east side. Then the heat, not the summer kind, but the Fed kind, put too much pressure on Middleton. The city council had a big turnover. They fired the crooked chief of police and hired an honest one. Soon after, the long serving county sheriff was voted out of office. I guess the city and county got religion. But no matter what do-gooders want, you can't strangle the underlying desires of most people. There is plenty of riff raff left to go around."

Gramps got that far away look again and said, "You best stay away from the broom factory, too."

A few days later Rollie said, "Jeez, first The Hurd House, then the ravine, and now the broom factory. There's no place left to go. We can't go to the sand pits where they make cement blocks. We got run out of there."

I said, "I still would like to get into that broom factory. They might have some leftover brooms. We could take them to a witch convention and sell them just before Halloween."

"Funny man," retorted Rollie, "but, let's go look anyhow. Summer will be over and all winter we will wish we had investigated."

It was off to the Broom Factory the next evening. We ditched our bikes in the weeds a few blocks away and ambled up the street to the factory. We didn't bother with the back steel door. Instead we found a side window that was boarded up. Whoever did the work must have been cheap; there were only two nails in each board, one top, one bottom. We worked the lower nail free from a couple of boards and were able to swing them open to climb inside.

We looked around the first floor and found little except disturbed dust and tracks that lead to the stairs. On the upper floors we found a few raggedy blankets, balled up wax paper and food containers, and several empty beer cans. We guessed it was railroad hobos or teenage kids.

Then we found a stairway that lead to a basement. In spite of the dimming light we slowly crept down the stairs. The basement was almost bare.

"Hey, look," whispered Rollie. He picked up a small pie tin and showed it to me. "Doesn't this look like the one we found in the ravine dirt pile back at Gramps Strang's?"

"Yeah, you know I remember I've seen pie tins like this before. You know, my dad used to work at the Middleton Bakery. They used small pie tins like this for the pies you see in the neighborhood stores. After the little pies were baked and cooled, they were slipped out of the tins and into cardboard shaped ones, then put into bags. Most of the little pies went to a distributor called Lakes Bakes. They put them in stores for a dime a pie. On Saturdays, when I sometimes went to work with my dad, we did the pie route. We delivered full sized pies to a lot of bars and restaurants."

By now, bored out if his mind with the pie industry, Rollie interrupted, "So how did the little tins get from the ravine to here?"

"Let me finish. There was a guy who owned a bar and restaurant, The Blue Darter. Some guy called The Pie Man owned the place and bought at least two dozen small pies a week. He insisted that they be delivered in the original tins. My dad said he paid through the nose for that. His favorite was pineapple, a dozen of those were always pineapple. We collected the used tins but never got all of them back."

"Did you ever see the guy?"

"Yeah, once. He was old, a big guy— tall, fat and almost bald. He looked scary as hell. He just glared at me."

We looked around some more and found a door in the basement wall. It was steel like the back door, and it too was held shut with a shiny padlock hasp. By then it was getting too dark to seeand was time to head home. We had to use our bike lights and were late getting home. Both of us got grounded, except for baseball, for a week.

After we served our week sentence, we had to tell Gramps about the broom factory. He wasn't in his house when we got there. We often worried about him, and since there was only a screen door to keep us out, we went inside to see if maybe he was hurt or keeled over on the floor.

There was no one on the floor, but there was much of interest on his table: yellowed newspaper clippings of headlines about missing girls. One was from 1950 about the O'Brien twins we had heard people talking about. Another was from 1953 about the sisters from St. Ann who had disappeared. "Look at this," said Rollie. "Here's a story about The Pie Man. See, it says he was a person of interest in the disappearance of the girls from Lake Park and the O'Brien twins."

Near the clippings was a white piece of something that looked like a bone. It was arced like a rib bone. Just then Gramps walked in and yelled, "What are you doing in here? You know you are not to enter when I am not here."

We both jumped at the same time, mumbling on about how we were worried he was inside, hurt, lying on the floor.

"We called your name and got no answer," I said.

"Usually when you're gone the inside door is shut," Rollie added.

Gramps calmed down and said he was sorry he yelled. "But, you boys are not to enter if I'm not here. OKAY?" We nodded yes.

We went outside where it was cooler. Gramps sat in his old oak chair. We sat on the ground in front of him. Gramps said he had been out making flower deliveries and that's why he wasn't around.

"Wasn't that a bone on the table, Gramps?" I asked. "It sure looked like one."

"Oh, that." He paused, frowned and then, smiling, said, "Yeah, it's a bone." Another long pause. "It's an animal bone I found in the load you brought me from the ravine. I figured it must be a squirrel or rabbit. But most likely a stray cat."

Changing the subject, he asked what we'd been up to lately. We told him that last week we rode our bikes over to the broom factory. "We got inside," Rollie piped up. "You know what we found in the basement? Another pie tin like we found in the ravine, and we found another locked steel door in the basement. It had a shiny new padlock on it."

Gramps jumped up and yelled for the second time, "Boys, I told you to stay away from both the broom factory and the ravine. You just don't understand. You can't keep messing around in those places, and in The Hurd House, too. They're dangerous places."

"Yeah, we know," I said, "but who is The Pie Man? I remember my dad used to deliver pies to him, and we saw your article on the table. It said he was a person of interest in those cases about the missing girls."

"Listen, Rollie and Stu, The Pie Man is a big man in this town. He has more money than God. He owns many, many businesses. He is powerful enough to make law enforcement look the other way when they try to tie him into anything. You don't want to mess with him. Stay away from him."

"How can we stay away from him? We don't even know him," blurted out Rollie.

"He owned the broom factory, the old building is still his."

"How come there are new doors with locks on them," I asked.

"Yeah, and why is he called The Pie Man?" Rollie joined in.

"Some say it's because he eats those little pies he has special ordered. Others say it's because he has his fingers in every pie in town. He even finds a way to get his fingers in a piece of other people's pie.

"Just stay away from him and his property. You probably don't know it, but he bought The Hurd House and the 600 acres of field to the west. The ravine is part of all of it. Don't bring me anymore dirt. I won't pay you anymore."

We left Gramps and went to the baseball field and sat against the backstop. Rollie said, "You know, Gramps was looking at those newspaper stories and that bone. That doesn't look like an animal bone to me. What if it's human?"

"Sure," I answered, "He had those stories of the missing girls and the one about The Pie Man. What if that is what happened to The Hurd Girls."

"Stu, we need to go back and dig some more in the ravine."

"Rollie, Gramps said he won't pay us for more dirt."

"We aren't going there for more dirt; we're going there for more bones. Maybe we can solve a murder case. We'll get our own pictures in the paper. Maybe Gramps will keep a clipping of us, too."

It was decided. We would search for more bones early in the morning before anyone would be up. The next morning at five I heard the milkman's truck rattling the bottles and got up. I found Rollie already waiting. With shovels and the pickaxe we started rooting up the bog. We found nothing but lumps of damp dirt. We quit when we saw a car stop across the field near the baseball diamond. Two men seemed to be looking our way and pointing. We remembered Gramp's warning to stay away. So, we picked up our gear and high tailed it in the opposite direction.

"That didn't work so well," a white faced Rollie mumbled. When his color returned, Rollie said, "We aren't quitters. Tonight we go back after dark. We bring flashlights and wide forks. Forks will work better than spade shovels. We wait until everyone is asleep and sneak out."

That night at midnight we each escaped out of our bedroom windows and met in the alley. From there we made our way, spreader forks and flashlights in hand, to the ravine. After an hour we hit pay dirt, bones. Some of them were bigger. "Look at this," Rollie whispered. "This is a skull."

"Oh my…" I never got all the words out before a deep voice boomed over our bone pit. "DON'T MOVE A DAMN INCH." A bright flashlight was flipped on and the shape of two men moved the light toward us. Each was holding what looked like a pistol. The light from the three quarter moon was enough to see that one was The Pie Man. I recognized him from my dad's pie route. It was the same man as in the picture in the news story on Gramps' table.

The Pie Man rasped, "Boys, you're too damn nosey for your own good. First, The Hurd House, then here, onto the broom factory, then here again. We're going for a ride to another swamp where you won't be found by other nosey nellies with too much time on their hands."

"NO," screamed Rollie. "If you're going to shoot us, do it here. We are not moving a damn inch."

With a laugh and turning off his flashlight and dropping it, The Pie Man took a long piece out of his pocket and screwed it onto the barrel of his pistol. The other man followed suit. In the moonlight I could see The Pie Man begin to raise his pistol. A loud crack shattered the night air. As The Pie Man dropped, his pistol flashed. I heard Rollie scream, and then I heard another crack. The second man dropped on top of The Pie Man. We could see Gramps Strang rise out of the high grass of the ravine. He had a single shot .410 rifle in his hand.

He got to his feet and walked over to a moaning Rollie. He checked Rollie's bloody arm. "It doesn't look too bad, boy. You'll be able to show off your combat scar at school." Gramps took a bandana out of his pocket and bound up Rollie's wound.

The three of us sat there on the ground and looked at the stack of gunmen. "Don't you think we should take their guns?" I asked.

"Single Shot Strang never misses. They won't move again."

Confused, I looked at his single shot .410, "But I heard two shots, and two of them are down. How did you reload so fast?"

"I didn't. Go look in the tall grass over there for my other .410. I figured I might need to deal with more than one thug. So, I cleaned my old one and brought it along. Good thing for you boys I did."

Rollie's arm seemed to have stopped bleeding. Puzzled, he asked, "How did you know we were out here?"

"I know you two. You don't listen. I know you can't leave well enough alone. So, I kept track of you. I saw you out here this morning, and I saw that car by the ball diamond watching you.
"I knew you wouldn't quit. I got here at 11:00 and waited in the tall grass. I guess I got caught up in what you were doing. I must be slipping. I didn't notice those two until they stood up and yelled. It was time I got The Pie Man."

By this time the field was crowding up with cop cars, red lights flashing. Gramps told them to get Rollie to the hospital and send the meat wagon for the two goons. Gramps suggested that, come the next morning they might find some answers to missing kids by digging up this side of the ravine.

Rollie was carted off to the hospital, red lights flashing. He was in his glory. Gramps and I were questioned by the city cops and the county for hours. The next morning the FBI had its turn. Our parents, who were drawn to the ravine by the gunshots and the flashing lights, were relieved that Rollie and I were not seriously harmed. They were relieved but extremely peeved by our sleuthing behavior. I knew the rest of the summer would be hard labor.

A week later Rollie and I were both granted limited parole. We were allowed to visit Gramps Strang in thanks for saving our lives. We each had gifts from our parents for him. My mother sent a dozen of her famous bread rolls and a pound of cheddar cheese. Rollie's mom sent him toting a huge blueberry pie.

Gramps was happy to see us but did lecture us. "Boys you've got to learn to do what you are told." As Gramps shared his largess with us he told us about The Pie Man, whose legal name was Alexander Gumwalt. Many years ago, Gramps had worked for The Pie Man. When he figured out that The Pie Man was a crook, he tried to quit. The gangster was not about to let Gramps move on. After a year of constant nagging, The Pie Man finally agreed, but told Gramps, "Strang, if you ever breathe anything you know to the cops, your family will pay the price you wish was paid by you, not them."

Gramps said that was why he never ventured away from the relatives who owned The Greenery. He watched over them for thirty some years.

"The Pie Man was big during prohibition. That's how he got his pile of money. He knew mobsters out of Minneapolis and St. Paul. That got him connected with the filth out of Chicago and K.C. The Pie Man bought up all the local moonshine he could get, including Minnesota 13, then resold it to the big guys."

Gramps went on about how all that money went to buying up businesses and properties in Middleton. After prohibition The Pie Man got into prostitution, especially young girls.

"You know the broom factory you boys broke into was owned by him. It was an escape route and entrance. You remember that locked basement door you found? The tunnel leads to an underground pleasure palace that I hear was still used on some weekends and other special occasions. Out of town money, businessmen and politicians came in for the girls he provided. On the other side of the underground pleasure palace are tunnels that lead to the Middleton Hotel and a few business places.

"Thanks to you boys that was all uncovered by the FBI. After the ravine thing, they found it easier to get search warrants."

"What about The Hurd girls?" I asked. "Were they found in the ravine?"

"No. It hasn't hit the papers yet, but both were found in an old barn near Ironwood Lake. Both seem to be physically okay, but they must be really messed up. The body of their mother was found buried near that barn. No one knows where the father is. The filth keeping the girls hostage was killed by the FBI in a shootout. The FBI dug up a lot more bodies near that barn.

"When all those girls around here disappeared, I wrote a letter using my left hand and wearing gloves. I told the cops they should look at The Pie Man, but they never could pin anything on him. If I hadn't shot him, I bet he would have had his high price lawyers get him out of what he was about to do to you guys.

"When you boys started messing around at The Hurd House and brought the dirt to me with the bone in it, The Pie Man paid me a visit. Told me if I didn't stop you boys, he would. Then I, too, would cease to exist. That's why I was following you after you told me about the broom factory."

After we ate and cleared off the table, Gramps brought out some new non yellowed news clippings about The Pie Man, his crimes and property ownership. There was a big photo of Alexander Gumwalt, all 6'4", 300 pounds of him. There were more stories about finding the bodies of many missing girls. The search for who they were now included the five state area.

The best story was about Herbert "Gramps" Strang. The article related the midnight shootout at the north side ravine. It detailed The Pie Man's attempt to shoot the young sleuths, Roland Klein and Stewart August. The majority of the story was on Gramps and his heroic rescue of Rollie and Stu. A big picture of a smiling Gramps accompanied by his .410 shotgun highlighted the article. The caption read, "Dead Eye Strang dropped the culprits with a single shot each from two separate .410 shotguns." School headshots of Rollie and I were also included.

The stories said that the investigation would go on for months, if not years, in the "slicing up of The Pie Man by the two preteens and an octogenarian."

Gramps said now that The Pie Man was no longer to be feared, he might move to a new house and out of the flower garden business. "Maybe I'll open up a school for ten year old boys who need to learn to listen to their elders."

I hadn't been back to Middleton in many years. The river walk along the Mississippi was new. From downtown I took it north for about a mile to the end. There I sat on a bench facing the river. At my back was Sainte Marie de la Tourette Hospital where I had worked my way through college. As I watched the river flow, memories of the past surfaced.

The first time I met him he was pushing a rubbish wagon in the sub-basement of St. Marie's. He was so short I could hardly see him. I was pushing my empty laundry cart to the clothes chute to exchange it for a load of dirty hospital linen. As we were passing each other he stopped, smiled and said, "Hello, I am Jacques. Who are you? I don't think I know you."

"I'm Gus. I just started part-time in the laundry."

"I'm happy to meet you." He resumed pushing his wagon. I wondered if I had just met a gnome who stepped out of someone's garden. He could not have been five feet tall. His neatly combed hair was snow white, the same color as his burly, neatly trimmed mustache. The curled up ends extended beyond his angelic face. His ears seemed oversized and looked more like flaps. He wore dark green, cuffed work pants. These were held up by red suspenders over his matching dark green, button down shirt. On his tiny feet were a pair of brown, well-worn work shoes with red laces. I wondered where he was able to purchase shoes and work clothes like that. Surely no children's shop handled such items, and I couldn't imagine a fleet store having work clothes that small.

He was old. His big smile and blue eyes couldn't hide his many wrinkles. His gnarled hands gave evidence to many years of hard labor.

I turned to look again to be sure I wasn't off in some daydream. But there he was, slowly moving away, humming or maybe singing a song.

Every Saturday and Sunday and in the few days I worked after school, I encountered cheerful Jacques' smiles, hellos, and lilting tunes that at times seemed to have words, words I could not decipher. Mostly I heard humming. He was always pushing his cart to or from the garbage room or cleaning that room with its dumpster and incinerator.

After the first few months on the job, I asked around about him. The answers were always the same, "Jacques? Oh, he was here when I started here." "Don't know much about him." "All I know is he always smiles and says hello." No matter whom I asked, the answers echoed each other.

Those who worked at the hospital twenty years or more seemed a little elusive. "I really don't know." "Can't talk now." My quest for information told me he had always been there, pushing his rubbish cart, humming, smiling, friendly and kind to everyone. All seemed to refer to him as an old man.

The Dominican nuns who owned the hospital and provided many of the leading staff members were of little help. The younger nuns could only tell me he was there when they came to work there. The older nuns were evasive at best. Even Sister LuRella, who was older than all of them, perhaps even older than Jacques, evaded my questions. She and I had become friends over the five years I worked there. She did tell me that his name was Jacques

LaVeau, but when I asked where the French name came from, she said she had to tend to her chores.

A year and a half later and now in college, I had moved up the food chain from the sub-basement sorting dirty wash to the basement Central Supply Department. I was a clerk with free range of the entire hospital, from the sixth floor surgery to the main floor emergency room. I checked and supplied the nursing stations and retrieved used equipment.

I was issued starched, white pants and side snapped white jackets, ala Dr. Kildare, the TV hero of the time. I had full access to the men's lounge with a locker that held the hospital laundered and pressed uniforms. The lounge was back in my old haunt, the sub-basement. Many evenings of my 2:30 to 11:00 shift I would see Jacques and be greeted by his friendly hello and smile. His living quarters were near the lounge. I never saw what was behind his door but learned he had two rooms: a bedroom and a small living room. He ate his meals in the cafeteria. I was told he did have a small refrigerator.

Jacques' room was at the far south end of the hospital, but the hallway continued. It marked the entrance to a tunnel that connected the hospital to the nursing school affiliated with the hospital. The school was a five story affair that housed the classrooms, but consisted mostly of dormitory space for the student nurses and assorted med-tech types ranging from lab techs to x-ray. Of the nearly two hundred students, about 98 percent were female. The males were housed off campus. The seventeen to twenty-two year old students were constantly passing through the tunnel, especially in winter or rainy weather. The students ate their meals in the hospital cafeteria and pulled intern shifts in the hospital after their freshman year. Lucky me, as a young college student I got to know hundreds of young women in my years at St. Marie's Hospital.

Perhaps even luckier was Jacques. I often saw him sitting outside his door in a chair he had pulled from his room. He was usually humming. As he sat there, he greeted every passing student with a smile and a hello. The girls often stopped to chat before passing back to the dorm or onto work. Some evenings I saw Jacques passing out pieces of wrapped candy to the girls, usually a candy kiss. On a few occasions one of the girls would give him a bag of hard candy. He liked lemon drops.

Jacques whittled, he was pretty good. One lucky student nurse showed me a loon he had carved out of a piece of pine. It was beautifully done. Others of his favorite girls were rewarded with similar gifts.

The lack of information about Jacques and the stories about where he came from fed the imagination of many. Some of the older hospital workers in the boiler room and the laundry said that no doubt he was the result of a carnal encounter between a Dominican nun and a priest. I disregarded that. If such an event had happened, it had to have been long before anybody in Middleton ever heard of him. He had to be at least eighty, meaning he would have been born in the 1870s or 1880s. St. Marie's Hospital did not exist until 1928. Others responded by saying, "Yeah, but the Dominican Mother House, only ten miles away, was built in 1883." Then I asked these rumor mongers to account for his French name and the sound of the indecipherable songs he tried to sing.

I asked Jacques how he had come to work and live in the hospital. I asked him where he was born. "Gus, so long ago. I don't remember."

"Didn't anyone ever tell you?"

"Tell me what, Gus?" Off he went on his rubbish haul.

I gave up trying to get him to tell me. Everyone referred to Jacques as, "Slow, a nice guy, but slow."

One of the older nurses who had worked there for more than twenty years thought that the nuns had given him sanctuary. Maybe it was political, or he had run afoul of the law.

Another said he was a foundling. The nuns took him in, and since most nuns rarely worked with babies, they fell in love with the child. They had to keep him, too attached to let him go.

Adding to the mystery was the ever reminder of the French sounding songs and his name. A few of the student nurses who had taken French in high school spoke to him in that language. Each time one of them did this he stopped and smiled from ear to ear, holding the smile for a long time. Then the smile was replaced by a confused frown. During these transactions he kept looking at the face of the girl who spoke, as if trying to place her face. Then, with a look that suggested he just remembered, he would mumble in what sounded like French, turn and quickly walk away with tears running down into his grand white mustache. After such an encounter Jacques would not be seen at his usual post in the hallway for several days.

After a few such incidents, the student nurses were told they could no longer speak French to him. The mystery darkened. Who was this gentle man?

A few days after his disappearances from his evening post at his door, he would return with a smile and a bag of candy kisses or Tootsie Pops. The young women loved it.

The students tried to find out the date of his birthday. Again no one knew, or would not say if they did know. That didn't stop the students. Every three months for several years on a certain day the students would repeatedly say, "It's Jacques' birthday." Then in the early evening they would knock on his door, sing happy birthday and present him with a big sheet cake frosted with HAPPY BIRTHDAY, JACQUES. The girls came equipped with paper plates, plastic forks, a knife and napkins. Jacques would blush and say, "No, not my birthday, oh no." Then he would turn back into his room and drag out a small table for the cake. He returned to his room for his chair. He spent the rest of the evening smiling and passing out cake to each of the girls as they came out of or went into the tunnel. The celebration lasted until all the cake was served.

• • •

In the spring of my senior year of college the mystery of Jacques LaVeau remained. The love affair between Jacques and the student nurses was still in full bloom. Then the skies darkened. Weeks of heavy rain and the resurfacing of the parking lot between the hospital and the nursing school cast a dark shadow. Heavy road working equipment had been left in the parking lot which had been stripped of its tar. The rains pounded down. The work had been halted for several days. The construction company had not been made aware of the tunnel connecting the two buildings. They had parked their heavy equipment over the path of the tunnel. On a Tuesday night at about 11 o'clock, when the student traffic was heavy with the comings and goings of the afternoon and midnight shifts, the resurfacing equipment from the parking lot collapsed the tunnel. The machines sank down a foot or so but did not fall completely into the tunnel. Instead, much broken concrete and gravel fell into the tunnel in two separate places. A dozen or more of the girls who had not yet reached the first cave-in retreated back to the nursing school. Two others came flying out of the tunnel into the hospital behind the second cave in. They pounded on Jacques' door and told him that four girls were trapped in the tunnel. They had been only ten yards behind them. One girl, Barb, ran to get help. The other student, Nitz, stayed to help Jacques.

    Jacques moved as quickly as a spry man his age could. He entered the tunnel, and when he reached the cave in, he began to tear at the chunks of concrete and tar. The light from behind allowed him to see. Like a badger he dove into the gravel, and using his hands to scrape, he pushed dirt behind him. Barb, who had run for help, was now back with a few hospital workers. They looked into the tunnel and watched the white haired Frenchman and Nitz both digging. Then Jacques sent Nitz back to get a crowbar and a flashlight. Soon an orderly found a flashlight and a crowbar in a janitor's closet. Nitz grabbed them and ran back into the tunnel. Everyone else seemed reluctant to join in. Jacques took the crowbar and began to pry a chunk of concrete aside. Nitz helped him work the lever. The hospital workers at the tunnel entrance hollered for them to come out. "Let the professionals do it. They're on the way," they said.

    The two inside continued working and managed to wedge a concrete slab far enough to the side opening a hole. More sand and gravel poured in. Jacques dug more with Nitz holding the flashlight. The hole reopened into the pocket of the tunnel that was still holding. Before Jacques could crawl into the opening Jean crawled out, "Betty's leg is trapped under a piece of cement," Jean cried. "Judy and Taffy are trying to free her. They both have their night duty flashlights with them. But they need help." Jacques, crowbar in hand, tunneled his way into the hole. Nitz, with the flashlight, followed close behind. They found Judy and Taffy trying to lift a chunk of concrete that had pinned Betty's leg. With the crowbar Jacques and Nitz were able to raise the concrete slab just enough for Judy and Taffy to free Betty's leg and drag her back to the opening. Nitz had crawled ahead and pulled Betty through the hole. Jacques sent Taffy and Judy next. While Taffy, the last one, was four fifths of the way through the opening, there was a loud rumble collapsing the rest of the tunnel behind her. Nitz and Judy used their hands to dig Taffy free and pull her out of the tunnel. Now the space between the two closed sections of the tunnel was completely filled, covering the body of Jacques LaVeau.

Hospital workers had already taken Betty up to x-ray. Nitz, Taffy and Judy, whose uniforms were mostly torn off their bodies had cuts, blood, bruises, and caked mud covering them. They shouted to the others to come and help save Jacques. "He is still in there." All three of them, along with Jean and Barb, rushed back in and began clawing at the wet gravel trying to reach Jacques. Several orderlies and security personnel pulled them away fearing that they would suffer the same fate as Jaques LaVeau.

Rescue workers and construction company laborers, who had been called back to the job, worked for three hours before the body of Jacques was recovered. Betty's ankle was put in a cast and the other girls were treated for cuts and bruises. The head of the nursing school organized a head count. All the students were alive and accounted for.

• • •

That summer Betty, now free of her ankle cast, along with the five others who had worked with Jacques in the tunnel, raised money for a memorial for Jacques LaVeau. They raised enough to purchase an ornate rose granite bench with an engraved plaque dedicated to:

### 'THE HERO OF STUDENT NURSES: JACQUES LAVEAU'

On August 15th, graduation day for the senior nursing students, a dedication and memorial service for their hero was held on the lawn behind the hospital near the river. The Middleton Times covered the event. The president of the nursing class gave a moving speech about the love that all the medical students at St. Marie's had for their friend Jacques. She said, "He was a giant of a man whose worldly possessions could fill a janitor's closet, but he had a gigantic heart filled to overflow with love for everyone, especially the students who traveled the tunnel of which he was the guardian. He gave all he had every day of his life to all he met. To the student nurses, whom he loved, he gave his life."

After the blessing of the granite bench by the Bishop, the hospital and nursing school hosted a reception. Hundreds of people, mostly present and former hospital employees and graduated student nurses, had punch and cake. Since no one knew exactly when he was born, a dozen frosted sheet cakes proudly proclaimed August 15th as Jacques's birthday.

I sat at a table in the nursing school eating cake with Sister LuRella. She was in her late eighties and had been at St. Marie's Hospital since it opened. We were friends. In spite of painful arthritis and a handful of other old age aches and pains, she always wore a smile and had a kind word. On hot days in the unairconditioned hospital she would bring me a kettle of lemonade with an ice chunk floating in it. Even at her age she worked in the hospital. At night she tended the cash register in the cafeteria. She kept the collection of snacks and sandwiches plentiful and the coffee urn filled. She was there every night. Her greeting brightened everyone's coffee break. Many evenings, before I made my rounds to check and deliver supplies, she would stop by my department and visit before going to work her eighf to eleven shift.

As we munched on Jacques' birthday cake I said, "Sister, you always told me you didn't know the story of Jacques. He's gone, Sister, I know you know. Tell me, please."

She took a deep breath and sat there for a full minute saying nothing. Finally, "Gus, for your ears only. Okay?"

"Yes, Sister."

"The Dominicans came to Wilson County in 1883 from Canada. We have convents in several provinces of Canada and several more in the United States. We followed in the footsteps of Father Marquette and settled here.

"Sometime in the early 1890s, in a small town north of Montreal, lived a Catholic family of ten—husband, wife and eight children. They said the husband was basically a good man, but he was flawed. He could not avoid the brandy bottle or stay with only one glass of wine. He was skilled with tools, but his drink made it impossible for him to hold jobs. He had trouble housing and feeding his family. In a drunken stupor, he was said to have found his own solution. Using a shotgun, he proceeded to shoot his wife and seven children before putting the gun under his own chin and pulling the trigger. His drunken state more than likely accounted for his failure to realize he missed one child. Two days later the neighbors investigated. Their children went to school with some of Jacques' brothers and sisters and reported that no one had seen a member of the LaVeau family for days. The authorities found nine bodies. The search for the tenth began. Jacques, about four years old, was found in a cupboard. He was catatonic. He may have been playing a kid's game of hide and go seek with his brothers and sisters, or he may have hidden in fear of his life.

"The parish priest took the boy to the Dominican nuns. The boy did not talk, smile or play. He would do small chores if instructed to do so. He would sweep the floors or shovel some snow. He was a tiny little guy.

"Because of the notoriety of the brutal massacre, the big city newspapers, Montreal, Quebec, Toronto were always coming to the little town. They said they heard there was a survivor of the family carnage. They wanted the story. They wanted to see the boy, talk to him. They wanted their story and would not be denied. The Dominicans moved Jacques to a Montreal convent. It took less than a year for the press to sniff out his whereabouts. Then it was onto Sault St. Marie, Ontario, then Marquette in northern Michigan. The trail ended in Wilson County. Jacques was not traced here.

"By this time he was eight or nine years old. He seemed more relaxed. He learned to smile and soon was speaking some

English, which got better and better over the years. He liked to play with the carpenter's tools, I guess he got that from his father.

"He was always comfortable with the Sisters. Perhaps this was because his mother and sisters loved the baby boy so much. They said that the father, in his state of drunkenness, often physically abused his wife and children. I suppose the family females protected the baby boy. Jacques was always at ease with girls and women. Perhaps that is why he loved his student nurses.

"He grew up ten miles from here and became the convent's handyman. Except for his ability to fix things his mental development was limited. Socially, he was fine, but seemingly at a childlike level. He came here to the hospital in 1932 and has been here ever since.

"Since the nursing school opened in 1948, and especially after the tunnel was built in 1951, he loved the girls. He was never aggressive or out of line. He seemed to respond to them more as a child responding to a mother or loving sister. I guess the student nurses had more appeal than us matronly nuns in our black habits, wimples, and veils. At least here in the hospital the black habits were replaced with white ones."

She sat back in her chair and sipped some punch. "Not as good as my lemonade," she said with a smile. "Keep the story, Gus. No one needs to know."

I got up from Jacques' bench the better for having recalled the story and headed back downtown.

I've kept that story for fifty years.

*Nov. 19, 1989*
*Dear Gus,*
*I love it here. I landed in New Mexico in an art colony area not far from Santa Fe. Art schools and camps, art galleries, and plenty of tourists to buy my pieces give me all I need. Sorry it has taken so long to reconnect.*

Rummaging through old folders and files, as retirees do, I unearthed a letter I had forgotten. It tapped a wellspring of memories. When I had returned from my four-year adventure teaching in São Paulo, Brazil, I was fortunate enough to land an English teaching position in a small suburban school. At forty-two I was one of the youngest on the staff. The population of the school district aged, yet the homeowners remained. School enrollment dropped. The district was almost all middle-class demanding high educational standards. Teacher attrition, when it occurred, was usually due to retirement. It felt good to be a youngster at forty-two.

As the staff continued to age a few real youngsters were hired. Katchia Kacee, an idealistic, energetic twenty-two-year-old was the first hired. She was an art teacher in the middle school who also taught one high school class. Because of shrinking enrollment, the high school and middle school were housed in the same old, large edifice.

By far the youngest on the staff, Katchia had no one her age with whom to form friendships and alliances. I, too, found myself in a similar situation, an outsider. The cliquey staff had long ago formed its alliances and social structure. I remembered what it was like my first-year teaching, the struggle of long hours and confusion about a new profession. I made it a point to seek out Katchia, offering a friendly smile and a helping hand, if needed.

After a month in the classroom Katchia sought me out and said she could use some help in navigating the ways of her new life. I suggested an after-school supper at a good Italian restaurant. A frown formed on her forehead. Having known the financial struggles of a young teacher, I quickly added, "On me." The frown turned to a smile followed by a nod yes.

We met at Pino's. Katchia said, "Everyone is nice, but I feel so alone, so isolated. I'm not part of the everyday banter. In group meetings my comments and suggestions are met with condescending smiles, then ignored." We talked about how hard it was for both of us to be outsiders. This was the first of many such dinner chats, all on me.

*Things are easier here. There is only one bank in town.*

I laughed as I read. At the first supper she suddenly shifted the conversation and asked, "What if a person deposited money in the wrong bank?" I must have looked puzzled. "I mean, if a person filled out a deposit slip to put money in a checking account of a bank they didn't have an account in, would they lose the money?"

"I don't think you could do that. The cashier would catch the mistake."

"No, they wouldn't. I just did it. I signed my paycheck and filled out a deposit slip for the bank on the corner over there. I thought it was a branch of my bank. As soon as I ran out the bank door on my way here, trying not to be any later, the sign on the window of the bank across the street flashed in front of me, First Federal Bank. I looked at my bank deposit slip. It said Federal Savings and Loan. I turned and ran back to Federal Savings, but the guy just locked the door, smiled, pointed to the clock and turned away as I pounded my fists on the glass.

"It's Friday and I don't have enough money in my account to cover anything, I have no groceries and no cash for the weekend."

As tears began to roll, I suggested that on Monday she call both banks to salvage the situation. Meanwhile, I lent her cash to get through the weekend.

"As my mother used to say when I did stupid things, 'Gotcha, Katchia.'" As she wiped away the tears, she said, "Thanks. I have never been good at adult things." She paused in thought, then began to blush, "At least most adult things."

> *Yes, it is so much easier here. Gathering my own materials is a breeze. In the city I had to hunt for everything. Here everything is close, and for the most part free for the taking. The variety of plants is endless. I harvest from fresh flora of the rivers and valleys to higher and drier plateaus, and then it's off to the driest of deserts. I have access to every plant I can think of to use in my dyes. Then the earth pigments, too, are endless. Stratified river and plateau dirt and rock, and all the minerals of the desert give me so much access and so many options.*
>
> *Remember how the kids in middle school loved how I dressed and how the staff and some parents hated it? Here nobody cares what color my hair is or what clothes I wear. Nobody cares how much or how little skin I show. I don't have to worry about what is appropriate for what occasion.*

While the staff acceptance of Katchia didn't much improve, her teaching was a hit with the students. They loved her. Her appearance was middle school friendly. Her hair color varied, sometimes from day to day. The girls asked who did her hair. "I do it myself. I make my own dyes. I make dyes for my tie dye t-shirts as well." Even the boys were intrigued by this and asked how she did it. Her ever changing Henna designs became the talk of the high school girls who were in the photography class she taught.

Some of Katchia's class projects not only involved the students making their own paint colors, but she had them constructing their own brushes. She convinced a local slaughter house to save and donate pig snout bristles. The kids used the brushes and paints for their own projects.

> *There are no formal interviews here, only friendly visits. I don't even have to worry about getting to job interviews on time here. For the most part this area of New Mexico has adopted Native American time. "Things start when you get there." This works well for me. By being me and looking like me, I was able to get a teaching stint at Six Days of Creation Art Garden. They also sponsor a few of the many area art camps. I have found work at several of them in the two years I've been here. The Art Garden classes are twelve-week semesters. At the camps the classes are from one to ten days long. The students range from age six to sixty plus and come from all over the country. The camps are most popular in summer.*

Another Italian supper popped into my mind. "You know how I got this job? I had an interview set up at this fancy private school. I thought I would fit right into their progressive philosophy. I got to the interview early. Then I found out that the interview wasn't at their upper school campus but was ten miles away at the main office on their lower school campus. I rushed to get to that location on time and ended up with a speeding ticket which delayed me even more. I was so shook up when I got to the parking lot, I drove over the curb. I got the car parked and tried to dash off in my high heels.

"I was only 15 minutes late. From the beginning I could tell things were not going my way. The interview was really short. As I was dismissed and left the room, I noticed that the windows overlooked the parking lot. I could see my mis-angled, old junker taking up two parking spaces. They must have witnessed my grand entry.

"As I left the building my reflection in the door window revealed a piece of my torn dress hanging down in back. I must have caught it in the door as I rushed to be on time. I just bought that dress for the interview with money I didn't really have. Another, 'I gotcha, Katchia.'

"After that I got an interview at your school. I dressed in my only decent pair of slacks and borrowed a good blouse, no heels this time. I got to the interview early."

*I also work with the area Native Americans. I teach my methods and introduce modern materials to them, and they teach me traditional styles using traditional materials. Somebody asked me if I volunteer on the reservations. I told them I barter knowledge and skills for knowledge and skills.*

*Everybody tells me to specialize, but I can't. I want to do everything. I still sculpt and paint, but now I throw pots and weave. Oh yes, I still have my cameras and shoot as much as I can. The desert and the Anasazi caves are so rich in shades and shadows. I do mostly black and white, but the changing colors of the badlands reveal so much beauty.*

*I even convinced a local carpenter and a blacksmith to give me time in their shops. I barter some of my works, so I can make frames and do welding and iron work. You should see the muscles I am developing. I'll arm wrestle you when you come out to see me.*

> *At least here no one hassles me when I use "men's" equipment. No one challenges me about my right to weld, use a saw or a joiner. I have not been told directly or indirectly, "men only."*

Another Italian supper drifted back to me. "Gus, I need your advice. You know I make my own frames for my paintings. I showed my kids. They want me to make frames for them. I got the shop teacher, Mr. Bass, to help them make their own frames in his shop class. I got a lumber yard over in Nordeast to donate some scrap lumber for those kids who can't afford their own. I got permission from the principal and Mr. Bass to use the shop outside of school hours to make patterns for my eighth graders. Mr. Bass usually leaves right after the last bell, so I thought I would have the place to myself. Well, three or four older male teachers, some from the high school, evidently have been using the shop as their private lounge, drinking coffee and discussing hot women.

"The first time I went there, I interrupted their chat about some girl's 'desirable bod.' They didn't like a female witness within earshot. Right away one of the good old boys began with the cheap shots. 'The shop is for men. What are you doing here, girlie?' On another day I got, 'Why don't you get your pretty butt out of here?' And then a few days later, 'Don't cut off anything you want to keep.' After two weeks it was, 'Can't you take a hint? You don't belong here.'

"The worst one was Roy Klack, he was 90 percent of it. He even got up close and in my face. What should I do? I don't want to cause trouble, but I can't take it anymore."

"Katchia, you have to report this. Make a list of every date and everything they did and said. Get their names. Report all of this to principal Larson."

"But, I don't know all their names."

"Figure it out. Ask around."

Katchia did as advised. Roy Klack was called in for a conference with the middle school principal and the district superintendent. Accusations of sexual harassment were presented to him without him being told who complained. He was reminded that this was not the first report of such out of line behavior, and that any more complaints would end up in formal action being taken.

Katchia said she was told that Roy Klack just sat there, denied nothing and nodded that yes, he understood he could be fired, end up in court, or both.

*I don't even have to threaten anyone here with a sexual harassment suit or present evidence to anyone. I don't even have to join a union.*

That was another point of contention between Katchia and much of the staff. She refused to join the teacher's union and was incensed when she was assessed fees for salary negotiations. "I'm not political, and I don't argue over money. If I don't like what I'm paid, I leave."

After the dressing down of Roy Klack, things seemed to get better for Katchia. She used the shop less but still received cold stares from the good old boys.

In spring Katchia had gained permission to use the shop on Saturdays to make easels for her students' artwork, which was to be displayed at a special school art show. The sale proceeds and the donations collected at the art show were to be used for transportation for Katchia's middle school students for a field trip with guided tours at The Art Institute. A picnic lunch on the Institute's vast lawns was to follow.

On Katchia's second Saturday of easel construction she encountered Roy Klack and two cronies. She entered quietly. They hadn't noticed her as they selected lumber from the school supply and moved it to a table saw. Roy Klack said, "Since I got the first poker table, Kenny, you get this one."

"Then they noticed me and became irate, yelling sexual obscenities I had never heard before, not even from drunk football players."

When she got home she called me and gave me all the details. "Katchia, write it all down, every detail, even about the lumber. Write down what they said verbatim."

On Monday I saw Katchia after school in the cafeteria. There was a reception for two retiring teachers in the school district, one high school and one elementary. The reception was attended by staff from all the schools. The place was crowded. I think it was the cake and ice cream that drew most. Listening to the speeches was the price of admission.

Off to one side eating our treats, Katchia told me she was scared to death. She didn't turn in her statement about what she saw and heard until the last hour of the day. As we ate she asked me to look across the room at the three men staring at us. "Who is the third one, the bald guy, on the right? I know who the other two are, Kenny Zerby, and Roy Klack, but what's the other guy's name?"

Very confused, I said, "Katchia, that's Roy Klack. How can you not know that? The bald guy is Roy Klack.

"Are you sure?"

"Katchia, I have known Roy Klack for three years. Yes, I am sure. We teach on the same floor."

Katchia got up and ran from the room. I followed her outside into the parking lot and suggested we sit in my car and talk.

"Gus, what do I do now? I accused the wrong guy by name. This doesn't make sense. How could Roy Klack not even defend himself when confronted by Ms. Larson and the superintendent? He isn't that dumb, is he?"

"Look, students and faculty members have complained about his behavior for years. He wasn't falsely accused of sexual harassment in general. That's how he acts. What you reported about who you thought was him is true to his nature."

"But why hasn't he been fired?"

"No one has ever made a formal complaint in writing, documenting it. No one wants to be the one to testify at a school board meeting or in court. Klack has been warned over and over. When accused, he must have assumed he was guilty. I don't suppose he catalogs his transgressions."

"What do I do now?"

"You have to find Ms. Larson and clear this up. I didn't see her at the reception. The guy you should have named is Earl Steid, another high school teacher. In all likelihood Larson hasn't acted on your report yet."

We both went into the building and learned that Ms. Larson was meeting with the superintendent. We went to his office and got his secretary to interrupt. The secretary escorted Katchia into the lion's den while I waited in the outer office.

After 45 minutes a tearful Katchia emerged. We adjourned to a nearby coffee house, and Katchia gave me the details of her embarrassing confession. But ever resilient youth soon had her chattering about how maybe the promised land was in the Southwest. She said, "I can't stay here after this misadventure. Besides, I can't thrive here. I need to be somewhere where I am allowed to be me without harassment of any kind."

Her letter to me confirmed that she had found a thriving environment for her art and teaching gifts.

As for Roy Klack and Earl Steid, Klack continued in the classroom for a few more years and had student complaints about looking up their skirts and down their blouses. Meeting with the principal, the superintendent and a union lawyer, Klack announced his retirement.

Steid had beaten Klack to the retirement punch right after the shop room scandal. Before any action against him was taken, he retired to fishing and using his new poker table.

Twenty-five years later, as I reread Katchia's letter I was hit with the same emotions as I felt back then. Should I laugh at this absurd fiasco, or should I cry? This misidentification and its implications reeked of comedy of the absurd. Roy Klack's ever present behavior had him so used to being confronted that he failed to realize that he wasn't even a player in that particular drama. What a punchline to a bad joke.

I also want to cry. Sexist behavior of years ago is still present. How sad is that? Sexual harassment has a long history. In recent years society is much more aware. More is being done to prevent it, but it is still with us.

I raised my eyes from the letter to the wall in my study. I looked at two landscape paintings, one of the desert badlands and the other of the Anasazi caves. The colors, shades and shadows were magnificent. Recently, in preparation for drawing up a new will, I had them appraised along with my other world travel acquisitions of rugs and paintings. The appraiser sent photos of Katchia's work to a Santa Fe art gallery. They knew her and her work. Each painting was valued at between one and two thousand dollars.

> *Gus, I'm so happy here. I would never have survived that one ugly, yet fascinating year without your help. I'll send you a few pieces of my work over the next few years as soon as I do something really special.*
> *Love,*
> *Katchia*

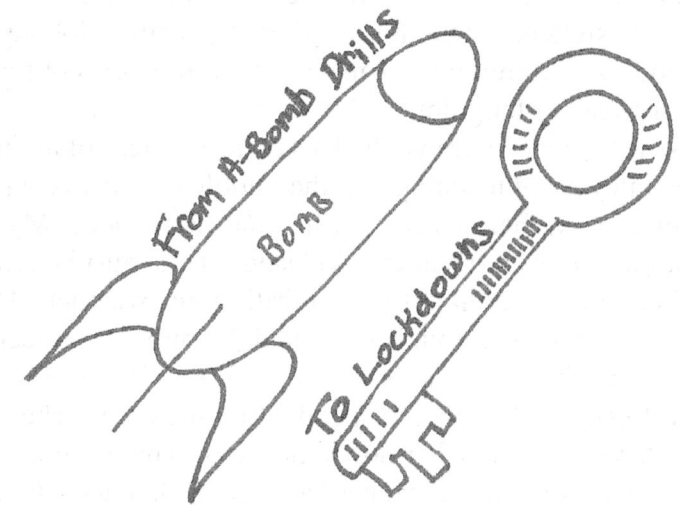

*From A-Bomb Drills Bomb To Lockdowns*

"Oh, my God. You're a teacher? Aren't you scared? I know I would be. All those crazy school shootings. Lately, I've been hearing about teachers assaulted in classrooms and hallways. I couldn't do what you do."

The words came from the guest of the groom at a wedding reception I had attended recently. That wasn't the first time I had been told that. My name is Stuart August, and I have spent over forty years in the classroom as teacher and coach. The worst I have suffered is torn rib cartilage from an errant sneeze.

They question me about how the supposed threats to teachers and students have changed over the years. At the Class of '62's monthly luncheon for those of us still in Minnesota, or those visiting, the chatter, as usual, turned to "remember when."

Bob piped up, "Remember those A-BOMB drills? The horn would sound. We crawled to the wall or ducked under our seats and prayed."

Peggy chuckled, "Yeah, I can imagine how those old oak desks would've kept us safe from collapsed walls, roofs and radiation."

"But we did as we were told and shuddered. In the 1950s we lived in fear of the bomb," Mike resonated in a preaching tone.

Paula sighed, "Then those endless fire drills. Nobody took them seriously, nothing more than a waste of time except for getting out of class for ten minutes."

Now the classroom vet had a say. I told them of an incident in my second year of teaching. "In the middle of January with a temperature of five below zero, the fire alarms sounded. My kids looked at me and each other. One kid said, 'This must be real. The principal can't be that dumb to call a drill in this weather.' The entire student body, K through 12, exited the building in record time sans coats, hats, or gloves, including Lori Walz, who was an 80-pound freshman destined to spend a lifetime on crutches. My instructions were to carry her down the steps, which I did. Each hour of the day some male teacher had Lori Walz duty. The exit was orderly and successful and surprisingly quiet.

"We no more than cleared the building when a junior boy, Herb, ran up to the principal and said, 'I caught my shirt sleeve on the alarm. I didn't know what I caught it on and yanked. The glass broke. I'm sorry.'

"As the fire house alarm sounded down the street, we saw the volunteers rushing to the fire station. The principal yelled to the janitor to shut off the alarm and for all of us to slowly re-enter the building. Maybe fire drills do pay off."

I went on to say that people often criticize teenagers, but over the years when the chips are down, I found high school students to have more common sense and better behavior than most adults I know.

"Yes, but the exception proves the rule." The retired lawyer, Dennis, in his modulated voice extorted. "Can you support that with additional evidence?"

"Yes," I countered. "Twenty years later at the suburban school I was at, the fire alarm sounded. This time it was a fine October day. Some kid yelled, 'It must be the real McCoy.' None of us got wind of a planned fire drill.

"Sure enough, as we exited from my second floor classroom a sharp acrid odor wafted up the stairway as we descended. Talk quickly spread that there indeed was a fire in the science room. Fast thinking and level-headed Mr. Klein stayed behind and worked the fire extinguisher smothering the blaze. The entire high school and junior high quickly and orderly cleared the building. We all sat on the lawn over one hundred feet from the building and enjoyed the recess. The fire department arrived and did its thing. Within an hour we were all back in class except for one science room. No one ever solved the mystery of the flaming wastebasket. In a crisis I want high school students on my side."

Another member of the class of '62, Charlie, a former elementary teacher, spoke up. "I'll add further evidence to dependable kids. About fifteen years after I started teaching, tornado drills were added to the list of alarms. I remember one time we were on a tornado warning. We had the kids in the basement sitting on the floor of the inner hallways. There were heavy rains, thunder and lightning. Then the power went out. We were there for over an hour. The kids had begun to get antsy. A couple of teachers started singing old songs such as The Itsy-Bitsy Spider. Soon the kids joined in, I guess they thought it was more fun than going back to class. We sang until we got the all clear and, hand in hand, we all escaped the dark basement. Kids do well under pressure, especially when they can take a musical tour of Old McDonald's Farm."

Then Judy jumped in with, "Now you can add bomb scares and lockdowns into the drills. My grandkids always complain about them and how hokey they are."

"We had bomb scares back in the early 1970s," I replied. "In my fifth year of teaching we had a call come in saying there was a bomb in the building set to go off in an hour. Again, the evacuation was orderly. The principal's voice came over the intercom telling everybody to exit the building via fire escape routes. Town kids and those with cars were instructed to go to the fire station, and bus students to meet their buses on the east side of the parking lot furthest from the building. No cars were to leave the parking lot. Again, everybody rallied to the task and exited the building without panic.

"Turned out that the call was a hoax traced to a recently expelled junior."

"Funny they didn't add bomb drills then to keep the paranoid conspiracy folks satisfied," sarcastic Randel J, the ex-DJ threw in.

"Oh, but we had them then," I interjected. "When I taught in Brazil in the 1980s, we had bomb scare drills. It was after Ronald Reagan ordered the bombing of Gaddafi in Libya. For a while we had a couple of armed Marines from the U.S. Consulate at our gates. In our bomb drills the regular school bell rang continuously, a signal for all to leave the building and gather on the soccer field by homeroom. Teachers had to take attendance and keep all close by, calm and orderly. We were lucky only to have the drills and not the real thing."

Charlie said, "Then Columbine changed everything. After that we had lockdown drills. At first, we had so many of them kids just groaned and said, 'Oh, not again.'"

"I know," I responded. "My high school students shouted out, 'Drill. Drill. Drill,' when the lockdown coded announcement sounded. When the all clear code was announced: 'Mr. Johnson has left the building,' The kids shouted, 'All clear.'"

"But," grandmotherly Kathleen rebutted, "Sandy Hook and Parkland has reminded us that schools still need to keep my great-grandkids safe. It's so hard to grow up in today's world."

Art, the leader of the class of the '62 luncheons, questioned, "Charlie and Gus, did either of you ever have a real threat that required a lockdown?"

By this time the entire crowd of about thirty had gathered two deep around one big table, as at a campground fire pit.

"No," said Charlie. "I can offer my thanks for that."

All eyes turned to me. "We had one serious incident."

I then told them that it was during my prep time. A student was in my room working on some research for an independent study class. Then Micky, a recent transfer, darted in knocking over a chair. She raced to the corner where I was sitting at my desk. She dropped to the floor behind me while saying, "I'm not here." I just sat there for a minute or two. Tony, the independent study kid, looked at me and shrugged as if to say 'I don't know, do you?' I didn't.

Micky was put into my creative writing class about four weeks earlier. I was told she was in her third school that year. Apparently, her single mother was having job problems, as well as boyfriend abuse issues.

Micky just sat there gasping, repeating, "I'm not here. I'm not here."

Then a shaggy-haired man with a two or three-day stubble filled the doorway. He was wearing washed out jeans and a tight t-shirt that gave evidence to his weight lifting. His t-shirt said, 'I eat nails for breakfast.'

"Where is she?" He snarled.

I told him, "If you are looking for someone you need to check in at the principal's office. They will be able to direct you."

He stepped into the room, "Dammit, where is she?"

I replied, "There is no one here that you can't see."

His chest puffed out, and he blared, "You got that right, Buster. I can see her dirty blonde hair poking out from behind your chair. Micky, get your ass over here. We are leaving now."

She sunk closer to the floor, sobbing.

"You little bitch. NOW," he shouted, taking two steps in our direction. I stood up and moved between my desk and the window. Micky was behind me with a desk, a walled bookcase and me boxing her in.

I sternly said to him, "Mister, I don't think it's worth your trouble, but you need to come through me to get to her. She stays where she is until I get a proper authority to release her to you."

Then I reached for the phone on my desk.

As I dialed the principal's office the jerk could have tossed me out the window, but he seemed to reconsider his options and backed out of the room. I tossed my keys to Tony and said, "Lock the door."

As he locked the door, the principal's secretary answered my phone call. I said I had to speak to him now.

"He is dealing with major issues and not available right now."

I told her, "Tell him one of his issues is in my room on the floor safely behind my desk. His other issue is loose in the hallway."

After I hung up, the lockdown alert came over the intercom. I closed the curtains and told Tony to sit on the floor next to the bookshelves away from the locked door and the narrow window on that side of the room. I told Micky to stay where she was and as low as possible. I sat down next to her and held her hand. Micky mumbled, "thank you," amid her continued sobs. All else was quiet in the room. The whole second floor was church quiet.

Ten or fifteen minutes later there was a knock on my door.

The thirty-some members of the class of '62 seemed to move closer. I felt like I was holding court. All eyes were on me. I continued the story.

The voice of the principal, Mr. Skjei, said, "Mr. August, I am unlocking the door and coming in. Don't be alarmed." He entered with a chunky, blonde woman.

Micky stood up and ran to her saying, "Mom, Mom." As they embraced, both burst into tears. Leading both Micky and her mom out of the room, Mr. Skjei turned and said the all clear would soon be announced and classes would resume for the day. He told both Tony and me to come to his office after school for a police statement.

The crowd around my table started to break up, but was halted by Edy as she boomed, "Well, what happened to the guy?"

I told them as soon as the school went into lockdown the police arrived. The station was only half a block away. The guy must have headed to the rear of the school toward the gym and locker rooms. All the lockdown practices must have done some good. The doors he tried were locked. In desperation he exited the gym into the parking lot where he met two armed policemen who carted him off to jail. They found an army buck knife in his boot.

"What happened to him and the girl?" the ever curious Edy queried further.

"He was arrested, jailed, and tried for, among other things, attempted kidnapping and child molestation. He apparently had his car packed with two of his suitcases and one for Micky. The guy was also charged with domestic assault. Micky's mother had served as a punching bag as she tried to protect Micky from him more than once.

"I even got to testify at the trial. He did time in prison. As for Micky, I wish I knew what happened to her. I never saw her again, not even in court."

Kind hearted Judy, who by this time was sniffling and wiping tears from her eyes, softly voiced, "You know, we were a lot better off in the days of the A-Bomb drills than the kids in today's lockdowns. I never believed the bomb would get us, but now I fear for all of today's kids, not just my grandkids and great grandkids."

What to do with Astrid

Books to inventory, tests to score, final grades to do, would I ever get it all done? There was even more work at my apartment. I had to pack all that I had not yet shipped home to Minnesota in two Bunyanesque suitcases and a carry on. I was returning to my old school after a five year leave.

São Paulo, Brazil and a Catholic American school, Escola Aparecida, had given me a five year thrill of a lifetime. New close friends, challenging students, enjoyable teaching, travel, and more than a few adventures made it a five year scenic cruise. However, the ship was in danger of sinking after ten weeks. My first adventure almost sunk before the port was out of sight.

These thoughts were interrupted by a just-graduated student. The pretty blonde bounced into my room and blurted out, "Mr. August, how can I help you? I know you are going back home and leave Brazil tomorrow. You must have so much to do. Here, let me help you with those books."

I had known the girl since she was in the eighth grade. She took two full years of English with me and became a favorite student and friend. After we checked and stacked away all the textbooks, she helped score final tests. I rarely gave a multiple choice final, but the school required a final test and demanded grades within 48 hours. Instead of the usual essay final it was much easier to correct a multiple choice test. I covered the names, and my new assistant scored all of the exams. I worked on totaling the rest of the final grades while she worked.

As we chatted away the day, she said, "You know, your classes were hard, but they became fun. I learned so much. I wish my younger sisters could take your classes."

"We did have a good five years," I said. "I really enjoyed working with you. We got off to a good start."

"I bet that when I started eighth grade you never would've guessed that I would still be here to graduate, or that English would be my favorite subject. You even gave me an A last year, an A for the full year."

"I guess it must have been your blonde hair, Swedish accent, and that you are no longer a skinny little girl that made me do such an insane thing," I said, laughing. She gave me a fake dirty look.

"I worked hard for that A," she retorted. "After a trip back home to Europe, I will start school at Victoria University in Toronto, Canada next September. My final GPA here should be 3.4, and I scored well on my TOEFL (Test of English as a Foreign Language). My first semester here at Aparecida my GPA was only 2.0. My mom is so happy. I know I will do well next year. Do you think you had anything to do with that?" she smiled.

"I hope so. But you really didn't need me once you got started, once you used your stubbornness and tapped into your excellent Scandinavian brain."

The two of us finished the books and tests. She asked if I needed help packing at my apartment; did I need a ride to the airport?

I told her that because of all the time she had saved me, I could handle the rest. "Thank you."

She rushed up to me and gave me one of the biggest and most heartwarming hugs I ever received. The hug lingered for a long time as she repeated, "Thank you, thank you, thank you."

She slipped a piece of paper into my hand and said, "Here is my college address. Write to me." Then she kissed me on my cheek and fled the room.

As she said, her mom would be happy. It was her mom who almost sank my overseas teaching vessel. Ten weeks into the semester we had parent teacher conferences. A tall, broad shouldered, blonde, expensively and stylishly dressed, strode into my room. She towered over me as I sat at my table. In a commanding voice she demanded, "Mr. August, what are you doing with my daughter?"

I was sure it was all over, and I would be on my way to the airport the next day. I would not get to finish teaching students from thirty some countries in a prestigious American school in São Paulo, Brazil.

Indeed, what had I done to her daughter, Astrid? On the first day of classes my last period was a global collection of eighth graders. Among the eighteen was a short, blonde haired kid, skinny, wearing a bulky turtleneck sweater. The sweater, no doubt, was a bow to a São Paulo winter, a chilly, damp sixty degrees. I didn't know if the slender short haired blonde was male or female. The name Astrid told me little. As far as my knowledge of all the new names represented in the many languages and cultures of the school's enrollment, I didn't have a clue.

Astrid sat in the back near the window. During the entire fifty minute class period my new riddle never made eye contact, never interacted with any of the other students, but did frown a great deal. Foreheads tell accurate stories.

The second day of class repainted the first day's picture. I asked around. Who could tell me about Astrid Johansson? By the third day of class I had sleuthed a few things: #1 Astrid was female. #2 She was Swedish. #3 This was her first year in an American school. She had attended a Swedish school for seven years and took the required English classes there. #4 She hated being in an American school, but the family faced a choice of sending her back to Sweden for further schooling, or enrolling her in an American school so she could attend an English speaking college. #5 And most telling, she absolutely hated speaking English, which she did poorly.

What to do with Astrid? After the third day of class, I stopped her as she was about to leave the room. It was easy to catch her alone as she was always the last student to leave. She still avoided classmate interaction.

I put my hand on her shoulder and asked her if she had a few minutes for me. She nodded yes. I directed her to a desk and sat in one next to her. "Astrid, you seem to have some difficulty understanding all I say. Is that so?" Again, a nod yes. "Astrid, how about this? I'll move you to the front near the window. That way you are closer to me. I'll try to speak slower, and if you don't understand what I am saying, just raise the finger next to your thumb like this. Nobody will know you are telling me you don't get it. I will go slower and use different words to say it again. Can you do this?" Again the nod.

She got up to leave, and I walked her to the door. I put my arm around her shoulders and gave her a hug while I said, "Astrid, since this is the last period of the day, I can stay and help you with any problems you are having." I gave her a squeeze and a pat on the back as she left the room.

This seemed to work. An index finger raised, I reworded. Eye contact made, accompanied by a smile, something new— I connected. As the days passed Astrid often asked for help. This went on for weeks. Each day was the same. Astrid was always the last to leave. I always walked her to the door with an arm around her back or shoulders, always a pat on the back after an improved vocabulary quiz score or a good test result on a story read for homework. Her last words as she left the classroom each day were, "Have a good evening, Mr. August." On Fridays it was, "Have a good weekend," or, "Will you travel this long weekend, Mr. August?" I noticed too that she seemed to have made some friends. She smiled more and seemed happier.

Before I came to Brazil, occasionally a student teacher would say to me, "You take a lot of risks. You do something we are told never to do, touch a student." My answer was two part: one, I have to be me, and two, I gave a long lecture on the importance of touch in communication. The lecture usually ended with studies that demonstrated how touch was a major factor in communication. Now my touching was about to bite me. My inner monologue kicked in, Oh no, Astrid must have told her mother I was hugging her. "Mr. August, what indeed are you doing to my daughter?"

"What is the problem Mrs. Johansson? What do you think I'm doing?"

"That's just it. I don't know. My daughter is not a very good student. She dislikes school, always has. She hates studying English. She was not happy when we enrolled her here, yet every day for the last eight weeks she shuts herself in her room for two or more hours every evening. I finally insisted she let me into her room and made her tell me what she was up to. You know what she was doing?" I told her I had no idea.

"She is studying English. She hates English. She showed me the vocabulary root words she was memorizing. She showed me the stories she read and told me how many times she read each one.

"Now look at this, a C in English on her report card. At the Swedish school the best grade she ever had in English was a D."

"Please, Mrs. Johansson, sit down." I then told her what I had been doing with Astrid, about the talking to her, the hugs and pats on the back. I told her that Astrid's grade was on the rise, little by little. Her grade of C was legitimate. The better her grades were the more hugs I gave her and the longer our after-class chats were. If she keeps improving she will soon be getting Bs. I also told her Astrid was spending more time making friends and seemed so much happier in class.

Mrs. Johansson rose. The Swedish accent thickened. "Mr. August, you yust keep doing vat you're doing." She left the room. I did keep doing what I was doing. Astrid's hug that last day was a beautiful return on my investment of hugs for her. I did write to her in Toronto. She got her degree and moved onto a career, marriage, and family. I am sure she is still giving out hugs.

The old man

The old man dozed on and off, the radio playing easy listening music. Some called it elevator music, but he was sure old Otis himself would be proud of the designation. He was dozing off more and more during the day. At eighty-four, aches, pains and the loneliness of people his age gave him an understanding of his grandma's advice, "Don't get old." He was still living in his own apartment in a seniors only complex. He worried about how long he could continue to do that.

As he dozed, his fleeting dreams were haunted by the theme of Father's Day. Perhaps the radio station had aired a commercial to guilt someone into buying things for dear old dad, things that most dear old dads didn't want or need. If dear old dad wanted or needed it, he already had it. If he couldn't afford it, chances were his kids couldn't either. Then again it was the thought that counts, or so he had endlessly heard. However, for the old man there never had been thoughts of that nature. That he had deciphered this meant that he was now fully awake.

He glanced at his nearby calendar. Yes, it was early June. The calendar had marked Father's Day as June 16th. He wondered if the celebrating of that event and others like it was a creation of Hallmark or others to sell cards and gifts. No doubt the economy owed much to such events. Christmas, Easter and Halloween could not by themselves sustain those commercial enterprises.

Yes, it must have been the radio that planted the theme in his head, but what did it mean? Did it have any meaning for him anymore? His dad had been dead and buried for almost thirty years. He had given cards and gifts to his dad. But what did it mean? Had he done so just because he was supposed to? He guessed that was all there was to it. He was expected to.

He got out of his recliner and checked the newspaper for the time of the Twin's game. Now he had to get his supper. Today it would be the sloppy joes that he had made on Sunday. Sunday was the only day he really cooked anymore. Chicken breasts, pork loin or Italian macaroni hot dish usually lasted for a couple meals during the week, better than a cold cut sandwich or a can of chunky soup.

As the hamburger with a tomatoey, smoky taste warmed, he thought about his dad. He remembered when he was five or six and wanted to go fishing. His dad took him to Rascal Lake and rented a boat. The boy wanted to catch a northern, so his dad rowed him around the edge of the lake three times. His dad had no motor. The old man at last realized the physical effort his father must have endured to make him happy. Those old wooden boats were not easy to move. The boy did snag a two-foot long, skinny northern pike. A great day for the boy, but a great deal of labor for the dad. Perhaps that was a good reason to celebrate Father's Day.

The old man was 79 years too late. As he ate his sloppy joes, supplemented with good Gedney baby dills, he wondered what his doctor would say about consuming so much salt. As he once told his then eighty-seven-year-old grandma, who wanted to go out in her garden on a hot summer day to pick raspberries, "Why not? What is the point of being eighty-seven if there is no fun allowed anymore?" The old man remembered the hell he had received from his aunts for allowing grandma to put on her bonnet and fill with berries the tin can which she had tied around her neck.

The old man smiled and reached for another dill pickle. Another smile followed. He should have given his dad a Father's Day card for the great dill pickles he canned each summer. Gedney had a ways to go before they matched those. Then there was his dad's canned beef, better than the sloppy joes for his sandwiches. Yes, his dad gave the old man many legitimate reasons to honor his father. His dad worked two jobs much of the boy's growing years. The part time work, baking doughnuts from four to seven a.m., came before his regular job, or in other years he worked six to nine p.m. piling lumber after his regular job. This allowed his dad to clothe his eight kids, feed them, and see that there were Christmas gifts and a few summer picnics. There were many reasons for celebrating Father's Day. The old man felt depressed. He had never really said thanks.

As he cleaned up his supper dishes and grabbed the two chunks of his daily chocolate ration, he began to feel even worse. In 84 years he himself had never received a Father's Day card. He had never had any children in his seven to ten years of marriage, as he put it. He always said seven to ten years because it was over after seven, but not legally ended until the tenth. He recalled telling his wife that if they had children, he felt he would have to quit teaching. He said he didn't think he could spend eight hours a day meeting the needs of his students and have anything left over to properly give enough to their children. After the divorce he regretted not having had children. At least he would have had something more than good memories to show for his married years. But he knew it was selfish to think that way.

His ex-wife wanted to travel and live all over the world, Europe, Asia. He told her he would go wherever she wanted. She told him no, she couldn't be responsible for his leaving teaching. She said she knew how much he loved it and how good he was at it. She left for England. He remained in Minnesota to continue teaching.

Even with the nap the old man had a tough time lasting through the entire Twin's game. The Twins were at home and helped him stay awake by avoiding a bottom of the ninth. There was not much else left in his life other than a Twin's game to bring him happiness.

That night his dream was still on Father's Day. In his dream people asked him about his children and grandchildren. They kept bugging him about how many kids he had. In the dream he gave the answer he had often given in real life, "A few." When pushed for an exact number he laughed and said, "Four or five thousand," and waited for a reaction. After the attempt at humor failed, he said that he was an English and speech teacher who retired after thirty-seven years, but continued to coach speech for twenty-seven more. He told them that the official count was somewhere between four and five thousand kids in his life.

The next day was his house cleaning day. Oh, he had a cleaning gal who came in every two weeks, but he tried to keep up on his cleaning chores a little so he could have more time to visit with her. Some days she got little cleaning done in her three hour stay, but she seemed to enjoy his stories. As he pushed the noisy vacuum cleaner, he thought about his nonexistent children. He remembered that, in an education class, a point was made that a teacher was *in loco parentis*. What did that mean? He shut off the vacuum cleaner and got out his two remaining dictionaries. The Oxford American Dictionary defined the term as "in the place of parents, responsible for child protection." Protection, interesting word, he thought. He had stood in for parents. He had been legally responsible for the safety of those in his charge. He knew that, in the last twenty-five years of teaching, laws had been enacted to require teachers and coaches to report known or suspected cases of child abuse. They were legally required to report erratic or self-destructive behavior, or hints thereof.

Well into the afternoon he decided to forgo his usual nap and read. He still read mystery novels, but today he browsed through his poetry books looking for poems of parenthood. Robert Frost, Emily Dickinson, Carl Sandburg, and T. S. Eliot offered little on the subject. He missed his collection of five thousand plus books. Surely if he still had all of it, he could have found something. Instead he reread most of the Robert Frost collection. That still left several hours before the Twin's game. They were now on the West Coast; it would be a late game. Maybe he could make it through the fifth inning.

He didn't cook that evening. He was still chewing on *in loco parentis*. Ice water, Bing cherries, and salted in the shell peanuts preceded the two Dove dark chocolate bits for his supper. He always like to read the message on the inside of the Dove wrapper. One of them said, 'Help the children.' He guessed he had done that. He had protected his children. There was the girl who ran into his room to hide from her mother's abusive boyfriend. He stood between the girl and the husky aggressor who could have ripped him apart. Instead the man retreated from the room. He reminisced about how he went to Sandy's aid. She was a sophomore whose locker was directly opposite his classroom door. She was shy, naive, and not one of the brightest of his kids. She was also tall and pretty, the perfect prey for the likes of a bully, sexist male whom he observed for several days getting into Sandy's personal space and putting his suave moves on her. She was visibly uncomfortable. The old man intervened and told the hulk that, since he didn't have any classes on that floor, if he saw him again he would personally make trouble for him.

The old man didn't see the kid around after that. He asked Sandy if the boy was bothering her elsewhere in the building. She said no. Her friends told her that the boy said, 'That skinny,' here she stopped and mouthed the word 'bitch, was not worth it.' Her friends told her that the boy's cronies said he didn't want to mess with "that guy up there." The old man smiled.

Two home runs by the Twins in the first inning against the Angels added to the smile. The old man dozed off in the fourth and woke up in the eighth with the Twins ahead 4 to 1. He headed to bed hoping his dreams would be about baseball rather than Father's Day.

His dreams were not about baseball or Father's day. A restless night of tossing and turning was punctuated by jerking awake from dreams that were more like nightmares. In each one he was in some type of trap or predicament that he couldn't extricate himself from. When he was faced with the worst of it, he woke up feeling helpless. He eventually drifted off and found himself in another dangerous place.

The next morning, working the daily crossword in the newspaper, he rehashed his trap dreams. Maybe he had been wrestling with Father's Day issues. When he was a kid, who had he always gone to for help when he needed it? His dad. Kids went to their parents for help at least until they were teenagers. Teenagers, if they went for help at all, often turned to teachers or coaches.

Many of his students had come to him when they found themselves trapped. Vicki came into his office crying because the counselor had told her to forget about college—she would flunk out anyway. The old man told her to follow her dreams. He then quoted John Greenleaf Whittier, "The saddest words of tongue or pen is that it might have been." She did, was admitted to a private college and got her degree.

Then he thought of Rosario, the Mexican girl he had in class while teaching in South America. She too came in tears and asked what she should do. Her mother and her mother's new boyfriend wanted to send her back to Mexico to live with her sister. "My mother and her boyfriend don't want me around, and if I go back with my sister, her husband will come to get in my bed again." He advised the girl to tell her mother and her sister. She said she told her mother, and the mother called her a liar. Rosario said she could never tell her sister; how could she hurt her sister?

The old man had informed the counselor and principal of the private school. It was a few days before Christmas break. When school resumed four weeks later, he found out that Rosario's mother had pulled her out of school and asked that her transcripts be sent back to the school she had formerly attended, apparently back with her sister.

Maybe he didn't deserve a Father's Day card. He failed to protect that time. But what could he do in a foreign country when the girl had been sent to another country?

Rosario's story led him to Cynthia's tale. She asked to speak to him privately during his prep hour. At the time the old man was about forty years old. He could still hear her words, "I have come to you because you are the only one around here who will listen and not be judgmental. I can't go anywhere else. I think I'm pregnant. I don't know what to do. There is college, my parents, my boyfriend's parents. I don't know what to do?" The old man just sat there for a few minutes, both in silence.

Finally, he asked the girl to list what she thought she might do, to write down her options. The girl did. Then he asked her about the pros and cons of each option. She made a column for each. After some silence, Cynthia said, "I guess my first step is to find out." He offered her money if she needed it to find out. She said, "No, both of us have money to find out." She then smiled and left. About two weeks later she said there was no problem.

He didn't solve the problem directly. However, he listened, which helped her sort the issues and pursue her own solution. The old man guessed that was a parental responsibility: LISTEN.

The old man's summer was moving along. To pass the time he sorted through some old yearbooks. He ruminated on some of his speech teams and plays he had directed. He looked at senior pictures and marveled at the memories, how much those seniors had changed and grown from grade nine. Some of those he remained in contact with over the years, but the years saw those numbers dwindle to only a few. He had outlived more than a few of them.

Yearbooks nudged his stream of consciousness to thoughts of his "goody file." He moved to his old oak desk which his aunt Mary had rescued from the Standard Oil junk pile when they cleaned out some old offices. That was 64 years ago. He located the wrinkled manila folder and began to revel in the jewels of his teaching career.

First were the letters from college deans and admissions offices. The letters were sent to inform him that so and so had listed him as the most influential and inspiring high school teacher.

The second pile contained letters from parents for his work in helping their children to achieve excellent writing and speaking skills. One single mother said, "You turned Marci's life around. She was a lost, angry teenager who hated authority figures and inflicted her anger on any and every one since her father's death several years before. I was so worried about her. She was forced into an independent study with you because of a scheduling conflict. You would not put up with her crappy behavior. You told her to use her excellent brain. You cajoled her, pushed her, nurtured her. You told her you cared about what she became. You both won. I remember the day she told me, 'Mom, I didn't know learning could be so much fun.' She was so happy when she came back from a reading at a local bookstore with the autograph from the author she did her project on." Marci was a success. She had turned into a star basketball player who lead her college team, graduated and became a teacher and coach.

Another letter thanked him for having taken her sad, moody, depressed ninth grader and somehow convinced her that, in spite of being a terrible speller who didn't know punctuation marks existed, she could be a good student. The letter said, "Not only did you guide her into being the editor of the school literary magazine, but you got her to join the speech team. The shy, scared, quivering-voiced daughter of mine won a speech conference, first place. She went from baggy sweatpants and sweatshirts to hide herself to wearing clothes that allowed the world to see the beautiful, confident girl that she is today."

The old codger smiled and thought to himself, 'Maybe that was my best effort.' The last he heard of the girl was that she wanted to pursue a Ph.D in linguistics.

He guessed the dictionary had missed a great deal in defining parent. All of the dictionaries listed biology first, then mentioned rearing and responsibility for secondarily. Didn't fostering come into this? Wasn't that a vital part of raising children? After all, that was such an important part of his growing up, becoming a man, a teacher. Fostering. That was what he got from his best coaches and teachers. They convinced him he could do things, be somebody he never thought he could be. They would not accept less than his best effort to be and do, but they convinced him he could. Yes, fostering.

Perhaps instead of *in loco parentis,* he was a foster parent.

As he got up out of his curved back oak chair that was also retrieved from the scrap heap, an envelope fell to the floor. His aching knees and back didn't make it easy, but he rescued the envelope and took it with him to his recliner. He needed a nap now so he could make it to the end of the Twin's game that night.

Comfortable in the recliner, he opened the envelope. Inside was a card. He opened it and read:

*Dear Sir,*
*    I am sitting in my room, the night before my first college classes. I just wanted to say thanks. I know I wasn't your top student and your classes were so hard. I never had to work so hard in any other class. I worked hard because that is what you demanded. You told me, actually all of us, that we could do it. You made us work and learn. I did it. I only got Bs from you, but all the kids said that a B from you was like an A from anyone else. I took all of your classes I could.*
*    I know I'm not so smart, but in your classes I felt smart. You made me feel smart. I want to be an elementary teacher and make kids feel smart.*
*Thank you so much,*
*Tara*

A big smile on his face was sprinkled with a few tears as he drifted off to sleep. He drifted so deeply into his sleep that he never awakened.

He had received a Father's Day card over 35 years ago. It was on his very last day that he finally recognized it.